A FOOL'S DEATH

A FOOL'S DEATH

PATRICK CODY

CROWN PUBLISHERS, INC.
New York

Copyright © 1993 by John Cooney

All rights reserved. No part of this book may be reproduced or transmitted in any form or by any means, electronic or mechanical, including photocopying, recording, or by any information storage and retrieval system, without permission in writing from the publisher.

Published by Crown Publishers, Inc., 201 East 50th Street, New York, New York 10022. Member of the Crown Publishing Group

Random House, Inc. New York, Toronto, London, Sydney, Auckland
CROWN is a trademark of Crown Publishers, Inc.
Manufactured in the United States of America

Library of Congress Cataloging-in-Publication Data

Cody, Patrick.
   A fool's death / Patrick Cody. — 1st ed.
     p.   cm.
   I. Title.
PR6053.0529F66   1993
823'.914—dc20
92-34308
CIP

ISBN 0-517-59123-5

10 9 8 7 6 5 4 3 2 1

First Edition

For the Murphys of Majuro

The real world is not easy to live in.
It is rough; it is slippery. Without
the most clear-eyed adjustments we fall
and get crushed. A man must stay sober;
not always, but most of the time.

—Clarence Day

A FOOL'S DEATH

1

*M*ESQUITE Charlie knew he'd die a bad death, but I doubt even he thought it'd be quite this nasty. Alligators got him. The three hundred pounds per square inch of pressure in those massive jaws crunched up poor Charlie like he was a candy bar.

A client's in my office on the second floor of one of the old, weathered frame buildings on Duval Street in Key West. He's whining about a wife who vanished, but I'm not paying a hell of a lot of attention. Charlie's grisly death is preying on my mind. It doesn't seem real somehow. My good friend dead. And he checked out like a simpleton.

If the gators were a little hungrier, Charlie's whereabouts wouldn't be known for sure. His right hand and his foot in his right shoe were found on a strip of ground in the shallow, shimmering waters of the Everglades. His rusty, battered old Chevy was parked by the Flamingo Lodge, which is a couple of miles from where the bits and pieces of Charles Wayfield Donne were noticed by a fishing guide.

For the past couple of days, the press has made a big deal out of Charlie. He was the first person ever killed by gators in the Everglades National Park. A hell of a distinction.

When Martin Huff gets here, I should learn a little more. I don't know whether Huff is aware the victim was my friend, but he wants me to work on Charlie's case. He phoned last night, saying he has a client who wants to get to the bottom of what happened. That strikes me as peculiar, but I'm grateful. My own sense of loyalty leaves me no choice but to look into Charlie's death. Besides, I already promised the women in his life I would. There's no way I could charge them. At least now I'll get paid for my efforts.

Meanwhile, I try to focus on the problem of the poor son of a bitch with me. His name is Harold Thompkins, and he's not unhandsome even though he looks like a pig. I worked with a cop once who said an easy way to remember people was to think of the animal they look like. He was right and I never forgot it.

Thompkins is all beefy and ruddy the way certain private-school boys get, and his nose is tilted back a bit so the nostrils are perfectly round Porky Pig holes. He's about thirty-five years old and from Sharon, Connecticut. Clean-cut, he's dressed in khakis, loafers, and buttoned-down everything. Sitting in one of the two wooden chairs in front of my desk, he speaks with an Ivy League drawl and a dismaying edge of sanctimony as he rattles on about his runaway wife.

"She just turned thirty." A wounded expression creases his big pink face. "I can't believe Beverly's done this to me."

To him, the situation is a tragedy. To the guys back at his office, it's gossip to snicker about. To me, it's a source of money, always in short supply.

I swallow a yawn. Another end-of-the-road case, as I call the people who run from their lives in colder climates and wind up down here, the last stop ever on U.S. 1. Criminals, nuts, and assorted others find their way to Key West to shed their old selves and take on new ones. A fair number of people feel they can be butterflies rather than the moths they've become, if they only find the guts to take a chance. Sometimes it works.

A FOOL'S DEATH

From his half-angry, half-dopey look, Thompkins seems dazed and unsure of himself. I charitably guess it's to cover nervousness that he irritatingly drums his fingers on my desk while giving the particulars.

"This will help you," he says, taking a photo from a large white envelope and handing it over.

The picture is of an attractive brunette with a sadness in her eyes that belies her vivacious smile. With her lean face, high forehead, and flared nostrils, she looks like a colt. She's wearing a plaid skirt, white turtleneck sweater, and navy blazer.

"I made sure she lived very well." Smugly he holds out a batch of photos that are testimony to a yuppie lifestyle: a house like a little Cotswold cottage, a BMW sedan, a Volvo station wagon, a dog like Lassie, and a smart little day sailer. Despite these affidavits to prosperity, his wife up and left without any warning. At least none he ever picked up on.

"Five days ago, she sent a postcard from here saying she won't come home," he says, starting that damned drumming again. "I don't know what came over her."

He hands me the postcard and I almost laugh. The lady has a sense of humor. The front is a replica of a "Get Out of Jail Free" card from Monopoly. The writing on the back is firm and emphatic. "Harold, I will not be back. Beverly." I feel like telling Harold to save his dough. This woman isn't going to second-guess herself. But why throw away found money?

Not too many years ago, it was just about all women looking for runaway husbands, but today it's half and half. That doesn't matter. Once you know your way around this little bit of America, finding people of either sex who don't want to be found isn't all that hard.

"I'll locate her if she's on the island," I say encouragingly.

"That's what I'm paying you for," he snaps.

I'm tiring of Harold, so I fine him for being a twit by doubling my usual lost-and-found fee. "You pay half now, and the rest when I find her. The one qualifier is my standard 'squirm-out clause,' as I call it."

"What's that, for God's sake?"

"You agree not to press me to tell you where she is if she doesn't want you to know." It's kind of odd, but some people run away to call attention to themselves. Those that do want to be found.

"But that's not fair. After all, I'm paying."

"Take it or leave it, Mr. Thompkins," I say, pushing the agreement and a pen across the desk. "That's the way I do business."

Tightening his jaw, he grabs the pen and signs. Naturally, none of them ever like my condition, but then they don't have much choice. I'm the only game in town.

"Where are you staying?" I ask.

"The Marquessa," he says, naming an expensive renovated inn.

"I'll call you there in a day or so."

Thompkins takes off and I find myself again preoccupied by Charlie. What does Huff know? Who hired him and why? Someone who has enough dough to hire a lawyer like Huff to look into Charlie's death makes no sense at all.

As the morning squeezes toward noon, stifling heat oppressively fills the office. I'll have to buy an air conditioner with Thompkins's advance. Mopping my brow, I check my watch. Huff is running late. Maybe his plane's behind schedule. Maybe he went to my old office by mistake.

I moved to this one just a month ago, part of my now ritual migration to the higher numbers of Duval Street as renovators keep driving up rents on the lower numbers. My first office down here had a water view if you leaned out the window and bent your neck like a contortionist. That was before fancy hotels and shops catering to well-heeled tourists began replacing cheap office space off Mallory Square.

From the little office refrigerator, I grab a beer and pop it on the way back to the desk. Out of morbid fascination, I start rereading the day's account about "Gator Fodder," as a sicko national tabloid headlined the story of my unlucky buddy.

The picture of him the paper used isn't very good. Charlie's standing in the cockpit of his fishing boat. In the photo, he looks like a collie. He looked more like a lion, thick in the shoulders and with shaggy, light brown hair and a gentle demeanor that could turn ferocious when pushed.

Huff's footsteps finally draw near, the resigned trudge of a man who spends so much of his life in high-rise office and apartment towers that he's almost forgotten what to do when he comes across stairs. He's with Carruthers, Rushmore, Cowan, a posh law firm in Miami. A minute later, his head shadows the opaque-glass door-pane emblazoned with the name of my firm:

MASON COLLINS & ASSOCS.
PRIVATE INVESTIGATOR

There are no associates. Never were. When I first went into practice, I foolishly thought I could afford a secretary. The large, healthy girl I hired suggested the touch, which she assured me would make people think I was big-time.

A tentative knock comes.

"Enter if you dare."

Huff warily pokes his head in the door, getting the lay of the land. Though it's a good eighteen months since I last saw him, he seems the same: a sad, thin face, a little beak of a nose, and the alert, empty eyes of a chicken. A shy fellow, Huff was born looking fifty-six years old. His graying brown hair is always a little mussy, and he wears gold, wire-rimmed glasses. Though his conservative, charcoal silk suit is expensive, Huff still manages to look like a defensive high-school teacher.

"Marty, how are you?"

"Fine, just fine, Mr. Collins."

That's the way it is with us. We've been doing business for ten or twelve years, but it's Marty/Mr. Collins.

Edging wearily to the chair Thompkins vacated, Huff mops his face with a hanky. All the while he glances around with a trace of dismay, which he does whenever he first sets foot in one of my offices. There isn't much to see. The desk and fridge, the chairs and a couple of filing cabinets, although stacks of paper on the floor attest to the way I usually file stuff.

"Want a beer?" I ask, trying to be polite.

He winces as if I asked him to do something obscene in public and pointedly looks at the still-morning hour on his watch. "Do you have any water?"

I trot over to the fridge and open it. "No water." I hold up a bottle of orange juice and jiggle it his way. "This okay?"

"That will be fine."

There's a nice cold bottle of Stoly in there. I wave that at him too. "Want to goose up the OJ?" I ask helpfully.

"No . . . thank . . . you." Closing his eyes, he seems to be counting to ten.

When I sit down again, Huff wears the pained expression he usually adopts when in my company—the earnest teacher trying to get through to an incorrigible student and knowing it won't do much good. I try to look upright, but he sees through me and scowls as he dispenses with pleasantries.

"The officials first believed the hand and foot were probably Mr. Donne's because his name was on the owner's card found in the glove compartment of an old car that appeared abandoned near the boat landing. Then they matched up the fingerprints with Mr. Donne's military records in Washington."

It's strange hearing Charlie called anything but Charlie or Mesquite Charlie. Nobody here ever used his last name. I think I'm one of only a few people hereabouts who knew what it was. And until I read the newspaper stories, I always thought Charlie spelled his last name with a *u*, not an *o*. So much for my powers of observation. I must've seen his name stitched over the left-hand pocket of his fatigues just about every day when we were in Nam, a half a lifetime or more ago.

"We want you to find out all you can about how and why Mr. Donne died."

"Who for?"

"I'm not at liberty to tell you right now."

"Hell, Marty, why would anybody pay good money to find out what happened to Mesquite Charlie?"

"I'm not quite sure yet myself." He adds, "I'll send you a copy of his will when I get one from Philadelphia."

"Right." We've both been around the block more than a couple of times on estates. When someone dies funny, see how much dough they had and who gets it. But except for his fishing boat, which has mortgage payments due until some time in the twenty-third century, Charlie didn't have much more than the clothes on his back.

"Why's his will in Philly?" I ask out of curiosity.

"Apparently that's where his family is."

Family in Philly. A new one on me. The case is getting weirder. One of my best friends gets eaten by an alligator and now one of the fanciest law firms in the South wants me to check into his death. Why is the identity of Huff's client a secret? Something else bothers me. Why did Huff bother flying down here when he knows so little?

"We could've done this on the phone, Marty."

"There's one matter that must be taken care of in person." He opens his briefcase, pulls out a legal form, and hands it over. "You'll receive a retainer when you sign this."

How could it have skipped my mind? Huff always has me sign one of these things, even though I don't think I've ever been able to fulfill the terms of the damn contract. I scan the document, which is full of the usual impenetrable legalese, a mind-popping number of *wherefore*s and *party of the first part*s.

"What is this?" I ask innocently.

He scowls again and replies testily, "A confidentiality form. As *always*, we don't want you discussing your findings with anyone but us."

I shoot him a you've-gotta-be-kidding look, grab a pen, sign, and toss back the paper. I hold out my hand for the check.

Huff quickly examines my signature, as if I might've put down a phony. It did cross my mind. Now I wish I had. He digs into the briefcase again and extracts an impressively oversize blue check and drapes it across my fingers.

Holding it up to the light, I make a show of carefully examining the amount and the signatures on it. Huff gets up and leaves without even a good-bye.

■■■■ 2 ■■■■

THE Monroe County medical examiner headed out of town, but he promised to leave word that I was to be given every courtesy. Huh!

The older I get, the more I realize how open to interpretation language is. I've been here at an air-conditioned hospital freezing my heels for nearly forty minutes while waiting for the acting coroner to see me. It's so cold that I'm pacing up and down, rubbing my arms to keep the circulation going. What are the poor patients doing? Building bonfires? It reminds me never to get hospitalized.

Autopsies are makeshift sorts of things down here. For what little there is to do on Charlie, the coroner booked Fisherman's Hospital on Marathon Key, which is about fifty miles from Key West. Usually, he just lines up any old funeral home where he can do his job.

Finally, the office door opens and a toothy guy with a pale, rabbity face and sullen eyes emerges. He brushes past me and collars a young Latino orderly.

"Why didn't you tell me the room wouldn't be finished?" he yells.

A FOOL'S DEATH

The orderly's dark eyes flash. "No . . . I try tell." The poor kid sputters in broken English, but he's so nervous he can't get out what he means to say.

After carping at the guy a little longer, the coroner irritably says, "Oh, what's the use," and turns away. The youth glares after him, obviously debating whether to make him a more permanent resident at the morgue. After this high-handedness, Toothy turns to me. He doesn't bother shaking hands or even using my name.

"I'm Dr. Swanson. I'm filling in as coroner. What do you want?"

Though I know he knows, because a receptionist told him twice while I was waiting, I rattle on for thirty seconds about Charlie. Rudely glancing at his watch, he listens with obviously bored impatience.

Doctors become pathologists for two reasons. The good ones love challenges. Finding out about death is a big challenge, especially if there's a crime involved and your research can help set the stage to help catch the criminal. The bad ones know the dead can't sue. I don't doubt which camp Swanson falls into.

Why is this creep here? The sad truth is that the regular coroner has a tough time finding somebody to fill in for him when he goes on vacation.

"Follow me." He uses the same irritating tone he used on the orderly and turns his back on me.

I grab him by the biceps. Squeezing his arm, I spin him around. The smug look on his face is replaced by a nice grimace of pain and fear.

"I'm a taxpayer, you little shit," I say softly. "As such, I pay your salary. If you don't show some common courtesy, I'm going to break your goddamn arm. We clear?"

He looks around frantically. We're the only two in the corridor. The receptionist is gone. The Latin kid is mopping up a room and steps back so the doctor can't see him. I dig harder into the soft flesh.

"Yes!" he squeaks.

As I let go, he spins on his heel and walks briskly down the hallway to the elevator. The rattling of his leather soles on the tile floor reveals his inner fury. Redness rises up the back of his neck like a quick sunburn.

I take my time so he has to hold the elevator door for me. The orderly flashes a smile that's all white teeth. During the ride to the morgue, Swanson doesn't look at me. The redness never leaves his face.

Bringing out the body parts a few minutes later, he places them on a white metal gurney. He's watching through half-closed lids to see how I'll react. A smirk flirts with the corners of his mouth. The coroner must have told him Charlie was my friend. Half-wits take their fun in peculiar ways.

What I confront is a kind of desecration. When all is said and done, Charlie's remains fit into a couple of little freezer Baggies. Truth to tell, when first examining the contents, I'm sort of curious. The one bag isn't any help. It holds a foot and an old Adidas running shoe. Hell, half the thirty thousand or so souls who call Key West home wear shoes like that at one time or another. Besides, who the hell can identify somebody else's foot unless there's something weird about it.

The hand is another story. It's Charlie's all right. *L-O-V-E* is tattooed across the knuckles. The missing left hand bore the inscription *H-A-T-E* and is probably still giving some gator indigestion. When he got drunk, Charlie used to do the number Robert Mitchum did in the movie *Night of the Hunter*. He clenched his hands together as if they were beasts locked in mortal combat and ranted about various things. Unlike Robert Mitchum, he usually quoted poetry too. One of his favorites was a bit of Robert Browning:

> *Dante, who loved well because he hated,*
> *Hated wickedness that hinders loving.*

Drunk or sober, Charlie was like the rest of us. He had a tough time figuring out how to love well. But he was exceptional in that he tried harder than most folks. As a result, he succeeded and failed more often. Charlie married four times.

A FOOL'S DEATH

A couple of days ago, right after people learned what happened to him, Amanda Kay, who was wife number three, phoned all teary voiced and asked me to find out what happened. I told her I'd give it a try. Then Betty, number four, followed by Marlene, number two, rang up and asked the same thing. Only Virginia, whom I know the longest and who'd been number one, didn't phone up within an hour of the others. It took her almost half a day to call. She was in California visiting her son by another marriage who's on a baseball scholarship at UCLA. Nobody could reach her right away.

Besides being the only PI they know, the wives called me because, on more than one occasion and usually in public, Charlie made me swear that I'd check out his death if he ever died like a jerk. The ladies were pretty sure being eaten by a gator qualified.

"If I die like an ass, promise me you'll find out if it was truly an accident," he would say.

I'd dismiss his ranting by giving him the fish eye, but he was serious. For the most part, Charlie was a careful man. He took chances, but calculated ones. He never took out his boat when it was stormy. He didn't drink and drive. He wore a helmet with his motorcycle. He loved women who loved him back.

He had a real thing about that asinine or "obscene" exit, as he sometimes called it. He usually wound up quoting poetry, something about dignity in death, which is far from the way I see it. Death just makes even bigger clowns out of all of us. For me, especially, it will just be the last layer on a fallen cake. But Charlie was so goddamn sincere in his pleading that I always broke down and said I'd do as he asked. He put a good bit of faith in my abilities. More than I ever did.

Fortunately, he wasn't alone. The people in south Florida are a trusting lot. They're too distraught or too ignorant or too used to people telling the truth when they seek my services to believe I'm anything but the genuine article. Or maybe they don't expect too much.

I'm just like a lot of people in Key West, a big part made up and a bigger part best forgotten. But you do something long enough and it doesn't matter much whether all the t's are crossed and i's are dotted on the credentials saying what you are or even who you are.

I guess I should mention here that each of the women think Charlie "met with foul play," although only Amanda Kay actually used that quaint phrase. I assume they feel that way because Charlie knew his way around the outdoors better than most men know how to find the bathroom from their beds. And he had more than a healthy respect for alligators.

Betty has another reason, which bears special consideration since he was still living with her when he died. She says Charlie had no reason to be near the Everglades, this being high season for him. His sport boat was chartered solid through the next month. Besides, he wouldn't have gone off without telling her what he was up to. He especially wouldn't lie about going on a fishing trip.

Given the circumstances, maybe it's despicable, but I liked being able to tell the women that I would indeed check into his death. Shamelessly, I assured each of them that I was only doing it for her peace of mind.

Charlie always married smart, good-looking women, and I was half in love with each of them. Not that I ever acted on it. I have a rule that I never mess around with a friend's woman, even after they're divorced. There's always some deep feelings, complex variations of love or hate, left between exes. Interfering with that is a sure way to bust up a friendship.

Charlie had a quality that I always found both remarkable and completely unfathomable. The phone calls bore it out once again. He had a knack for walking out on a woman and leaving her with her dignity intact. None of the women hated him. He once told me he had some kind of internal alarm clock that went off when he gave a woman all he had to give. He got out before everything turned bitter and sour. The women appreciate that.

Other than trying to boost my image in the eyes of Charlie's wives and make money from Huff at the same time, I'm anxious to live up to the strange promise my pal exacted from me. I owe him that much and more.

Charlie and I first knew each other in Vietnam. We were mates on a supply boat making runs up and down the Mekong River. There were few of us on board and we got to know what counted in one another. Charlie had a selflessness that was appealing in wartime or anytime. I won't go into details, but he saved my life.

We lost track of one another until fate brought us both to Key West within a year of each other. I had lost a cop's job up north after getting my head caught in a political blender. My private life exploded as well. Charlie had the decency never to probe. He was trying to put something behind him too, and it must've been pretty bad. I didn't ask either. Our friendship took on a special dimension. Not just because of what we shared in Nam and the good times we had down here. We each knew the other was building up scar tissue over old psychic wounds.

Not only was Charlie the type who stood by you when you were in trouble, but even rarer, he was genuinely glad when something good happened to you. My life has been kind of short of the latter for quite a while now, but there are still moments when something decent happens to me. Take the time I won the sport-fishing contest at Islamorada, as Plantation, Windward, and the Matecumbe keys are generally known. Charlie arranged the celebration when I got back home. He was runner-up.

Another side of Charlie suited me just fine too. He read a lot and talked about ideas. There aren't all that many people in your life who can do that intelligently.

As I stare at the severed hand, the impact of Charlie's being gone forever finally strikes home with an unutterable sense of loss and loneliness. I lean heavily on the gurney and tears fill my eyes.

For an instant, his face is as clear to me as if he stands before me. He wasn't good-looking and he wasn't ugly, an ordinary-looking lion. Five foot nine or ten. Maybe 165 or 170 pounds. For some reason, what I remember most is that women were drawn to him because he knew how to be playful with them, how to make them laugh. But there was more to their attraction than that. He made them feel protected. Once I asked a girl why she liked him.

"His eyes," she said. "He has wonderful, warm eyes that make you feel safe."

The pale blue eyes of a man who'd seen the world and knew its good and its evil and would always try to shield a woman from the bad. He let them feel that the bogeyman wouldn't get them. For an uneasy moment, I wonder if he didn't get Charlie instead.

3

W E'RE skimming across the shallow glades in an aluminum speedboat owned by the National Park Service. The guy sitting in the rear driver's chair is Sgt. George Weller. I wish he weren't.

The sergeant is in his late thirties, with the stringy build and the hard, bony face that DNA stamps out in droves in Appalachia. He looks a bit like a wolf. His crisply ironed tan uniform is as sleek as his wraparound sunglasses.

Weller strikes me as a hardass. Judging by my phobic reaction to Swanson, I'm turning into at misanthrope in my middle years. Unfortunately, the sergeant works at confirming my impression. We've gone a while without rain in south Florida, and the Everglades is shallower than usual. Weller's avoiding what river channels there are and whips over the parched shallows so that mud splatters up high enough to hit me but not him.

I debate about giving him the finger but decide against it as I glance at him. It's not personal. He's not even fully conscious of what he's doing. The nastiness is natural, like breathing.

Hell, I'm just wearing a pair of jeans and a T-shirt. A little mud won't kill me. Besides, he hasn't told me yet what he knows about the case. Most of all, I need him to get back. With a little provocation the son of a bitch would probably strand me out here, and there wouldn't be much I could do about it. He's the one with the gun. Instead, I stretch out, ignore the mud bath, and enjoy the scenery.

There's nothing like the Everglades in the whole world. It's a constant source of wonder. Florida dangles off the U.S. like a dick that's seen better days. More than halfway down is Lake Okeechobee, an Indian word that like most Indian words comes right to the point. It means "big water"; the lake is the nation's largest body of fresh water in the South. Below that is the Everglades.

The glades stretch out 750 or so square miles. The shallows are generally less than a foot deep, but there are spots where a man can wade up to his armpits. The place is so vast it's intimidating but intriguing too. The glades have their own charm. Everywhere you look you see floating water lettuce, scrubby trees, and thick reeds, but more than anything else there's the saw grass. Brown and green, the saw grass ripples on forever.

What's heartbreaking is what you can't see. The Everglades is dying. We've drained, ditched, and diked the state in the name of progress but messed up the ecological balance in the glades and elsewhere. Runoff from dairy, sugarcane, and other farms fed an explosion in the growth of plant varieties that clog open waterways, robbing them of oxygen and crowding out animal life. Fish in most parts of the glades are unsafe for eating because of mercury poisoning.

The disaster's like lung cancer. If people could see what their lungs look like every day, they wouldn't smoke. If we could see the environment get uglier every day, we'd change our path of destruction.

But nature can hide her problems. Everything looks just fine. Blue heron on their stick legs stand around on the stretches of islands, graceful egret and white ibis dart around the miraculously

A FOOL'S DEATH

clear blue skies. Bass break the surface, splashing, making me yearn for a rod and reel.

And there're the gators, nasty things moving slowly, menacingly through the waters or sunning themselves on the banks of islands. Those fearful-looking, primitive, armored creatures have toughed it out since prehistoric times by eating just about anything, as Charlie's death sadly goes to show.

When you see gators lazing on the shore or floating like black logs, you wonder how they could ever get close enough to anybody with all his wits about him to kill him. But they're smarter and faster than they look. A gator's stealthy when he wants to be and can move like a jaguar when he wants dinner, outrunning a horse for twenty yards or so, clocking forty to forty-five miles per hour. Every once in a while you read about a child being snatched up by a gator, a horrible thing. But Charlie wasn't a little kid, and he knew more about alligators than I ever will.

The roar of the engine eases up and the boat slows as Weller pulls up to an island. He points to a spot about six feet inland from the water.

"That's where they found the hand and foot." His harsh twang bespeaks generations of hill people for whom possum was a nightly entrée.

I look about carefully. No gators are around, but we passed a mess of them coming in. I take off my sandals, so as not to muck them up. Jumping ashore, I hit the marshy ground with a squish. With my first two steps, my toes sink out of sight in the warm, oozy mud. Then the ground firms a little as I walk up about two yards, point down, and turn quizzically to Weller.

"Little more to yer left."

Moving over, I carefully scan the terrain. The park police were over the place, of course, but you can never tell. Other footprints are still in the soft ground, and I'm careful not to mess them up.

"All these shoe prints from police?"

Weller shakes his head. "Some. Others are Donne's and maybe two other guys who came across his body parts but didn't bother reportin' what they found. Prob'ly poachers."

A FOOL'S DEATH

That's a little odd. By one of the few sensible acts of government, the poaching problem was eliminated in the glades in recent years. The gator population grew so much that park rangers need help in paring down their numbers, much the way the deer and wild-horse herds have to be thinned out up north.

Who'd the park cops turn to for help? Why, the poachers. The rangers knew just about all of them from arresting them. So they deputized the poachers and put them in the category of legal gator-getters or some such thing. So why wouldn't legal gator-getters tell the authorities when they saw what was left of Charlie?

"You take casts of all the footprints?" I call out.

"Somebody did."

Walking around, I squish on something hard. Part of it glitters. Squatting, I nonchalantly cup and pocket the muddy object while pretending I'm looking at the footprints. A moment later, I walk in a few ever-widening concentric circles, hoping something else crops up.

Before coming out, Weller told me that there was no sign of the boat that had brought Charlie out this way. Maybe it sank. Maybe a gator got that too. Those powerful jaws can shred an aluminum boat like a candy wrapper.

But where did the boat come from? That's one of the issues confounding the authorities. None of the rental places in the area reported a missing boat. The cops think Charlie brought one up here with him. No way. Charlie was like most Key Westers, who tend to be lazier than most people. He would've rented a boat rather than haul one around with him all day.

Which brings me back to "Why the hell did he come up here?" He liked to bass-fish in the glades, but if he was thinking about coming, he most likely would've asked me along. We were that tight. Anyway, he wouldn't screw off when paying customers were lined up to go on his sport-fishing boat with him. He needed the dough to make his boat payments, and he always set money aside to live on when times were lean. And he sure as hell wasn't a poacher.

19

Something else is odd. Weller says that nobody around the dock remembered Charlie's arrival, and he didn't have a room at the Flamingo. The former was more than a little curious. It's just about impossible to take that ugly old 1948 Chevy of Charlie's anywhere without drawing a fair amount of attention, mostly critical.

The trip back with Weller is uneventful. At the landing, I help him tie up the boat. He's finicky about the way he does it, careful that nothing dirties his uniform. "Damn," he yelps when a drop of water from the line gets on a pant leg.

"Where's your investigation go from here?" I ask, hoping to get a line on what the hell I can do too.

Arching his eyebrows, he bends down and straightens the crease in his trousers. " 'Vestigation? Why, Mr. Collins, this here's pretty much an open-and-shut case as far as we're concerned. Yer friend was out fishing, prob'ly got drunk, got out of his boat to unsnag a line or something, and was so careless a gator got him."

"Then where's his boat?" I stare at him. "Where's his pole?"

Weller shakes his head at the obvious juvenile level of my questions. "Boat could've drifted fer miles or maybe sunk. The pole could be in it or . . ." He pauses as his long arm sweeps the entire glades, and he laughs at the dismay that creeps across my face. "It could be buried in muck out there."

"Well, thanks for the help." I try for a tone of pleasantness that I don't feel because of his making stupid judgments about the death of a man he didn't know.

"Say," he says with an edge. "You got yerself all muddy out there. Hope it weren't my driving. You look about as bad as your buddy's hand and foot."

I eyeball the son of a bitch. A friend had given me a lift to Marathon Key to see the coroner. From the hospital, I went out to the airport and hitched a ride with the owner of a private plane who was flying to Miami. From the Miami airport, I took a cab out here. I told Betty I'd drive Charlie's car back down, so I don't need a ride back to the Park Guard headquarters in Weller's jeep.

A FOOL'S DEATH

"Well, I din' say noffin'," I say, aping his accent, " 'cause that boat looked like it were too much fer a cracker like you."

Weller goes into a slow burn. "Watch yer ass, cocksucker, or I'll make you wish the gators got you steada yer asshole buddy."

I wink. Hell, we're back on land now, even if he does have that gun. He's wiry and mean and probably as tough as a hickory tree, but I figure he won't shoot me. There'd be too much explaining to do. Though I wish he'd take a swing at me, he probably won't. A fight would dirty up that crisp uniform.

I give him the middle-finger salute and a big smile. "Go back to Dogpatch, son."

Looking as if he wants to kill me, he spins around and heads for his four-wheeler, muttering and taking his hand off and on the butt of his gun. Once in the driver's seat, he yells, "Come back agin and see what happens."

Oddly enough the threat is comforting. I'm all keyed up and ornery over Charlie's dumb death. That's why Swanson bothered me so much too. I want to lash out at somebody, anybody. A good fight wouldn't be a bad way to get rid of a lot of the hostility I feel. Anger at the nameless gods that take away friends.

Approaching the Chevy, I think Charlie must've slipped into the park after dark for nobody to have noticed the car. There's nothing stately about the make, wasn't even when it was new. A big boxy thing with a split windshield. Then I notice something real wrong. Charlie always parked ass backward, so he could drive out nose forward. I'll have to back the car out.

Troubled, I get the key from under the front floor mat where Charlie always kept a spare and climb onto the old spring seat. Sitting here is depressing after all the times I rode in this antiquated vehicle beside Charlie. I almost feel his presence, telling me there's more to his death than meets the eye.

The engine purrs to life as I press the foot starter that juts out of the floor near the gas pedal. The old Chevy might look like hell, but she's perfect mechanically. Pulling out the choke a little, I put her in reverse and back out. I drop her into first and watch Weller pull out and tail me.

A FOOL'S DEATH

I stay five miles below the speed limit, knowing the son of a bitch is looking for any excuse to nail me. Just as I leave the park, the big jeep tooling along behind me turns off. Key West is about 150 miles away. I'm glad to be heading home, but I'm uneasy. The wives all think Charlie was done in. What if they're right?

With Weller gone, I pull onto the shoulder of the road and grope in my pocket for whatever it is I picked up while mucking around out there. Scraping off the mud, I find myself looking at a coin, very old and maybe gold by the looks. Once the muck's off, it's obvious it was recently polished. Strange.

■■■■ 4 ■■■■

THE coastal highway is mostly a two-lane road, and for the most part it's monotonous. Sea and trestles for the road and more sea and the junkier parts of the islands are the scenery. Before facing that long journey I need a break. I pull into Alabama Jack's, which looks like an old bait shop with a weathered deck and bar. It's so ramshackly a good blow would probably send it slowly creaking and collapsing into the water.

Even so, Jack's has its own scuzzy charm. The booze is what you find anywhere and the fare is only bar food. But Jack's is one of the first bars you hit before that long, hot stretch of road. It's also an anthropologist's dream. Unstudied primitives hang out here. Hell's Angels types. They in turn draw tourists who want to gander at mean-looking bikers.

If I owned the place, I'd increase business by staging a show, but nobody would know it was make-believe. A burly, rotten-looking biker would grab a virginal tourist from one of the tables and haul her out over his shoulder while ripping her clothes off. They'd roar off into the night on his Harley. That's what I suspect most folks who come to Jack's secretly want to see. "The

Biker and the Virgin" routine could be held every couple of weeks, but tourists would stampede down here nightly hoping to be titillated.

It's midafternoon. The only other customer is a displaced person who looks like she made a wrong turn on the way to the country club. Well tanned and in her forties, she has the gaunt features of a Weimaraner or professional dieter and the sad eyes of a professional lush.

On her table is a sea of empty margarita glasses and side shots of Cuervo Gold. With her expensive tennis outfit and fingers full of diamonds, she must be on a temporary pass from the Ocean Reef Club, the weird enclave of condos for the rich that's nearby and, according to the FBI, the nation's "most secure resort." With its armed guards and encircling wall, it's hard to tell whether it's a rich prison or a place people actually want to be.

Ordering a beer, I ignore the lady, who glances over, hopeful she's found a drinking buddy. Lonely and bored, she's probably here by herself all week until her husband flies in on the weekends from some cold place, when he bothers to come at all. Tennis and booze fill the days. Drunken pickups take care of nights. Shutting her out, I look west over the clear water, thinking again how insistent the wives are that Charlie was murdered.

My reverie's broken by the roar of cycles, raucous whoops, and the stomping of booted feet. Padres enter, and it feels like a bad Halloween party. I know some of them. Padres is a gang that roams south Florida. A menacing-looking bunch, bristling with studs, chains, hair, and tattoos, Padres are okay during the cracks in time when they're not tanked up or drugged out. I have nothing against bike beasts, except the tax dollars spent scraping them off highways.

Grunts of recognition erupt from some of the thundering herd. I grunt back.

"Mason, how the fuck are you?" hisses a biker who looks like Jesus only 130 pounds heavier from pumping iron. He also looks like a tiger because of his watchful eyes and the rippling, muscular way he moves.

A FOOL'S DEATH

"Could be better, Snake."

"Yeah, I read about Mesquite Charlie. Too bad. I know how tight you guys were."

Though he doesn't look it, Snake is a very bright man. As a former client, he once told me a bit about his background. When not loco, Snake can talk knowledgeably about everything from architecture to zoology. A National Merit Scholarship winner at a high school in Orlando, he's maybe the only kid out of a Florida trailer park ever to win one.

With the exception of some elite schools, education isn't much to brag about here. Now one of the fastest-growing states, Florida's schools are bursting at the seams. Education is best summed up by a bumper sticker: "If You Can Read This, You Didn't Go to School in Florida."

As for Snake, he studied physics at MIT for three years before dropping out when schizophrenia hit him. He took to punching out strangers in bars and elsewhere if he thought they were looking funny at him. Since he's big, he did a lot of damage. He bummed around, getting into jams. But one man's sickness is another's yardstick of well-being.

He picked up with the Padres after he beat the hell out of a couple of them in a gas station. Inevitably, his combination of brawn, brains, and nuttiness made him the gang's leader. He came to be called Snake about two years ago, shortly before he hired me. He was in a brawl and his throat was slit. There was a lot of damage to the vocal cords, so he hisses when he talks. Don't feel bad. He actually likes the end result.

"My voice terrifies people," he says.

Hell, he's a walking nightmare anyway. Six feet four, 260 pounds of muscle, and long, flowing golden hair. A jumbo Jesus with an iron cross tattooed in the middle of his forehead.

Snake came to me to find his sixteen-year-old sister. She ran away from home and holed up somewhere in the Keys. The Padres tried to find her, but it was like sending Frankenstein's monster to look for a missing baby. People were too afraid to talk to them. I eventually located the girl. She was shacked up with

A FOOL'S DEATH

a foolish stockbroker who was about forty years old. He didn't know how old she was, which was understandable when you saw her in a pair of tight shorts and a bandanna halter. He had his own plane and shuttled her back and forth between Boca Raton, where he worked, and Plantation Key, where he kept a cabin cruiser.

Snake arrived at the broker's boat one night. He retrieved his sister and gave her boyfriend not much of an option. He could be stomped to death or lose the worldly possessions that meant the most to him. The broker wept when the Padres sank his cabin cruiser and set fire to his Cessna. I never charged Snake, figuring that was good business.

"Bartender," I call, and motion for a round of drinks for the gang members.

They take my generosity for granted. People often try to bribe their goodwill. A big, ugly Padre starts dancing with the Ocean Reef lady to a slow song that comes on the jukebox. Two others jitterbug together when some 1950s rock 'n' roll comes on. Then various Padres slow-dance together. Funny, I always thought they only did that to shake up the tourist trade, especially when they ask tourists to dance with them and drag the terrified guys around the floor.

While the rest of them talk about the merits of various Japanese bikes, Snake turns to me. "Was Charlie stoned out of his mind out there in the glades or what?"

Frankly, drugs hadn't occurred to me. Charlie liked to get high on grass once in a while, but he wouldn't be smoking weed while fishing. "No way," I reply. "We got stoned on a fishing trip once, but being high wrecked the day's fishing for both of us. Besides, he never drove stoned and he'd have to drive back."

Suddenly, Snake says something curious. "You know a guy like you was nosing about Charlie six, seven months back?"

"What do you mean 'like me'?"

His scowl leaves me no doubt I'm slow on the uptake. "A private dick."

"What was he asking?"

Snake orders another beer while collecting his thoughts. "Like what's he like. Fishing, fucking, whatever."

"Remember who he was?"

"Lemme see. He was out of Miami. I don't think I even bothered getting his name. I hate to be so vague, man, but I just wasn't paying that much attention."

For a moment, I find myself ashamed for wishing Snake would go into one of his schizy numbers. When in that mode, he's uncanny. He can remember everything from how many boat whistles he heard in a harbor to the license plate numbers of cars that passed by. He can tell you exactly what people looked like and the expressions they wore, recount conversations word for word, and what was on TV if one was on and what commercials were aired. Schizophrenia is like that for some people. Total recall.

"What'd he look like?"

"Dark, curly hair. Maybe six one, two hundred pounds. Thirty-three or -four. Dark complexion . . ."

For a moment, Snake's lost in thought. "Tommy Costello," he hisses. "That's the name the dude gave."

The news is disturbing. The PI business attracts a lot of low-life. In a way, that part of it's heartening; some of them make me look good by comparison. From what I'd heard about Tommy Costello, he has as much class as a palmetto bug. An ex–New York detective who left the NYPD under a cloud, he's rumored to have set up shop in Miami with mob help. Why the hell had that slime ball investigated Charlie?

■ ■ ■ ■ 5 ■ ■ ■ ■

AFTER dropping Charlie's car behind his house, I hike over to Precious Adams's. Precious owns a curio shop just off Mallory Square where he caters to the tourist crowd with better-quality bric-a-brac than most such stores sell.

He was in the forefront of the movement by gays to renovate houses in Old Town in the 1970s and 1980s. He also happens to be a transvestite who decides to dress like a man or a woman depending on how he feels when he wakes up. Once I saw him wearing chandelier earrings and mascara with a blue pin-striped suit. He couldn't quite make up his mind that morning. He likes it here because of the weather and the fact that, even if he's dressed like Little Bo Peep, people take him seriously on civic issues he's concerned about, such as conservation and historical preservation.

"Mason, Mason, Mason," he says as he looks at me with dismay.

Precious always gets on me about the way *I* dress. Glancing down, I realized that, from the boat ride, I look like I fell in a pigsty.

"At least I'm consistent."

"If that is meant to be funny, I'll take it as such," he sniffs.

"But even though you're mean, you can look at this. You may never see one again."

He hands over a $50 gold coin, which is heavy and bears the date 1915. The inscription states the *Panama-Pacific Exposition*.

"What is it?"

"Part of a collection a client wants me to sell. There were commemorative coins issued to celebrate the Louisiana Purchase, the Lewis and Clark Exposition, the Panama-Pacific Exposition, the McKinley Memorial, the Grant Memorial, and the Philadelphia Sesquicentennial."

Slipping the coin back into a felt-lined blue box, he holds it up for me to look at. Inside are two $50 gold coins, a $2 ½ gold coin, a $1 gold coin, and a 50-cent silver coin.

"This collection is worth about twenty-five thousand dollars today because it's uncirculated," he says.

The curio shop is Precious's bread and butter. His real love is numismatics. He's an internationally recognized coin expert, but he never has the dough or, I suspect, the ambition to get into it in a big way. Even so, when he comes across something he believes is valuable, people trust his judgment. I've been in his shop on occasion when he had auctions going over his four telephone lines. One time the bidders for a rare coin were from New York, San Francisco, Hong Kong, and Rome. I wonder what they'd have thought if they knew the auction took place in this shop cluttered with Haitian masks and Mexican water jugs and other weird stuff.

Groping in my pocket, I pull out my find and put it on top of his glass case of coins. He picks it up, examining it carefully. Thoughtfully, he runs his fingers through his long, wavy hair, which is sort of like an old-fashioned actor's. With his little mouth and usually sleepy manner, Precious looks like a well-fed old house cat. He's chunky, and though in his fifties, his face is practically unlined until he frowns. He's frowning now, but with a strong sense of curiosity and, if I'm not mistaken, even a bit of excitement.

"Well?" I ask.

"Would you let me keep this for a few days?"

"Sure, what do you think?"

"Definitely Spanish. Apparently quite old. Possibly quite valuable."

He looks at me curiously. "You know, Mason, I'm not one to pry. You don't have to tell me where you got this."

In short, he's dying to know. From the caliber of wealthy people he deals with, I know Precious is discreet. Yet I don't want to tell anybody just yet where the coin turned up. It has nothing to do with Huff's confidentiality statement but practicality. The bottom line is that I deal in information. Why give away my stock-in-trade before it might prove profitable?

"I'll tell you when I can."

Precious winces. "If *that's* the way you want to be," he says as a dismissal.

I don't want him mad at me. After all, I came here for a favor, but I don't know how to tell him about my reservations without hurting his feelings.

"Tell me a story," I say instead, knowing that's maybe the one thing he finds irresistible.

Precious is one of our local historians. He collects the oddities of this odd island and will tell you this or that at the drop of a hat. He stops sulking and his eyes light up. He plops down on the high wooden stool behind his counter and faces me once again.

"Have you ever heard of Elena Hoyos?"

Sounds a little familiar. "Nice name. One of our Cuban girls?"

"Well, yes, but she lived a while back. A beautiful, beautiful girl as only those Cuban girls can be. She had wonderful long hair and the exotic eyes of a flamenco dancer. But she was tubercular and dying when Karl von Cosel came to Key West."

"Who's he?"

"Von Cosel was a learned man who had studied engineering, philosophy, physiology, and a lot of other ologies. He claimed to be a count who had grown up in a castle in Saxony. But who knows? He was in his sixties and did speak with a German accent. He also roamed around town with a cane and wore a monocle and tennis sneakers with no socks, which was not at all the style in those days."

"What days are we talking about?"

"Why, Key West in 1930, of course. He came to the island to work as an X-ray technician and fell in love with Elena when she came to the hospital. The count began pressing his attentions on her, but Elena was a good forty years younger than him, and she wouldn't go out with him.

"Poor Elena's condition got worse and worse. On Halloween of that year, her parents thought it would be nice for her to get some fresh air. They swaddled her in blankets and took her to the parade on Duval Street. When she began coughing desperately, she was rushed home. By the time a doctor came, the poor dear had died.

"The count faithfully tended her grave and eventually received permission from Elena's father to build a vault for the grave of the woman he loved. From all accounts the vault was the most ornate and beautiful in the cemetery. But secretly, and here's where the story gets ghastly, von Cosel took her remains to his run-down house. There he cleaned what was left of her worm-eaten body and tied the bones together with piano wire. Using plastic and wax, he rebuilt her and with cosmetics tried to give her a human glow."

While talking, Precious's eyes are focused on a wall. As if duplicating the old count going about his business, he flaps his arms and head around like an artist seeking perfection as he reconstructs the girl's corpse.

"He thought he could bring her back to life, and he even bought an old plane that he was going to restore so he could fly them back to Germany."

It's a hell of a story, and I remember reading a bit about the girl in a book called *A Key West Companion*. I recall the count got caught.

"Who found him out?"

"Why, Elena's sister. She had a creepy feeling about what was going on over at von Cosel's, but it took her eight years to get up the nerve to visit his house. You can imagine how shocked she was when she looked in the window and saw Elena in a wedding dress, with a wedding band on her hand, and half-sitting in a large bed. The lighting around the bed was very flattering."

"Thank God for that," I can't help interjecting.

Precious frowns severely. "The count told the authorities he was bringing the girl back to life. He expected her to marry him out of gratitude. There was a trial, of course, but the statute of limitations on the ghoulish business had run out. Nothing could even be done when it turned out that he had rebuilt her so he could have sex with her."

Precious wrinkles his nose at that, and I don't know what my face is doing as I take in the disgusting fact. A moment later, he finishes up the tale.

"Mason, she was put on display at Lopez Funeral Home during the trial. Hundreds of people came to look at her. I would have loved to have seen her. Wouldn't you?"

That's Key West too. The people here are an irreverent bunch and apparently always were. If they can turn something into a circus, they will.

"I don't know, Precious."

But even as I say it, I know I'm lying. Who the hell could resist seeing that?

"So what's the moral?"

He looks at me for a long moment and then smiles.

"Why, that everyone here has something to hide."

■ ■ ■ ■ 6 ■ ■ ■ ■

AN hour later, I'm cleaned up and at Amanda Kay's. She's the first of the wives to have called, so I decide to see her first. Also, when I think about it, I probably always liked her the best of them. It's evening and the air is heavy with the smell of Madagascar jasmine that comes from the fence around the cemetery that is right nearby. It makes me think for a moment about Elena Hoyos.

Amanda Kay's originally from Texas and as such is always called by both names. She lives in a little pink place on Angela, one of the streets where cigar workers lived back in the 1880s, when Key West was the cigar-making capital of the U.S. The Cuban factory owners bought up blocks of land and built these houses. Amanda Kay's is typical. A three-room cottage, each room behind the other. There's a little front porch and a white picket fence out front.

Approaching the door, I hear her singing a plaintive folk ballad. She has a pretty voice. I wonder if she's thinking of Charlie because the song is so sad. At the end, I rap on the door and suddenly she's on the other side of the screen.

"Mason!"

Her freckled face lights up. She seems glad to see me. I'm always glad to see her. Amanda Kay is in her thirties, a redhead whose long hair spills around her face and makes her startling green eyes appear even more so. Her cheekbones are high and her nose is curved a bit, giving her the fierce beauty of an eagle.

"Glad you found the place after all this time."

The exasperated look on her face makes me feel the guilt of neglect.

She pushes open the screen door. Amanda Kay moves lightly and quickly, like a dancer. She's already halfway down the corridor by the time I'm inside.

"Come out back and I'll fix you a drink," she calls over her shoulder.

I follow like a grateful donkey. Her trim little figure is hidden beneath a rose-colored sundress that nicely sets off her golden tan. She looks damned good as she grabs a bottle of gin and some tonic and a lime from the kitchen.

She teaches at the high school. In the yard, there are books and papers piled near one of the chairs, so I take the other one. Rushing back inside, she returns a moment later with a bowl full of ice.

Amanda Kay isn't a conch, as the people born here are called, but she may as well be. She's lived here off and on since she was a kid. Conch or not, like a lot of Key West women, she holds up her end when drinking with men.

"Well, Mason, do you believe Charlie was killed?"

"I don't know. The cops think the gators got Charlie because he carelessly got out of his boat."

"Do you?"

"No. But who knows . . . ?"

"Mason, all those times he talked about dying foolishly, he meant it. He was afraid that somebody was going to kill him one day. He wouldn't go into the whole story, but it had something to do with his family."

"What about his family?"

A FOOL'S DEATH

"I don't really know. He didn't want to talk about it. He was about as reluctant to mention his past as you are. I always thought one of the strongest bonds you two had was hiding out from your history."

Looking at her, I think about what Precious said. It's an easy conclusion to reach down here. It seems as if most folks on the island are looking over their shoulders, afraid their past will come flapping down on them like a bat out of hell.

"You make it sound sort of romantic. Maybe Charlie's past was, but mine sure as hell isn't."

She looks me straight in the eye. "Maybe I just try to make more out of people than they are. But I knew Charlie was more than he seemed to be, and I know you are too."

"I'm flattered that you think anything of me at all, Amanda Kay."

She flashes a warm, open smile that contains maybe just a hint that she considers me more than just an old pal. I smile back, glad I came over, and wondering, hoping really, that I'm right.

"Remember the time," she says, "you and that woman Rhoda and Charlie and I took that sailboat to Haiti for that big cosmetics manufacturer and got caught up in the voodoo ceremony?"

We both laugh and start swapping stories. Before long our reminiscing takes on a ritualistic quality. We drink and talk about Charlie the way he would have wanted to be remembered. Both of us had a lot of good times with him. The hours slip by quickly and night falls. Neither of us had dinner and the quart of gin registers dangerously low. I debate about seeing if she wants to go out to eat or if she has another bottle around.

"Charlie could be a real . . . Oh, I guess you should only remember the good, right?" Amanda Kay says strangely. "Anyway, you just borrow that kind of a man."

I don't know what the hell she means, but she sounds wise. If I keep drinking, what I say might even start sounding wise to me too. We're both pretty plastered and sit silently for a few minutes. The night's warm but not hot and there's no humidity; perfect. The moon's full and stars twinkle in the sky.

"What about you?" she asks suddenly.

"What about me?" I pour the remains of the gin into our glasses.

"Why didn't you come after me after Charlie and I split up? I could tell you always liked me."

I try to explain my philosophy, but when articulated at this stage of the evening, or through a dozen or more ounces of gin, it doesn't sound right. I'm not drunk enough to sound wise. It comes out kind of dumb as I ramble on about exes and not wanting to come between friends and whatever.

"That wouldn't have mattered to me or to Charlie either," she says when I finish. "When it was over with him, it was over. One day it just seemed as if he was a friend you'd always had, not someone you'd ever married."

"That right?" I feel like an ass because of all the wasted time I let slip by. Unfortunately, it's the kind of foolishness to which I'm prone.

"That's right," she says softly.

She gets up, climbs onto my lap, and kisses me. I kiss her back, letting my hands wander over her body. I slide my hand under her skirt and gasp with such delight that I think I might have a heart attack.

"Let's go inside, you dirty old bear," she says.

Rising, she leads the way to the house. Halfway across the yard, she lifts her dress over her head, and for a moment, she's trapped in a moonbeam. At that instant, I know the lightness of heart that maybe poets and a few other lucky souls get to experience. I'm thunderstruck. What a lovely woman she is! Her honey tan is unbroken from head to toe.

■■■■ 7 ■■■■

I'M an early riser, but Amanda Kay beat me to it. There's a note on the nightstand saying she went swimming before having to be at school at eight A.M.

A groan escapes me as I rise unsteadily to my feet. I'm not one of those people who get pleasure without paying for it. Despite feeling like I've been flung headfirst off a high building, I don't mind. Last night was one of the best nights of the recent arc of my life.

Somehow, I pull myself together. I go home and shower and change clothes. Twenty minutes later, I reach Pepe's to have breakfast and wait for the dull pain in my head to go away. I wave off a couple of guys who were up all night and want to chat. Pepe's is a little restaurant right across the street from a boatyard. There are always shrimpers around, coming off their jobs and revving up just as most everybody else is facing the workday with a sense of foreboding.

After breakfast, I walk up Caroline Street and head down Duval, going past Sloppy Joe's, the Bull and Whistle, and other bars that are largely tourist pits. Bars in Key West aren't what they used to be. The golden age of any place is usually right before I get there. Where pottery stores, fancy galleries, and cutesy dress shops now litter the landscape, there used to be bars jammed everywhere along with tattoo parlors and lots of strip joints, such as Delmonico's, which featured maybe the nation's only trapeze artiste who stripped while flipping and flying right above your head.

Then, of course, there's all the Hemingway crap. Papa spawned a cottage industry down here, everything from T-shirts and beer mugs with his face on them to tours of the house he lived in and bars he hung out in. Unfortunately, he left a reputation for fighting. There're always a million or two guys in town who think they look just like him and want to act macho. What most of them don't seem to understand is that the best thing he did was write.

Don't get me wrong. The town still has good bars and good people in them. A fair share of my income keeps them from hard times.

When I hit the office, I definitely feel improved. Memories of last night put me in an even better mood. But I don't want to dwell too much on Amanda Kay. Most likely last night was an aberration. She must've climbed out of bed this morning with an embarrassed shudder, wondering what the hell got into her when she looked down at the woolly, snoring wreck who shared her bed.

The glare coming in my front office window makes me wince a little more than usual, but my head's better than when I woke up. I want to think reasonably straight when I call Joe Clark in Washington. When I do somebody a favor, I don't expect anything back. But in the case of Joe Clark, my attempt at being a Good Samaritan has paid off in spades.

Joe was down here on vacation about four years ago with his wife, Connie, and two kids, Mark, who was then five, and Carol, who was two. After a day of swimming, Joe parked at the supermarket lot on Fleming. He and Connie locked the kids in for a minute while they ran a couple of quick errands. When they got back, little Carol was gone. After a frantic day and a half of searching and sitting around the police station, Joe came to me.

I found Carol happy and healthy on a houseboat on Christmas Tree Island, where much of the hippie tribe took to living. I may have alluded to the tolerance of people down here, but that isn't always true. Hippies used to cluster around the north end of Simonton Street, where they'd dock their houseboats and swim and sunbathe in the raw. Some upright types complained. Before you knew it, an ordinance was passed that banned poor boat dwellers from docking near Key West. So they headed out to Christmas Tree Island.

I'd heard that Carol was out there from a hippie friend who sometimes worked as mate on Charlie's boat. He explained that some months back one of the women had had a miscarriage and plunged into a deep depression. Her condition got so bad that she was talked into seeking professional help. The doctors were testing different mood elevators on her. But her behavior just got more irrational. One afternoon she showed up with Carol. Afraid the sick lady might get into trouble, he wouldn't tell any official what she'd done.

Not wanting to make money off a sad young woman's reaching out for the wrong kind of help, I refused any pay for finding the little girl. Even after I outlined what happened, the Clarks acted like I worked some kind of miracle. You can understand that. They were out of their minds with grief for nearly four days before they got their baby back.

In any event, it turned out Joe has a highly classified intelligence job in Washington. He told me to call whenever I needed anything, and he'd see how he could help. True to his word, he gets me information for cases I could never get any other way, including FBI records, some CIA data, and full military records.

I dial his number and he gives a hello.

"Joe, it's Mason. I hope the family's well, and I'm hoping you can help me out again. Would you see what you can get on a Charles Wayfield Donne? W-a-y-f-i-e-l-d. Donne is D-o-n-n-e. He was about forty-two or forty-four. You met him down here. Went by the nickname Mesquite Charlie."

"You mean he's dead," Joe half-stated, half-asked. There's an awkward pause. "I'm sorry to hear that. I know he was a friend."

"Yeah. He might've been killed. Also, Joe, would you see what you can dig up on a private eye in Miami named Tommy Costello. C-o-s-t-e-double l-o. An ex–New York cop."

"Sure, Mason."

We talk a bit more. He's coming down in another couple of months. With the kids older now, his and Connie's lives are programmed by the school year.

After cradling the receiver, I write up a sketchy little report for Huff. There isn't a hell of a lot to say yet, but I start keeping track of my expenses. Cab fare to the Everglades from the airport. Drinks for the Padres. My call to Joe. What it cost to fill Charlie's gas tank.

A couple of hours later, I'm giving some thought to lunch when Virginia calls, saying she's just back from L.A. "Come by my place this evening, Mason. I'm having the wives over. Maybe if we all put our heads together, we can help you with your investigation."

Virginia's that kind of woman. A doer. If there's a task at hand, she's already figuring out the best way to get it done.

A handsome woman about forty with a rich tan, she has short, dark hair and the big, strong body of the woman you'd want when you start the world over and need a helpmate. Suddenly, I feel a little anxious. Amanda Kay will be there. I don't want to get thrown out of her life in front of the other women. Even so, I'm glad Virginia asked me along. I sure as hell need all the help I can get.

■ ■ ■ ■ 8 ■ ■ ■ ■

*B*EFORE heading to Virginia's I stop for a bracer at the Full Moon, a bar where drinks are serious. It's funny but the prospect of being the only man in a room full of women makes me a bit nervous. I've felt this way since adolescence.

I enjoy the company of women, but I'm only really comfortable when it's one-on-one or in even numbers. I guess I have some primitive notion going on that when outnumbered, you're at a disadvantage.

Virginia lives on Fleming in one of the grand, faded white frame houses that she bought with insurance money when her second husband left her a widow. There are front and side porches, overhanging balconies, tons of gingerbread, and shuttered windows. Houses like this, and there are a lot of them here, were put up in the middle of the nineteenth century. They were built by jacks-of-all-trades, who were sailors, fishermen, spongers, and what have you. They tackled the houses the same way they did the ships they built. No blueprints. They just went to work.

I open the wrought-iron gate and hear the women talking.

Without knocking, I walk inside and find them in the living room, sitting under a lazy ceiling fan.

"Hello, everybody." I ease myself into a chair near the door.

The way they're seated around the floor makes me feel like I'm intruding on a sorority meeting. That's one of the odd things about Charlie's marriages too. The women are all friends. I don't think any of them knew one another before Charlie brought them together, but they remained friends once they met, which may not be so strange because they have so much in common. Besides being smart and good-looking, they are linked by having married the same man.

"Hello, Mason" echoes around the room.

I sneak a sheepish look at Amanda Kay to see if she's wearing the what-the-hell-did-I-do-last-night? look. Instead, she gives me a big smile. My whole body relaxes as I feel a sudden rush of relief. I must've been holding myself tight all day.

Virginia suddenly looms in front of me, looking as always like a sturdy but attractive bear. She's wearing a man's shirt that hangs outside her shorts and is splattered with paint. She's an artist who sells her designs to makers of sheets and curtains and that kind of stuff.

"I'll get you a beer," she says. "You look like you could use one."

"Heard you had a rough night, Mason," says Marlene.

The others all laugh.

Marlene's the youngest. A high-strung Arabian mare. She must be twenty-seven or so now. Charlie married her when she was a teenager. He admitted at the time it was pure lust, which is understandable.

Marlene is one of those smoldering, sensual Italian women like Sophia Loren. Copper hair, a strong, sultry face, ample breasts, and legs as long and shapely as a dancer's. She was on vacation from a college in New England when Charlie met her. They fell into bed almost immediately and were married two weeks later. Now she has her own sport-fishing boat and customers lined up for the next couple of years who don't give a damn if they catch anything as long as they can flirt with her.

"Is nothing sacred?" I ask indignantly. I give Amanda Kay a baleful stare. "What about my reputation? A guy's gotta live on this island."

"I'm so sorry," she says. "I only told the ladies here and the girls at school, of course, and . . ."

They all laugh at my expense again. Outnumbered, there's no way I can turn it around.

"You learned anything yet?" Betty wants to know.

"No. I'll tell you as soon as I do."

There are dark circles around Betty's eyes, which only adds to the vulnerability of her parakeetlike looks. She's obviously taking Charlie's death the hardest. Why not? Hell, he hadn't left her.

Her feathery blond hair is short and layered. With her trim figure and sharp, intelligent face, she looks a lot younger than her late thirties. An interesting woman. She remade herself so that you'd think she grew up on Park Avenue instead of a trailer park on Key Largo. She put herself through the University of Miami and now runs one of the major art galleries on the island.

Virginia hands me my beer and sits on the floor again. I become the focus of their attention. Funny how women are conditioned to do that when a man comes on the scene, even one like me. Men only do that if a woman's good-looking and they think they have a chance of getting laid, no matter how remote.

"Charlie told each of us that his fear of dying in some awful way had something to do with his family," Virginia said, naturally assuming the leadership role. "He didn't elaborate on that to Amanda Kay, Marlene, or me. He did tell Betty that his father and an uncle died hideous deaths."

"What else?"

Virginia looks troubled. "We also all realized that we took Charlie at face value," she says.

"That's pretty much what people do down here," Marlene says. "Don't we?"

"When we went over our lives with him," Amanda Kay says with a puzzled look, "we realized we didn't really know much about him at all."

■■■■ 9 ■■■■

I'M staring out the office window at a swirling, inky sky and blasting rain. Storms down here are an eerie business. Thunder roars. The sky rips open. Rain hurtles down in vicious sheets. Streets fill up like backed-up toilet bowls, and lush vegetation grows by the millisecond.

It passes through my mind that this is the hurricane the weather people forgot to mention. Maybe it's only the end of the world.

The weather rustled up just after I got back here from Virginia's. The women had settled into making dinner and were embarking on a gabfest that was revving up to last all night. It was time for me to move on. I had decided to come back to the office to tie up some odds and ends. When I was leaving, Amanda Kay followed me out to the porch.

"Promise you'll call," she said.

I was proud that I didn't crumple to my knees in gratitude. But I was honest. "It might become a habit," I warned her.

As the rain buckets down, a white stretch Mercedes stops out front. A dexterous chauffeur leaps out, opens the rear door, and simultaneously flips open an umbrella for a man who ducks under it. He's a blur of white suit and sunglasses. Why'd he stop?

I suffer an uneasy twinge or two. My last landlord wore white suits, but he didn't have a stretch limo, at least not the times he hounded me for late rent. He came around in a maroon Cougar that he confused with class because it had velour seats. I still owe him for several months.

One thing I know for sure: Mr. Dapper isn't my new exploiter. My new landlord is a she, a shrewd old dame who gutted me for two months' rent in advance and vowed I'll be out on the street the day after I miss a payment. She must've checked up on me.

A minute or so later, I hear the tapping of leather-soled shoes coming up the flight of stairs to the office. There'll be a pause before there's a rap on the door. People get hesitant when they're right outside and knock instead of just walking in. A friend explained the office looks uninviting and uninhabited. The knock comes.

"It's unlocked."

The door opens. In strides a dapper little person. He looks like a squirrel with thick eyebrows. His suit's Italian, and with his dark hair and complexion the guy may be too.

"Mr. Collins, I presume."

"Dr. Livingstone, I presume," I answer with mock solemnity.

His pointed features don't crack a smile. Once again I lament that we are no longer a literate society with common historical reference points. I want to tell him it's just a joke, a takeoff on what H. M. Stanley supposedly mumbled when he stumbled across David Livingstone at Lake Tanganyika.

But why bother? His face reflects the emptiness of living of someone in his early twenties. When I'm feeling curmudgeony, I believe most people under thirty were only schooled on what happened in the postnuclear era. Sadly, I decide to drop that little attempt at humor from my repertoire once and for all.

"Let's start over. Yes, I'm Mason Collins, and I'm pleased to meet you, Mr. . . . ?"

He takes the seat in front of my desk, lights a cigarette, and exhales a stream of blue smoke in my direction. "I was told that you are a wiseass, Mr. Collins. I don't know whether I'm pleased to meet you."

"Since we're getting off to such a swell start, why don't you just haul ass out of here, sonny, and shut the door behind you."

Exhaling another lazy stream of smoke, he purses his lips and squints as though he's looking at a bug. He debates whether to smile or be pissed off. Finally, the trace of a sardonic smile makes his face appear a trifle more lived in.

"It's not as simple as that. You see, I'd like your help. My name is Brian Donne. I'm Charles's brother."

In shock, I sink slowly down into my chair as I try to take in that the Squirrel is Charlie's brother. A brother in a fancy limo. And I just insulted the kid. The nimbleness with which I am able to put my foot in my mouth continues to astound even me.

"I didn't even know Charlie had a brother," I finally say.

He looks at me thoughtfully. "No, I suppose you wouldn't. We weren't exactly close. Charles left home before I was born. I only saw him a few times after that."

"Why are you here now, Brian?"

He stubs out his cigarette and pushes back a lock of black hair that fell across his left eye. He's a very studied young man, but beneath the faultless manners is an edge. The nails are manicured, but the fingers are strong. He looks wiry. Young Brian Donne could be a tough little squirrel.

He stares at me for a moment. There's more than a hint of worry in his eyes before he glances away as though embarrassed.

"I'd like you to help me stay alive."

There's only one reason he could think that. "That's not your everyday request. So you think Charlie was murdered?"

"No. I know he was."

"What makes you so sure?"

His composure cracks momentarily, and for the first time, I notice how drawn his face is. A corner of his mouth twitches, and his body tenses as he nervously lights another cigarette. Trying to keep his hands steady, he's almost successful.

"I guess the easiest place to start is to tell you something of

A FOOL'S DEATH

our background, so you will have a better idea of what you are up against."

"Hold on, Brian. I don't mean to be a spoilsport. I'll help you with what I can, but I'm already working on your brother's death for a client."

"Who?"

"I don't know. The job's through a Miami law firm."

That makes him anxious. Standing, he begins pacing about. He seems indecisive about what the hell he should do next. But he comes to a decision.

"I'll try to make your job a little easier by telling you what I can. I'd just appreciate your telling me what you can."

"Sounds fair."

He looks around the office as if he can't wait to get out. That's not unusual for visitors. Hell, plenty of days I look around and feel the same way.

"Have you had dinner yet?" he asks.

"No."

"I've been told that Mira is quite good and I made a reservation. Is that all right with you?"

The Mira's one of the best and most expensive restaurants on the island. "As long as you're paying."

"Of course," he says a trifle irritably.

The restaurant's kind of dressy, so I go to my filing cabinet, open the drawer marked A–F, and extract my blue blazer. On the way out, I lock up. By the time we're downstairs the rain has stopped. That's the way storms usually are here. Over in a flash, just the way they come on. The chauffeur opens the door and we sink into the kidskin backseat to cruise the few blocks to the restaurant. Mira's in a renovated old building, not far from where the wives are gathered.

"Mr. Collins, I'd like you to meet Tony Mongo. He's my chauffeur-bodyguard."

The back of the car's so roomy, I actually get up and lean way over to take the left paw the beefy Mongo extends around his thick neck. A gorilla with a blow-dry.

A FOOL'S DEATH

"Pleased to meetcha, Mr. Collins."

In the rearview mirror, Mongo sizes me up with a professional gaze. He's as tall as me but thicker and a good ten years younger. I can hear the creaky wheels in his mind clicking about how long I'd last with him if we ever went one-on-one. I can't help wondering what kind of moves he has. Is he just a lot of muscle or does a brain lurk under that blow-dry?

For the rest of the trip, Donne silently stares out the window, lost in thought. A brooder. He only comes to life again when the limo stops at Mira.

"Is the food as good as they say?"

I don't feel like going into the chronic shortages that humiliate my bank account, or how I could afford to maintain myself for a month on what he was going to drop tonight for dinner. "You'll just have to take 'they's' word for it. I never ate here."

We're ushered inside. Moments later a half dozen waiters glide around like they're on ice skates as they anticipate our wants. Mongo sits a few tables away, his back to the wall and eyes on the door.

For the next forty minutes, waiters bring dishes of rich foods, and I stuff myself like a goose being groomed to be the critical part of a pâté. Our conversation consists of small talk about sports, the weather, and what the fishing's like. That's fine with me. I don't want anything to divert my attention from the meal. We're into our second jug of Châteauneuf-du-Pape when Donne wipes his lips with his napkin and backs into why he asked me along.

"Do you know anything about our family at all?"

"As far as I know, Charlie sprang full-blown from the soil like a soldier from a dragon's tooth."

Pushing back his chair, he lights another cigarette. "Then you don't know how rich we are," he mutters.

What's going on here? I'd been thinking the kid might've hit the lottery and he's telling me the whole damn family is rich. Which meant Charlie was too.

He pauses as though considering just what to divulge and blows a smoke ring. "My father's name was David Donne. He and his brother, Gerald, had a salvage business. The headquarters is in Delaware, but that's merely for incorporation sake. The business was really in this part of the world. They came to the Keys to seek their fortune."

As if staring at something far away, he sits still as cigarette smoke wreathes around his head. There's a wistfulness about him, as though he wishes he could have been part of an adventurous calling in a simpler era. But he also seems to know that his yearning is a large dose of sentimentality for a life he doesn't really want. The kind where you're always living on the edge.

"There is no real dignified term for what they did. They made the most out of other people's misfortunes."

He looks at me for confirmation and doesn't get it. A bit irritated, he continues his tale.

"In certain respects the salvage business is the same as prospecting for gold. You look a lot and have varying degrees of terrible luck, but one strike can make the difference between riches and poverty. The Donne brothers had more than their share of good luck. They had a major strike. It quite literally set them up for life. With sound investments the fortune has not just remained intact but grown considerably."

"You still haven't told me a damn thing about Charlie," I said.

"Yes, Charles."

He utters his brother's name with a certain resignation. Other than that his response is devoid of emotion, which may be right for a brother he didn't really know.

"Charles was our black sheep. He was uncomfortable with our money. He was fifteen or so when the big strike came, so he wasn't born to it the way I was. In fact, Charles was with my father and uncle when they made their major find."

Brian looks at me expectantly. "You know being born to money or not makes quite a bit of difference in the way wealth is perceived, don't you?"

I'm still having a hard time digesting the fact that Charlie's family was rich, but I'm all ears for what young Donne is saying.

A FOOL'S DEATH

Why did Charlie never mention the family dough? What was wrong? Who might've known about it down here? Is that what got him killed?

"You're asking the wrong guy. I've always been envious and resentful of the rich."

"At least you're honest," he says. "I guess, in his own way, Charles was honest too. From what I've been told, he was ashamed of our money. He dropped out of school when he was seventeen and joined the Navy, and never really considered our home his again. After the Navy, he spent some time in the Southwest, which is where he picked up his nickname.

"I only met him several times. He came home for Uncle Gerald's funeral fifteen years ago and again when our father died seven months ago."

Fifteen years ago was about the time Charlie first showed up in Key West. I remember because it wasn't long after I got here. "How'd they die?"

Brian shoots me a sharp look. "My uncle drowned in his bathtub. He apparently suffered some kind of shock while bathing. My father's death was even more absurd."

"What were the circumstances?"

His mouth curls with distaste. "He kept a pool of piranhas on our property. He fell in."

"You believe their deaths were accidents?"

"No."

Reaching into his breast pocket, he takes out several folded pieces of paper and hands one to me. "After Uncle Gerald died, my father showed me this."

The paper is parchment and very old. I open it gingerly, afraid it might come apart in my hands. It's a map of Central America and the Caribbean. The markings are in Spanish. Handwritten in English across the bottom is: *It is folly to drown on dry land.*

"This came after my father died," he says, handing me another paper.

It's old too but not nearly as antiquated as the first. It's a map of the same area but with greater detail of the Keys. Across the

A FOOL'S DEATH

bottom, in the same spidery script, is: *Life itself is neither good nor evil; it is the scene of good or evil, as you make it.*

Reading the words, I get a chill and wonder about the tattoos on Charlie's fingers. What was the root of that strange, morbid hand-wrestling he did with himself? Combat between good and evil? I try to remember more exactly what Charlie used to say when he'd do it, but it doesn't come. I do, though, remember the strange look on his face. So weird that I'd laugh. I thought he was drunk and might get sick. Maybe I misread him completely. His face could've been a mask of despair. And my inability to see straight had kept me from helping him.

"My father tried unsuccessfully to find out who sent the map. I tried to do the same when my father died. I hired one of the nation's major private investigating firms. Charles said it would do no good, and he was right. He told me if I should ever need to go to a private investigator again, it should be you. 'A wiseass but smart. And good as there is at what he does' is the way he described you."

"So that was Charlie's assessment of me, huh?"

I'm not sure whether to be a little sore or a little flattered. Is that what a good friend says about you when you're not around? Just as we never know what's going on inside friends' heads, we never know for sure just how we impress them.

"Yes," the brother tells me.

"Wiseass, huh," I say, dwelling on the criticism. "What else can you tell me about him?"

"Besides Charles's not liking the trappings of wealth, I got the impression that he broke off his relationship with the family in order to avoid the terrible fate that he ultimately suffered."

"What makes you so sure his death is tied to your father's and uncle's?"

He hands me another map. "I received this yesterday."

Drawn in detail is the Gulf of Mexico, showing the straits between the Keys and Cuba. The inscription states: *There is no escape. The evil men do lives after them.*

Suddenly, my stomach sours. Charlie was murdered! What else

A FOOL'S DEATH

could these crazy sayings coming after the crazy deaths mean? With dismay, I begin to understand my friend's fear of a fool's death. Each murder was made to appear like a grotesque accident. Yet each reflects a moment of foolishness as if the victim caused his own death. Each crime was also done around water and, I am now convinced, by the same person. But why? The maps are obviously clues. The provocative maxims written by the hunter, which is the way I now think of the killer, are another.

There's still another potential clue, at least in the case of Charlie's death. Maybe it's a common denominator as well.

"Was a gold coin found at the scenes of your uncle's and father's deaths?"

Startled, he looks up. "What do you mean?"

"An old gold coin. Probably Spanish." I try to remember what's on the damn thing. "An eagle on one side. The other side has what looks like a fist full of arrows."

Brian reaches into his pocket and hands me a shiny gold coin. "Like this?"

I heft it and hand it back. "That's the one."

His expression clouds over. "It was found near their bodies. They were never without it and neither am I. This is a Spanish doubloon and quite valuable. They're from my father and uncle's successful salvage operation. Charles was the only one in the family who refused to carry one."

I think of the coin lying near where Charlie died. He wound up with one after all.

Angrily, Brian grinds out his cigarette. "My father was quite hurt when Charles refused his generosity. There was a lot of bad feeling between them."

That doesn't fit the man I knew either. Charlie was a pretty easygoing guy. There must have been a lot of misunderstanding or something worse there for him to treat his own dad badly. His father must have given him cause. I've met a couple of men who kept piranhas. That wasn't the only thing about them I didn't like.

Young Donne puts cash on top of the restaurant bill, which came in a huge leather folder like it was some grand document of state. "Well," he says, trying to sound nonchalant. "Do you think you can keep me from getting killed?"

"I'll do what I can, but, if I were you, I wouldn't stray too far from Mongo."

He nods and then he looks up abruptly, as if something just occurred to him. "I know my brother was married. There's the possibility that his wife may be in danger."

"Why?"

"My mother died at childbirth when she had me. Uncle Gerald, however, married late. His wife drowned in a sailing accident. I . . . I just don't know if her death was related to my father's or uncle's. . . ."

I get a sinking sensation again as I think of all of Charlie's marriages. Perhaps all the women were in danger.

We get up, and I walk Donne back to his chariot. Mongo is on our heels. "How about giving me photocopies of the maps?"

"Of course."

"Where are you staying?" I ask.

"Casa Marina," he says, naming the ritzy sprawling complex on the island.

"How long are you in town?"

He pauses and starts to raise his hands, but they fall helplessly to his sides. "I'm not sure. Charles's death has thrown me. I'm not ready to go back to Philadelphia, and I can't think of anywhere else to go."

I feel bad for him. Free-floating anxiety coupled with fear you're on a hit list is a terrible combination. My sympathy surprises me because he's rich. It must be because he's Charlie's brother. I manage to get through life without fretting about how people with lots of money are coping with life.

"Can we drop you anywhere?" he asks.

"No, thanks." I need a moment alone.

As they drive away, habit takes over. I mentally note the license plate, a Florida tag with a double X in it.

▪▪▪▪ 10 ▪▪▪▪

I walk back to Virginia's, hoping the wives will still be there. A poststorm calm is settling over the night. The heavy scent of bougainvillea in the air is like a rich perfume. Her house is quiet when I knock. Obviously, the others took off.

"What are you doing here?" Virginia asks a trifle suspiciously.

I get the feeling she's wondering if I've made it my mission to comfort all the wives in their time of distress. In the same chair I sat in earlier and with a duplicate beer, I fill her in on what I can. In the scheme of things, I figure it's better to break my word to Huff than keep Charlie's wives in the dark about what's happening. Perched on the edge of her chair, Virginia's sopping up every terrible detail.

"So be careful," I conclude.

"How much danger are we in?" Always the realist, she's trying to assess the odds.

"Frankly, I don't know. Maybe none, but maybe mortal danger. That's all I can say in honesty."

Nodding, she goes to a closet and pulls out an old shotgun. "I'll start sleeping with this."

"Good idea." It is.

"There were times I wanted to use the damned gun on Charlie," she says ruefully. "You know how exasperating he could be, Mason. The rationalizations he had for not wanting children. For treating women like they were boats to be traded in."

The twist in the conversation makes me uncomfortable. "Maybe this whole fear of a lousy death made him worry that his children would be subjected to the same thing."

"Maybe," she says dubiously, and shakes her head. "I knew you'd take up for him."

"He was a good friend."

Virginia rubs her eyes. "Mason, when you take on a friend, you only see the good in him. I guess that's what friends are for."

Wives have a right to have a certain amount of bitterness about husbands and vice versa. Everybody knows two people living together and trying to understand one another is a tough business. By going for four, Charlie deserved a medal for optimism.

"Want me to tell the others?" she asks.

"No, I'll do it. You get some sleep."

"Thanks, Mason."

Fortunately, all the women live in Old Town so I don't have to race all over the place. Ten minutes later, I walk up to Marlene's bungalow. Gangly night-blooming cereus, kapok trees, and hibiscus almost drown the house. The small pool in the side yard is illuminated and the lights on the first floor are lit. I bang on the door. Moments later the outside light comes on.

Marlene pushes the screen door open. "Mason, why are you here?" She adds mischievously, "You're more like Charlie than I realized."

"What do you mean?" I ask, following her inside.

"You need more than one of his wives to satisfy you. Sit in the living room and I'll get you a beer."

I watch her head down the corridor, followed by her brown-and-white-splotched cat Calico. She's wearing a white cotton robe. Judging from the way the kitchen light shines through the sheer material, that's all that's keeping mosquitoes away from her. Charlie mentioned once she always slept nude. Whenever I see Marlene, I remember.

She comes back with two beers. As she sits on the sofa opposite me, one beautiful leg juts through the V where the robe parts.

The cat jumps up beside her. Calico's like a dog and goes just about everywhere with Marlene, tagging along behind her. He even goes on her boat. Without looking, Marlene reaches over and strokes Calico. They both stare at me.

"So what can I do for you tonight, Mason, that Amanda Kay can't do?"

Marlene flirts with everybody. For a moment, I consider parrying her comment with something provocative of my own. But the idea makes me a little nervous, and my throat is suddenly dry. Cold feet rather than savoir faire governs a lot of my behavior with women. What if she actually takes me up on it? It's a long shot, a real long shot. She's seeing a rich restaurant owner, but women do some funny things once in a while. Look at Amanda Kay.

"Sorry, I'm a one-woman man." I think of Amanda Kay and realize there's more than an element of truth there.

"Then you're the only one on this island who is."

We both laugh. She shakes her head, growing thoughtful.

"Charlie was such a baby, wasn't he? Always running from one woman to another, never knowing what he was looking for but thinking it could be found in another woman's arms."

I start feeling uncomfortable again. Who the hell was Mesquite Charlie? Whose vision of him is right? Maybe we're all different people to everybody else and never realize it.

"Come on, Marlene. Charlie always knew when to leave a woman."

She looks at me wryly. "Of course he did. He was like Peter Pan always waiting to fly out the window on some goofy whim.

A FOOL'S DEATH

You couldn't hate him for it because he was like a big kid. I swear, Mason, there were times when I felt like his mother."

I sigh wearily and try to think of something to defend him with, but it's getting late and nothing comes to mind. "I came here only indirectly because of Charlie," I say instead. "Marlene, there's a chance you and the other wives might be in danger."

She leans forward, her right eyebrow arching in concern. Automatically, I peek through her half-open robe at the gorgeous breasts swaying there but force my eyes away, trying to concentrate on the issue at hand. It's tough.

"Each of you wives thinks Charlie was killed. So do I now. And because you were married to him, there's the chance the killer might come after each of you too."

"You're serious, aren't you!" Her words were shot through with alarm.

"I'm afraid so."

"Have you told the others?"

"Just Virginia." I swallow the rest of my beer and set it down. "I'm going to the other two now."

"Wait a minute."

Jumping up, she runs to the kitchen. There's a slam as the back door shuts, a clatter as the chain lock slides on, and a rattle as a window slides down. Then another. Rushing into the living room again, she shuts one window while I close and lock the others. The place is now tight as a drum, and she turns on the air conditioner in one living room window before the place gets too hot.

"I don't have to tell you not to let anybody in."

"You sure as hell don't. This is scary."

At the door, I turn. As I start to say good-night, Marlene stands on her tiptoes and kisses me. Her eyes are serious when she looks into mine.

"Amanda Kay's lucky, Mason. You're a good guy. If things don't work out, don't forget where I live."

Calico follows me outside as I exit through the screen door.

A FOOL'S DEATH

Looking back at Marlene, I get tongue-tied and start saying something asinine but recover just in time.

"Thanks" is all I manage.

The front door shuts. The dead bolt rams into place.

Walking away, I look up suspiciously. No, it's not a full moon. What's gotten into these women?

■ ■ ■ ■ 11 ■ ■ ■ ■

*F*IFTEEN minutes later, I look through Betty's front window, which is right by the front door. She's talking on the phone. Without knowing anyone is watching her, she appears sad. Finally, she hangs up. I decide it's okay to knock.

"What are you doing here, Mason?"

"I want to talk to you."

She's momentarily flustered. "The place is a wreck. Wait here for a minute."

A few minutes later, she lets me in and the living room looks fine. The place couldn't have been too bad. Charlie always said she was the fussiest of the wives. He put it down to her growing up in the close confines of a trailer, where, if a couple of things are out of place, a room looks as if a cyclone tore through it.

Betty's still wearing the black-and-white-flowered silk print suit she had on at Virginia's. She looks smart, like a businesswoman from New York or L.A.

"I suppose you want a drink?"

Looking at me awkwardly, she sits down wearily. "I'm sorry. I didn't mean that to sound the way it must have."

I laugh. She isn't a rude woman, and I know the strain she's under. I guess she tolerates me because I was her husband's friend. She's a bit shyer than the other wives, so there's always a bit of awkwardness between us. She and Charlie weren't married that long, so I didn't get much chance to get to know her better. Like all his marriages, it was a whirlwind thing. They met just five months ago and were married a month later.

I guess she married Charlie because he was always at ease with people. She parks her shyness somewhere when she works and cultivates the arty crowd and the rich crowd, which down here overlap a lot. From all accounts, she's good at what she does.

"Now what is it, Mason?" She sounds tired and a bit exasperated, sort of the way you feel when an old dog shows up and you wonder if you should feed him.

I run through the danger number once again. All the time, she sits looking at me incredulously.

"You expect me to believe that?"

"Why do you think I'm here, Betty?"

Her face reddens. "I'm sorry again, Mason. I haven't been myself since Charlie's death. Thank you very much for your concern."

She looks away, speaking again, more to herself than to me. "That's typical, isn't it. Charlie could endanger others and never bother to mention it to them."

Here we go again. I move to head off complaints. "I don't think he thought for a moment that you or the other wives might get harmed."

She folds her hands on her lap. "That's just the point, isn't it? He never thought about anyone but himself."

Betty rattles on some more about poor Charlie's failings. I extricate myself as quickly as I can. I'm only grateful that Betty doesn't say anything provocative or give me a sweet look.

By the time I land on Amanda Kay's doorstep, I'm dragging. The night's too long and too damned depressing. Her lights are out. I debate about whether to go home, but I have to warn her. And in my heart, I want to see her. My reluctance stems from half-fearing to do so. What if she realizes by now what a serious mistake she made? Suppose the women talked some sense into her after I left Virginia's the first time around?

Screwing up my courage, I knock gently but loud enough for her to hear. The lights come on, and the door opens a crack, immediately shuts while a chain lock is undone, and then opens all the way.

"I was wondering if you'd show up."

The bleakness I feel drops away like a cut-loose anchor when she grins up at me. Grabbing my hand, she leads me to the bedroom. The warning can wait till morning. She has her old bear to protect her tonight.

■■■■ 12 ■■■■

*S*HE didn't scream.

At least that's what Officer Mike Sanders says after interviewing neighbors up and down the block. "The coroner's report will tell us with a pretty good degree of certainty what time she died this morning," he adds.

Mike's about twenty-three years old. He's tall and gangly with the large eyes and wedge-shaped face of a giraffe. His blond hair is cropped short. He's very serious about his job and comes to me for advice once in a while because he's afraid to approach Will Griswold, Key West's formidable chief of police.

His assumption of the time of death is based on the fact that her naked body was spotted shortly before six A.M. by a man walking his dog. But then, she could have been there all night. Sanders points to the side yard, which is visible from the street.

"Mrs. Donne went into her yard and somehow tripped and fell into her pool. She must've hit her head or something."

Tears roll down my cheeks, and I don't even know it until Sanders offers me a hanky. Marlene dead. That vibrant, sensual woman erased from humanity. Another water death. Another presumed accidental death. Suddenly, the heavy scent of bougainvillea in the yard makes me want to gag. It smells like a funeral wreath.

It doesn't make sense. I know how frightened Marlene was. She certainly wasn't a fool. How the hell did the killer get her to open her door or come into the yard?

Returning to the office, I sit for a while in a groggy stupor. When finally thinking reasonably straight, I get up the nerve to call the school to make sure Amanda Kay arrived safely.

"She's with a class now," the operator says. "Is this an emergency?"

"No. No, I'll reach her later, thanks." The dread eases a little.

Next, I dial Will Griswold. Being police chief here isn't the picnic it seems that it should be. The cops do more than throw ersatz Hemingways in jail for punching out one another. There's robbery, murder, and mayhem of varying degrees. And because of the location, the cops have to keep an ever-vigilant eye out for drug smugglers. That's hard to do, and temptation calls the police like a siren to ancient mariners. Sometimes the cops get so caught up in the drug activities that they wind up getting arrested themselves on smuggling charges. Drugs are the century's miserable excuse for a gold rush.

Griswold owes me. Even so, he keeps me hanging on the line for a couple of minutes before picking up. That's the way he is.

"What do you want?" he demands.

Griswold's a lot like his name. Rough and a bit harsh. You're not sure where he's coming from. His saving graces are that he's fair and honest.

"Will, I want to see you. It's important."

I feel the annoyance on the other end.

"Pepe's in twenty minutes."

"You're on," I say into the mouthpiece as he hangs up.

Sitting in a wooden booth, I'm on my second coffee when Griswold heaves himself opposite me with the effort of the old bull he looks like. He's squinting at me, a disconcerting habit that's like John Wayne glaring at an outlaw whose jaw he's about to break. An irritated, distrustful look. Griswold distrusts everybody.

He orders coffee and plunges his right hand through thinning gray hair, a gesture that telegraphs dubiousness. Dubious that I truly have something worth dragging him away from important work. His fingers rake trails, revealing scalp the same mahogany color as his face and hands, which with his lined, worn face only adds to his cowboy look.

Griswold doesn't like me. Like a lot of cops, he sees practitioners of my trade as walking testimony to the shortcomings of traditional law enforcement. The attitude's right, of course. If cops had all the manpower and money they need, there wouldn't be much room for my kind. Even so, I'm often enough right about what I tell him that he pays attention.

The chief, however, doesn't limit his dislike to me or even simply PIs. Some of his officers swear he hates everybody, even his dog.

"Well?" Also like the Duke, he tends to be monosyllabic.

"I think Mesquite Charlie was murdered. I think Marlene Donne was murdered. And I think the three remaining Mrs. Donnes are on some lunatic's hit list."

"You 'vestigating Charlie's death for somebody?" His eyes narrow into slits again.

"I am. I have no proof yet. From what I gather, though, somebody's going to try to kill the rest of Charlie's wives."

"Why?"

Once again, I'm feeling a trifle guilty about the promise I'd made to Huff about not talking about the case to anyone. But once again it's a promise that can't be kept. "Some crazy thing from the past. Somebody felt burnt by Charlie's dad and uncle and has a vendetta against the family. Until Marlene died, I wasn't sure the killer would go after the wives."

"Coroner just said Marlene was an accident."

"That's how he ruled Charlie too."

He gives me the dubious scalp-scraping routine again. "What if he's right?"

"What if he's wrong?"

Exhaling a sigh of a man shackled to his duty, Griswold climbs out of the booth and shakes his head. "Can't spare men to be with the women full-time. We'll check 'em at their houses at night."

■ ■ ■ ■ 13 ■ ■ ■ ■

*I*N with the office mail is a plain white envelope with my name scrawled across the front. I open it and take out the photocopies of the maps young Donne promised me and a note saying he's leaving town. He doesn't say where he's going. There's also an envelope from Huff's law firm. It contains a copy of Charlie's will.

Now that I know there's big money in Charlie's background, I'm more curious about the will than I would've been. Much of it's pretty standard, but I find something interesting tucked deep in the dense pages of legal jargon.

> My estate shall be divided evenly among my children and their spouses and their children. This includes current wives and any wives from previous marriages. The former wives will have the same share in the estate as my sons and their current wives.

He goes on that he set up his will the way his father had done his; his father had married three times. The father's will simply provides for any wife, ex-wives, and children by any marriage to be treated the same as any children Charlie or his brother had by current wives. It isn't really complicated. All Charlie and his father meant was to make sure that everybody was treated equally, including all wives and kids.

What's immediately clear is that Virginia, Betty, and Amanda Kay all just became a little richer with Marlene's death. Ordinarily, this would make them all suspects. Not a pleasant thought, but one that even an old cynic like me can dismiss.

The red light's blinking on my answering machine. I hit the rewind and the play buttons while I scan the rest of the will.

Amanda Kay's is the first voice. "I know you must be very busy, but please call me at school if you can." Her words carom around the empty room like an eight ball on a pool table; the edge of fright in her voice gives a dreadful spin to everyday sayings.

After the ping, there's a call from the garage, reminding me that my jeep has been there two weeks. I haven't paid my bill for a rebuilt carburetor. The next message is from Joe Clark, apologetically saying he got jammed up and would get my information as soon as possible. The fourth message is from Virginia, thanking me for getting Griswold to watch her and the other wives. Precious is right after her, asking me to drop by when I get a chance.

Mike Sanders checks in too. "Thought you'd want to know I found Marlene Donne's cat under some bushes when I was checking her yard. Its neck was broken."

Now I think I know how the killer got Marlene to leave the house. Calico. The cat followed me out when I left her place. The killer must have made the cat cry out to lure Marlene outside. He must've known what the cat meant to her. That means he's been watching the wives for a while, knows their movements, their habits. The thought gives me the shivers.

Betty's is the last message. She sounds tense, strung out. "I came across something when I was going through Charlie's effects. There's a . . . an envelope he wanted you to have. I . . . I'm at the shop now."

Her use of the cold word *effects* makes me think what an awful disservice TV has done us, stripping us of a lot of what's personal as it takes over as our cultural denominator. She doesn't say his clothes or letters or fishing tackle or whatever. Just effects, the way TV cops call anything belonging to the dead, no matter how intimate or special it may have been.

I dial the school receptionist, who says it's better if Amanda Kay phones me back. She calls about five minutes later. "Honey, I'm scared."

"I know you are. I want you to stay at my place tonight. There's a key in the big clay flowerpot by the front door. Just root around about an inch down in the dirt on the right-hand side. Keep everything locked tight."

"Poor Marlene, Mason. Poor Marlene."

In my mind's eye, I see her small, scared face spilling hot tears. "I know, Amanda Kay. Please listen to me for a moment."

"What is it?"

"There's a brown leather flight bag on the top shelf in my bedroom closet. There's a loaded .38 inside. Get it and keep it in reach until I get home. Don't let anybody else in. Nobody!"

"Okay," she says, her voice wispy.

Next, I call Virginia. There's no answer, but I'm not too worried. She won't expose herself to danger. Right now, she's probably finding the safest place to be. I'm going to suggest to the women that they leave the island as quickly as they can.

As I close the office door behind me, I unconsciously start humming. Suddenly, out of nowhere, an unexpected chill goes through me, although the air is warm and humid. It's the kind of cold some folks say you feel when death walks close by. I stop humming and get angry with myself. The tune is "Ten Little Indians." I catch myself thinking "Then there were three."

Ruefully, I realize I somehow became the beneficiary of Charlie's life, his sole heir to the most important relationships he ever had. He bequeathed his wives to me, and I'm doing a piss-poor job of protecting them.

I have to keep the bogeyman away from Amanda Kay, Virginia, and Betty. I'm not up to the task at all.

■■■■ 14 ■■■■

*T*HE Duval Gallery, of course, is on Duval Street. From the sidewalk, you step into a serene courtyard spreading around a banyan tree, its thick trunk resembling dozens of boa constrictors laced together. In the open area between palms are modernistic bronze and cast-iron sculptures, each costing thousands of dollars. Huge arched windows as well as the gallery's doorway open onto the courtyard.

Her brow creased earnestly, Betty is inside talking to Peter Matthews, one of the island's well-known art patrons. Earnestness is as much one of Betty's qualities as her blue eyes.

Matthews is part of what passes for Key West's social set. Seeing him makes me a little jealous. Amanda Kay went out with him for a while not that long ago. In fact, he had a go at Marlene and Virginia a while back too.

He's a partner with a Miami brokerage firm and splits his time between here and there. I guess the word that best describes him is elegant. Today he's wearing a gray silk sports jacket, a black golf shirt, white linen pants, and Italian loafers without socks, looking, as usual, as if he just stepped out of a fashion mag. His graying hair never needs cutting. He's always courteous. He looks like a sleek greyhound.

He and Betty stop talking when I enter. I get the impression they were discussing a price. They both look a little flustered, so I guess they hadn't come to terms.

The uneasy silence that usually falls in such circumstances doesn't. Matthews gives me a serious smile that shows both concern about the terrible events and pleasure at seeing me. I guess that's what people who are charming can do. They make you feel at ease just about anywhere. Though I never thought about it before, I realize Matthews is charming.

"Mason, how are you?" he asks, stepping forward.

When we shake hands, he uses his left hand to cover the back of my hand, the way charming people do.

"I've already expressed my condolences to Betty, but I'd like to say the same to you, especially regarding Charlie, knowing he was your good friend. He was a good man."

"Thank you, Peter. That's real decent of you."

It's nice hearing somebody say something positive about old Charlie. I'm still feeling down about some of the stuff the wives dumped on me.

Turning back to Betty, he says, "I'll talk to you later. Maybe we can work something out."

"That will be fine."

Watching him exit, she wearily rubs her forehead. "I'd rather keep working. I don't know what would happen if all I did was dwell on these dreadful deaths."

She locks the door and pulls down the shade. Almost as if it's an effort, she walks back to where I am. What a terrible strain she's under.

Suddenly, her composure crumbles. She starts crying uncontrollably and puts her head on my chest the way a child might. Too exhausted to move, she stays like that even after the sobs subside. I'm glad she feels at ease enough to use me for that, although she probably would've turned to just about anyone for a little comfort at that moment.

Still leaning against me, she lifts her head and tries to pull herself together. "I'm sorry, Mason." Removing a tissue from her sleeve, she dabs her eyes.

"Hey, that's what friends are for."

She looks up and manages a smile. "Thanks for that too."

Gazing at her, I realize fully for the first time what Charlie found so attractive about her. Her clear eyes reveal more than determination and intelligence. There's a vulnerability and an innocence there as well that's strange for a woman her age. It makes her appear, well, beautiful. The kind of beauty that doesn't come from the slant of eyes, the shape of cheekbones or noses, or the fullness of lips. It's a kind of inner light.

Suddenly, I'm very conscious of the heat and soft contours of her body through her silk dress. As she presses against me, I wonder if she is too. Suddenly, our holding each other doesn't seem so much comforting as an embrace. Awkwardly, we step away from one another. I have a troubled feeling of disloyalty to both Charlie and Amanda Kay for what's crossing my mind.

"I'll be back in a minute," Betty says.

Keeping her eyes lowered, she goes to the back room. I know she doesn't want to look at me directly because of that erotic moment.

I understand a little of what transpired. Death makes life that much more precious. In the face of death, the living are drawn to the most vital and most primitive forces within them. Sex is one of our most powerful and basic drives: the desire to obliterate ourselves in that exquisite state where time and space dissolve.

When she returns, she's freshened up, but there's still a splotchiness around her eyes that makeup can't completely hide. She carries a manila envelope that she holds out to me. The front is marked: *Please Give to Mason Collins Upon My Death*. The initials under it are *C.W.D.*

Betty folds her arms defensively across her chest. Looking at me, she unconsciously takes a step backward.

"I found that in Charlie's desk along with his insurance forms, ownership papers for the boat, and his other important documents."

The envelope is a little bulky, but I know what's inside. Charlie and I had promised one another certain personal possessions if either of us died before the other. This is his statement officially handing over his fly rod and reel, that crumby old Chevy, and some other pieces of his life.

It makes me feel bad, and I don't want to open the package. Charlie had believed in death and I hadn't. I never even drew up a general will, let alone set aside a special addendum of odds and ends for Charlie. But then I have less to leave anybody than I once thought Charlie had.

As I make ready to go, I smile tentatively at Betty, not sure what to do. Neither of us are.

"Well, good-bye, Betty."

"Good-bye, Mason."

Tentatively, she touches my arm. Her hand rests there for what might be a millisecond or five minutes. All I know is that the heat of that touch is as erotic as when she pressed against me.

Finally moving away, Betty opens the door. If she didn't, I don't know what might've happened. Well, I do, and I'm not sure whether it would have been right or wrong. Just nature acting out the cosmic dance.

▪▪▪▪ 15 ▪▪▪▪

As I walk into his shop, Precious is talking to a well-dressed old lady who's holding a rose-colored vase. Though wearing a cool-looking green-and-yellow-striped shirt with white Bermuda shorts, he's obviously frazzled.

"Madam, I simply cannot sell it for that price!"

A grandmotherly type, the customer's reed thin, with wispy blue hair and a relentless gaze. Hunched forward, she has the vase tucked in the crook of her arm like a football. She's ready to straight-arm him and dash out of the store.

"I can get one just like it in New York for thirty-seven fifty and I'm not paying a penny more," she declares.

Precious's shoulders sag with resignation. Victorious, the woman eases her grip. Suddenly, his hand snakes out and snatches the vase away as if taking a bone from a bad dog. His face is crimson with fury.

"Out! Out! Out!" he commands, pointing at the open door.

Momentarily shocked, the lady's mouth drops open like a ventriloquist's dummy's. "Well, I never," she scolds, and storms away.

A FOOL'S DEATH

Precious roughly dusts off the vase as though she might've left a hex on it. "The public. The glorious public," he mutters. Raising his voice, he calls after her, "Bring back capital punishment for old witches!"

Turning to me, he pats his face, which is beading with nervous sweat. His expression is one of determination. "Mason, if I turn into a mean old thing, shoot me. No, don't argue with me. I mean it. Shoot me. If I wind up like *that* old thing, I'd rather be dead!"

"Okay."

Suddenly, he's crestfallen. "You would too, wouldn't you? I know. I know. Do the world a favor. Shoot an old fairy. Sometimes I really wonder why I bother going on. What's the use? People just want to shoot me!"

He flounces to the back of the store and disappears behind a colored beaded curtain into his storeroom.

I call after him. "You phoned. I assume it's about the coin . . . or do you want me to shoot you now?"

"Ha ha" comes from the other side of the curtain.

When he returns, he's holding the coin. He apparently decides to drop the issue of my personal guarantee for euthanasia.

"I thought I might be right about this when I first saw it. And I was. Well, I was, but I wasn't. You see, it might have been, but then I thought, 'Well, maybe it's not.' . . ."

Stepping back, I stare at him while he jabbers in that nutty mental shorthand a lot of people who live alone fall into at times. He doesn't fill in details for anybody who didn't go through his thought processes with him.

"In God's name, Precious, what the hell are you talking about?"

"Don't blaspheme, Mason," he says, finally noticing the exasperated expression I wear whenever he goes on like this. "Well, there's no reason to raise your voice."

Without letting me get a word in edgewise, he explains, "I said the coin was Spanish, which it is, but it was struck in Mexico. Mexico first had a mint about 1600 and coined Spanish currency until 1811. This is a doubloon and was minted in 1620."

He puts the coin down atop the coin case. "Look," he commands.

I stoop over. "So?"

"See the eagle facing right?"

The upright, fierce-looking eagle is spread-winged and has a snake in its beak. "Uh-huh."

"Well, before that, coins were printed with the eagle in profile facing left and leaning over with the snake dangling from the beak."

"What's it mean?"

"It means . . ." He pauses dramatically. "That little coin would fetch about three thousand dollars today. Very rare. Most of them around today came from ships that were carrying bullion back to Spain and sank. That means, my dear Mason, the chances are highly probable that your coin came from a salvage operation. Some daring souls found a sunken treasure."

That substantiates young Donne's tale. The origins of the family fortune. Now all I have to do is find the connection between seventeenth-century booty and twentieth-century murders. If there is one. I always keep a sliver of doubt open about anything or anybody. It's a quality that's generally good for business but particularly lousy for relationships with women.

"Any way of pinpointing which particular shipwreck this might've come from?" I ask.

Touching his lower lip with his forefinger, Precious considers the possibility. "What's logical is that the ship left Mexico in 1620 or 1621. Generally, it was newly minted doubloons that were shipped back to Spain. I suppose there is some way of finding the names of Spanish galleons that sank during that period, but I don't know how."

"Thanks for all the help."

"It was no bother really. Actually, it was fascinating. I've never had one of those coins in my hands before. Besides, this was little enough after what you did for me during that Willard Massey business." He shudders as he thinks again about that incident.

Willard Massey was a doctor from Chapel Hill, North Carolina, who contracted with Precious to sell off his coin collection, which was valued at $250,000. Naturally, Precious was proud to receive the assignment. Maybe he blabbed about it to too many people. In any event, thieves broke into his house and stole the coins.

I never saw Precious or maybe anybody else in such a state after he found the collection missing. He was so ashen when he came to my office, I thought he'd go into cardiac arrest. To make a long story short, the pair of robbers turned up drugged out on Long Key, where I retrieved the valuables. That was five or six years ago, and Precious has done plenty of favors for me in the meanwhile.

"Anything you want, Precious, just let me know."

He looks at me with concern. "There is one thing."

"What's that?"

"Please forget that business we were discussing about when I grow very old."

"I'm dismayed. You didn't say 'very old.' You just said 'old.'"

"Mason, you can be trying. 'Old,' 'very old,' what difference does it make? Just forget it."

"Okay, but remember."

"Remember what?" he asks irritably.

"You change your mind and you know where to find me."

His face turns crimson. "Out," he screams, pointing at the door. "Out! Out!"

Walking away, I ponder the human psyche as Marlene's death comes crashing back in. How could I even momentarily forget her tragedy? One reason, I guess, is that Precious hardly knew her, so I didn't think it necessary to mention her murder. But how could I forget even for a few moments? My feet begin moving in the direction of the Lopez Funeral Home. As an act of contrition, I renew my vow to catch the killer.

■ ■ ■ ■ 16 ■ ■ ■ ■

AT Lopez's, a handsome black woman resembling a sleek panther is holding down the reception desk in the office off the entry. Bent over a typewriter, she's wearing an orange sundress. Her eyes are slightly slanted and her hair is short. She's intent on what she's doing.

"Sis, is Doc Wilson in?"

Margie Collins looks up, scowling. "Mason, didn't I tell you my mama finds it insulting that you claim to be part of our family?"

"Margie, that's what my mama always said too."

Throwing back her head, she lets out a rich laugh. "You are *too* much."

Still shaking her head, she presses an extension button on her five-button phone board. "Dr. Wilson, there is a large, disheveled man here who would like to see you."

Lopez's is where autopsies are usually conducted in Key West. Claiming a variety of hokey reasons, the local hospital won't let the coroner do his business there. I think I know why. The hospital likes to distance itself from death. "The Big D" is bad for business.

Doc Wilson often fills in down here when the county coroner is away. When I walk into the mortuary a few minutes later, he gives me a grim look.

"I've been expecting you. Griswold told me what you said."

Without any frills, he launches into his findings. "There was alcohol in her system, enough that she could've lost her balance and fallen face first into the pool. There was a slight concussion. Most likely enough to cause her to black out when her forehead struck the edge of the pool so she couldn't move her face out of the water. There's no conjecture about this last part. She drowned."

He stares at me defensively. A short, compact man with an iron gray crew cut, he stoops a little and watches through horn-rimmed glasses that are too big for his face and make him look like a little old boy as well as a schnauzer. Joe's a decent guy who filled in off and on for the coroner for almost thirty years. Nobody ever thought much one way or the other about whether he was up to the job.

His inadequacy came to light in an embarrassing fashion a few months ago. He testified at a rape-murder trial as a witness for the prosecution, when the DA thought he had the goods on a young drifter. Wilson was the coroner who had examined the seventeen-year-old victim. An expert witness for the defense, a pathologist from up north, gave testimony on something Joe missed. The genetic breakdown of the semen found in the young girl's body was different from the defendant's. Joe has said he won't seek to renew his contract to do autopsies when it runs out in six months. Unfortunately, he did Marlene's.

"There's nothing unusual at all," he says accusingly, as though reading my mind. He pauses for a moment before finishing. "That is, other than her having died in an unusual way."

Indicating that our conversation is over, he turns away as though he has some important business at hand. Abruptly, he spins around, glaring. "Case closed!"

One look at my face tells him it isn't.

▪ ▪ ▪ ▪ 17 ▪ ▪ ▪ ▪

AT my office, I lean back in my chair and stare at the envelope Betty gave me. I'm not up to reading a last note from Charlie, so I push it back farther on the desk with my toe. Instead, I try to imagine what's going on in the killer's mind. He found Charlie and he killed him. He found Charlie's wives, and he killed one of them.

What's with the timing? Hell, he knocked off Uncle Gerald a long time ago. He did in Charlie's dad only seven months ago. Charlie four days ago. Marlene last night or early this morning.

The escalation in the rapidity of the deaths must mean something. Maybe the hunter is pressed. He feels time is running out. But why? He can't keep trying to kill the wives right now. Even Doc Wilson would have a tough time rationalizing such coincidences.

Maybe the killer doesn't care. Hell, his sending the maps means he must *want* people to know the "accidental deaths" are murders. Obviously he's crazy. Maybe he wants to come out of the closet, let people know how clever he is. Maybe he hopes to get caught. Maybe he thinks it makes no difference one way or another if the authorities realize the victims were murdered. Maybe having people terrified is a new twist on his fun.

The only clue I have is that the identity of the killer is buried somewhere in Charlie's past. That's not much of a clue.

I spend the rest of the day trying to dig up what background I can on the Donnes. A credit check on Donne Salvage Enterprise. A Dun & Bradstreet report on the company. The Maritime Association. I get hold of a detective I know in Philadelphia and ask him to nose around, and I ask him to get me whatever newspaper clippings there are on the Donnes and their company.

A lot of guys down here go treasure hunting, some as a hobby, some out of desperation to hit a jackpot, some as reasonable people willing to take an interesting long shot. I call one of those who is somewhat sane about it to find out who's still around who was diving for gold when the Donnes were.

While I work, I leave on the answering machine, so I won't be disturbed. Huff calls wanting an update. The garage calls again. Georgie Two Foot calls, leaving a terse message. "It's about the lady. The Empire Lounge. After eight P.M." A woman name of Gooden wants me to find her husband; she leaves a phone number with a 312 area code, which is Chicago. A man wanting me to give to "Save the Beasts" or some such organization dials up too. When Joe Clark's voice comes on, I cut in and talk to him.

"What have you come up with, Joe?"

"Nothing. That's why I called. I'm still jammed up and wanted to tell you. I'll try to get to it tomorrow, if that's okay?"

"No problem," I say, not sure whether I'm right. Joe's like that, very precise. He's a stickler for detail but can drive you crazy telling you he hasn't done something yet. I guess his job demands it. There are times he even has the president on his ass.

"I can fax it down to you when I get it. What's your fax number?"

"Joe, you know better."

There's a short laugh. "Mason, I forgot how out of step with the twentieth century you are down there. I guess it's progress that you have a phone."

"If you have the post office send it overnight, I'll buy you a drink when you hit town."

"Okay, but I expected that anyway."

I cradle the phone and stretch. Glancing outside, I realize how late it is. Evening has stolen the day away, and I remember Georgie Two Foot's message.

■ ■ ■ ■ **18** ■ ■ ■ ■

THE Empire Lounge is a distance from the office, so I take a cab. I like the place because it has a hint of lewdness. Even so, I don't spend too much time out here. For one, I'm not overly fond of lewdness. For another, I'm lazy. Most of my drinking is done within walking distance of my apartment.

Georgie Two Foot's at the bar and gives me a big grin. "Howdy, Mason."

"How are you, Georgie?"

"Good, Mason. Good."

"On the house, Mason." The bartender slides a beer across the bar.

"Thanks, Russ."

"How about me?" Georgie whines.

"How about paying last month's tab?" Russ retorts.

A notorious freeloader, Georgie pretends he didn't hear. Georgie doesn't look like much, just a poor frog. He's pudgy with a half-bald head. What's left of his black hair is slicked back over the collar of his western shirt. He wears a string tie, cowboy boots, a maroon shirt, and pants with saddle stitching. If it weren't for the clothes and the drawl that he picked up somewhere, you'd still take him for the Latino accountant he once was.

His nickname refers to his passion. On a dance floor, he's no longer a homely, little, middle-aged man but someone who moves like quicksilver and is enchanting to behold.

He lit into town a few years ago and never looked back to New York, where he last lived and worked. Work isn't important to him. Dancing is. He refuses to do any accounting jobs. He drives a kind of tourist train and fills in at a rent-a-moped place. He dances just about every night. And he's one of my tipsters.

The country and western music turns a little raunchy. Heads swivel toward the little runway behind the bar.

"Here she comes," Georgie whispers.

A good-looking brunette struts onto the stage. She wears a red sequin dress and red high heels. From the music and the patrons' yelps, you can tell she'll have her shoes on a lot longer than the rest of her clothes.

Sure enough, less than five minutes later she's shimmying, wearing only the shoes and a little red sequin bikini bottom. She's surprisingly good and has nice tits. I was right about her looking like a colt. Her rump is high and fine. I'm glad the smile on her face seems genuine.

I write out a little note, hand it to Russ, and take a table in a far corner of the barroom. A little while later, the lady comes and sits opposite me. Up close, she's prettier than her picture. Now she's wearing a navy silk robe and an expression of rock-hard determination.

"How did you find me?" she demands, staring defiantly into my eyes.

"That's not the point. What do you want to do now that you've been found?"

"Is Harold in Key West?"

"Yes."

A FOOL'S DEATH

Her gaze falters, but she recovers just as quickly. "Does he know where I am?" Suddenly, the belligerence collapses. She sounds afraid.

"No, and it's up to you whether you want him to know or not."

Confusion creeps across her features. She grips the edge of the table so hard her knuckles turn white. "What do you mean?"

"I won't tell him if you don't want me to. He's already agreed to that."

Her body relaxes and her face sags. Tears film her eyes. Her robe starts to open. It's kind of touching after what she's just been doing that she quickly pulls the garment around her before anything shows.

"Look, mister—"

"Mason," I interrupt. "And I liked your show."

"Mason," she says. "I tried and tried to make a good marriage with Harold, but it was impossible. He . . . he humiliated me."

Her voice breaks off and the tears flow. "He . . . he started hitting me. We didn't have children . . . there was nothing to stay for."

She seems like a nice woman and what she says sounds terrible. I'm not particularly fond of Harold myself.

"Beverly, would you mind writing a little note to the effect that you want Harold to leave you alone?"

"Of course."

She goes over to Russ, borrows a pen and notepad, and comes back. After a minute's consideration, she writes:

> Please leave me alone, Harold. It's really over. Nothing you can do will ever change my mind.
>
> Beverly

Handing me the note, she fixes her face. "I've got to get back for another number."

"I wasn't kidding. You're good."

"Thanks. I'm doing this until I can sort out what I want. Come and see me again."

"Definitely. And have a good life from here on in."

She smiles for the first time. "I intend to."

It's nice talking for a change to a woman who wasn't once married to Charlie. I don't have to worry about keeping her alive until she gets out of town.

■ ■ ■ ■ **19** ■ ■ ■ ■

*M*Y apartment is on the second floor of a worn building that has seen kinder days. Above me is Miss Julie, an aged actress who was once on Broadway. When she gets into her cups, she reminisces and acts out a lot of her old roles. You have to keep a close eye on her when she does, especially when she's on her porch. She plays a lot of characters who swoon, and she almost goes right over the railing.

Below me are two young cops. They're nice guys who give me classified information, keep burglars away because of their profession, and give me a little dope once in a while when they unexpectedly find themselves with a bit of contraband pot after a raid.

Once the house was grand. There are three stories topped by a widow's walk. Generous porches, lots of eaves, and intricate gingerbread are everywhere, and the yard is big. Today the house is moldering like Miss Havisham's wedding cake and is probably a lot like the place old Count von Cosel brought Elena Hoyos back to.

Hell, it might be the same place. Porch rails are missing, paint hasn't threatened the exterior for decades, and everything, including the floors, lists a bit to the east. The yard is so overgrown you could hide Long John Silver and his retinue of thieves in there and they'd never be found.

I like it just fine. The apartment is nice and roomy. There's plenty of sunlight. I've got my own porch, and best of all, it's highly affordable. I climb the flight of outdoor steps to my porch and see that Amanda Kay has dug in the flowerpot in the right place for the key. I let myself in and am surprised.

"Hello, Mason."

That salutation echoes twice more. All three wives sit around the coffee table in the living room. Safety in numbers. A bottle of gin, one of tonic, slices of lime, a bowl of ice, three tall glasses, and my .38 are in the middle of the table, all within easy reach of any of them.

"Evening." I get that slightly awkward feeling all over again with the awareness of being outnumbered. "Actually, I'm glad you're all here. I want to say the same thing to each of you anyway."

I head to the kitchen, grab a beer from the refrigerator, and take a chair that isn't my favorite because Virginia is parked in that one. The wives look at me expectantly, as if I know what the hell I'm doing and might say something profound. Under different circumstances, that look would make me grin.

"How about each of you getting out of town?"

Obviously disappointed, the women look at one another. Virginia reacts first. She stands up, hands on her hips. "Mason, I will not be run out of town! Some son of a bitch killed Marlene and Charlie. If he tries to get me, he'll wish he hadn't."

Reaching into the straw bag at her feet, she pulls out a .22-caliber pistol. "It's not big and it's not pretty, but it can do the job, and I've known how to shoot since I was thirteen. I've got this on me all the time, and I keep my shotgun by my side at home. If anybody comes around me, I'll blow his head off."

She's convincing. "Virginia, will you put that damned pistol away and sit down."

Betty doesn't stand or do anything else physical to make her case, but she's just as powerful. "I'm not leaving either. I hate to run from problems, and I don't think this is one that can be run from. If the killer wants us dead, there's nowhere to hide. He tracked Charlie down. He will track us down the same way."

She makes sense. Running might only buy time. But I have to be sure she'll be reasonably safe.

"Betty, you can't stay at your house. You're too vulnerable there."

"I know. I'm staying at the little apartment over the gallery. The only entrance is up one flight of stairs and there's a door at the top of the steps. I had a police lock put on the door this afternoon. Besides, the police, Virginia, and Amanda Kay will check on me. We're going to check on each other."

Turning to my right, I ask, "So that means you're staying, Amanda Kay?"

She has a temper, but she's not a woman who gets as quickly riled up as Virginia, nor is she as analytical as Betty. But she's a pretty strong feminist and I expect her answer to have something to do with sisterhood sticking together.

"I'm afraid so, Mason. Here we've got each other. If we leave, we've got nobody but ourselves to count on."

Then she gives me the full wattage of her smile, and I feel as if I'm basking in the sun. "And here we've got you."

Another wave of anxiety washes over me. So much confidence is being placed in me. What a hell of a guardian angel. I can barely fend for myself. Even so, I try to sound a little more reliable than a crack addict when I respond.

"I'll do whatever I can. But never go out alone. When you do go someplace, have the police drive you home from wherever you are. Griswold will go along with that. His men will check on you every night. Why don't you arrange some signal for the police when you're home so they know everything's okay?"

"How about a light in the front window?" Virginia suggests. "When the police see the light, they can routinely stop in and check on us as they make their rounds."

A FOOL'S DEATH

"How about two lights," Betty says. "Just to make them easier for the police to see."

"Good," Virginia says, adding gin to each of the women's glasses. "That's even better."

"You can't stay at your place either," I say to Amanda Kay.

"I've got a couple of other teachers who will drive me back and forth to school," she says. "I told them to pick me up and drop me off here."

"In for the duration, huh?" I'm pleased by what she just said.

"You better watch yourself," she answers. "I might make a habit of it."

Everybody laughs with a sense of relief. Maybe me more than anyone else. Things are happening so unnaturally fast that her being with me now seems natural. My being responsible for all three of them somehow seems natural too, much the way a hair shirt grows comfortable on a masochist.

"Before you came home," Virginia says, "we were comparing notes again on Charlie to see if we could find anything that might give us a clue to the killer."

The others nod.

"We decided the killer had to know Charlie before he ever came to Key West," Betty says.

"Why's that?" I ask, even though I'm glad they arrived at a conclusion similar to mine.

"He didn't make those kind of enemies here," Amanda Kay answers. "So it must be this family vendetta he talked about."

"Shortly after we were married, he ran up some big gambling debts," Virginia says. "We were almost wiped out, but we paid them off. There was a little threatening business from a bookie, but nothing ever came of it."

The heavy betting is news to me. The only gambling I knew Charlie ever did was the monthly poker game a group of us have in Josh Foster's law office up two blocks on Duval from my office. The stakes are low, and more talking among friends goes on than gambling.

I'm getting more resigned than depressed now that the wives

start griping about my friend again. There's so much I don't know about Charlie that I start wondering who the hell it was I knew.

"Something traumatic happened to him when he was very young," Betty says. "I don't know what it was because he would never discuss it. It used to infuriate me that he refused to talk about that or anything else that was bothering him."

"Don't I know that feeling," Amanda Kay says. "There were times when I wanted to kill him for not talking about what bugged him. I don't know whether there was a tragedy in his youth or not, but he drove me crazy when he just clammed up and you knew something was real wrong."

"Funny," Virginia says. "I'd almost forgotten that. He always made me feel guilty because I didn't know how to reach him when he was like that. That just made me all the madder."

I rub my eyes as I try to figure something out. "Could I please ask a question?"

"Go right ahead," Virginia says magnanimously.

"If old Charlie was so smothered in problems, why did you all marry him? Why the hell did two of you stay with him until he up and left one day? And why were all four wives concerned enough about how he died to want to find out why?"

The dead silence in the room lasts a full minute.

Finally, Virginia pipes up. "Mason, I've asked myself those same questions. It's hard for me to put into words. If I were painting, it would be a reddish gold glow. That's what Charlie did to me."

Betty nods her head slowly. "That's what it was, Mason. When he loved you, he loved you. It was the greatest feeling in the world."

"And you never stop hoping that someone will feel that way about you again someday," Amanda Kay says.

Betty glances around. "It's getting late. We should be leaving."

I call a cab and offer for me and Amanda Kay to go with them to make sure they get home safely.

"No," Virginia said. "You're not always going to be around,

Mason. I'll drop Betty off and check her place out. We've got to learn to fend for ourselves."

"Virginia's right, Mason," Betty says. "We'll have the cabdriver come into our places with us."

A bit later, the taxi horn honks, and Amanda Kay and I escort them downstairs. As she climbs into the cab, Betty looks up at me. "Did you go through what Charlie left for you?"

"No, not yet."

She looks a little disappointed, and I feel a tad guilty again. Here Charlie took the care to set something aside for me, and I sort of backhand him by not going through it right away.

"It's at the office. I'll go through it tomorrow morning."

Betty smiles wryly. "I'm sure it's nothing. It's just that when I saw his handwriting on the envelope, I thought you would want to go through it right away. It was silly of me."

Amanda Kay puts her arm around my waist. Guilt returns in spades as the cab speeds away. As we walk back to the apartment, I wonder if I can ever love her with the intensity Charlie did.

▪ ▪ ▪ ▪ 20 ▪ ▪ ▪ ▪

THE next morning, I hit the office early. My anxiety's in high gear as I check again with the school to make sure Amanda Kay arrived unharmed. Next, I call Harold Thompkins and tell him to come by the office.

After debating for a moment, I decide not to return the garage's call. Maybe I will later in the day. After paying the back rent on the apartment and the current rent on the office and a few other bills, most of my advances are gone. I'll use Thompkins's second check to ransom the vehicle. I'm not sure whether I'll keep my jeep or sell it now that I have Charlie's car, which looks a little worse than the jeep but runs better.

The packet bearing my name and Charlie's initials leers up at me from the desk, and I gingerly stretch my hand toward it. I don't really know why I'm so reluctant. I guess it's the prospect of reading the note inside. It'll be Charlie talking to me from the grave.

Disgusted by my procrastination, I finally grab and tear open the envelope. Inside is a sheaf of typewritten pages, which is yet another discovery about my friend. I never knew Charlie could type.

The dreaded note's on top.

I start reading and realize I'd made yet another foolish assumption. He hasn't left me an extension of his will. He hasn't left me any of his belongings. What the letter contains is an insight into a terrible part of Charlie's past. And he tells me who the killer is.

Dear Mace,

The note actually begins that way. The nickname is one that he called me on only one other occasion. I doubt if anybody other than the wives knew he did that because I swore to cause him bodily harm if he ever addressed me as that in public. Anyway, I guess he knew he could get away with it now.

> This is a story. A real one. I wrote it from a notebook I kept when I was a fifteen-year-old kid. If I died an obscene death, keep reading. Here you'll find out why I was murdered and who killed my father, my uncle, and me. I tried to get him before it was too late. But it was like trying to grab hold of the wind. I lost his trail, but I'm not sure he has lost mine.
>
> Thanks for taking on this last request of mine. Get him, pal.
>
> Have a good life,
> Charlie

What Led Up To My Death

I'll start with a little bit of background that led up to the salvage operation that destroyed my family. Here goes.

My father was one of those men in love with get-rich-quick schemes. We were always moving around the country. Texas and Oklahoma, where he tried to break into the oil business. Washington, where he tried fish hatcheries. A vineyard in California and land development in Florida. Uncle Gerry was always his partner. By the time I was twelve, I'd been in eight different schools.

My father was a great salesman. He always found financial backers for his schemes. I saw the way he charmed them. It wasn't really charm, but a zealous belief that what he said was true. He got consumed by an interest like growing grapes in California and read everything he could about the subject. He visited vineyards and wineries and got statistics that were always impressive.

When he spoke to potential backers, he was a man with a mission. They would double, triple, quadruple their investment in no time. He always made it sound as if there was hardly any risk because that was what he wanted to believe. People gave him hundreds of thousands of dollars, maybe a million or more over the years, to get his schemes off the ground. None of them ever worked out.

In a way, it wasn't his fault. He worked hard and invested the money, but he never grasped the variables of any business whether it was storms or a recession that could wipe you out, or simply the fact that money was often only made by trial and error and stick-to-itiveness, which was his shortcoming.

Inevitably, he hit upon gold. Soon he could think of nothing else. His passion was infectious. I saw him talk about it and other men's eyes lit up almost as brightly as his. He wasn't talking about mining but salvaging. We were in California at the time, and my father and Uncle Gerry had taken up scuba diving, which was then in its infancy.

Divers in the area spent weekends looking for treasure in old wrecks. It was talking to them that he heard about the Spanish galleons that used to carry hundreds of millions of dollars in gold and silver from Latin America to

Spain. A lot of the ships sank. The treasure has been waiting for centuries for men with the balls to take it. That was my father's kind of venture.

One day he announced that we were moving to Florida where he and Uncle Gerry were going into the salvage business. He had already sold most of what we had. We were supposed to sell the rest of our belongings and drive across the country one more time. My mother refused to go along. She told him he could do what he wanted, but she was taking me back to Philadelphia. When he came to his senses, she said, he could join us there and get a real job like a normal husband and father.

He and Uncle Gerry drove us to Philadelphia and we moved in with my grandmother. My father gave my mother most of the money he had. He promised to return for us in six months, eight at the most, and left with his brother for Florida.

By the time I was fifteen, my father and his brother, my uncle Gerry, had been in the Caribbean for the better part of two and a half years. Twice they had some minor scores, and my dad came up and visited each time. He gave us each a gold doubloon and bubbled over with stories about the treasures in the sea.

There were other sporadic visits. The rest of our contact with him was in the form of letters and phone calls telling us that they verged on a major discovery. The immediacy of the discovery kept getting delayed for one reason or another. My father wasn't lying. He wasn't like that. He truly believed he'd strike his fortune the next day. His enthusiasm never waned. In five minutes on the phone with him, you would believe he was going to bring up millions in silver and gold bullion, just like he said.

The spring of my sophomore year in high school, my father asked my mother to let me work with him and Uncle Gerry for the summer. With a great deal of reluctance and after a good deal of pleading on my part, she agreed.

A FOOL'S DEATH

You will never guess where he was living then. Key West! I flew into Miami and my uncle Gerry was waiting for me and drove me down here. He said my father was diving all day and would see me that night. I was more than a little resentful that he'd put the treasure hunt ahead of me.

Even though I'd wanted to come, I was angry at him anyway for putting this crazy business ahead of my mother and me for years. But his manic diving at all hours of the day and night, often day after day with little or no sleep, was just another indication of how much the gold fever had infected him. He was a man obsessed. But more about that in a little while.

The gorgeous aquamarine water, the clear sky that stretched on and on, and the sense that you were on an outpost of civilization made me fall in love with the Keys, especially because civilization seemed only as deep as a film of sand on a windshield. I loved Key West most of all as soon as I got here. Philadelphia was a stodgy city where young people didn't seem to have any place. Right away I knew Key West was where I could bust wide open and nobody would give a damn.

My uncle was the younger of the two. A quiet man who avoided controversy, he always wound up agreeing with my father, who would steamroller over him, the way he usually did my mother and most other people. When I asked Uncle Gerry how things were going, he replied, "Well, your father thinks everything's going great guns, Charlie."

Later I'd start asking him, "What do you think, Uncle Gerry? Not what your brother thinks. What do you think?"

But none of it really mattered. Not after what they were about to do.

Uncle Gerry drove to a marina. They were living on an old houseboat, which to a teenager who'd been living in a musty stone house with his mother and grandmother was exotic as hell. The houseboat fit right in with the dreams I had about swimming, fishing, diving, and yes, finding sunken treasure.

My father didn't get back until after midnight. "Tomorrow's the day, Charlie," he said when he grabbed me in a bear hug. "Tomorrow's the day we bring it up. And you'll be there to share it with me."

You can't believe how excited that made me and how sweet those words were. He and I sharing in this adventure. All the mad I felt toward him fell away. By the time I got to bed that night, I could scarcely sleep. When I did, I dreamed of sunken treasure.

The next morning we were up and off by dawn. My father and uncle had an old seaplane, and within minutes we were soaring over the Keys. I was amazed. From the maps I'd pored over, I had thought Key West was the last key. But from 2,000 feet up, you could see thousands of others dribbling westward along the 70 miles from Key West to the Dry Tortugas.

"Most of those islands don't have people living on them and don't even have names," my father said.

He pointed to the hardly broken line of reefs that ran along there too. "See that deep blue sea on the other side of the reefs? That's the Gulf Stream, the river the Spaniards used to carry their ships and their gold home just like it was a highway. They sailed north out of Havana until they saw these islands. They knew the reef was there and how dangerous it was. The islands were their checkpoints."

The galleons sailed these waters before the chronometer or the barometer were invented, so they had no means of telling longitude, nor any scientific way of forecasting weather. When a storm came up, those big old ships didn't stand a chance. You couldn't stop and you couldn't go in reverse. Sometimes entire fleets smashed into the reefs and went down. I'll bet every one of those islands took tribute from the Spaniards.

My father said the wreck we were going after was a galleon named the *Santa Lucia*, which was one of the biggest for the times, almost 600 tons. She sank in 1620.

"Think of that, Charlie," he said. "More than three hundred years ago and just waiting for us."

Uncle Gerry put the plane down near one of the uncharted islands and we taxied up to *The Doubloon*, their old tugboat that was operating as a salvage boat.

There were buoys in the water, which I learned marked the salvage site. One buoy was anchored to the reef the galleon struck, another to one of the ship's anchors they'd found, another to one of the ship's cannons. The problem as I later learned was that a ship's cargo could have been strewn for miles after it struck the reef and sank. But my father, the optimist, didn't like to take that into consideration.

"You'll meet the other man working with us now," he said.

"I didn't know you had a partner other than Uncle Gerry."

"His name is Nick Andalusia. He's got a small stake because it was his map that helped more than anything else in locating where the *Santa Lucia* went down. He's . . . he's a little strange, but he's okay."

The way he said it made me apprehensive. After I met Nick, I felt even more so. When we went on board, he had his back to us and was kneeling, fixing some gear.

"Nick, I want you to meet my son, Charlie."

He turned and was on his feet quick as a cat, which was amazing for a man that big. He was a good six three with massive shoulders, and muscular. He was completely bald and had a big, droopy Pancho Villa mustache. What struck you more than his physique was his eyes. He was the first and only man I ever met who had yellow eyes that made him look like someone damned. What he said didn't endear me to him either.

"This is a dangerous place, kid. Don't get in the way. You do and you go straight back. You get in trouble and

A FOOL'S DEATH

you get yourself out. You die out here, it's your fault and I won't try to help you."

My father glared at him but tried to make light of it. "I told you Nick was a little strange, but looking for gold will do that to a man."

We didn't find gold that day, the next, or the next. I didn't mind. The time passed quickly as we shuttled back and forth between the salvage boat and Key West. Usually, the shuttle trip was made by Uncle Gerry and me. My father and Nick stayed out at sea, diving night and day, both of them possessed by the same demon that drives men beyond the realms of reason.

For me, the whole venture was fascinating. I learned to scuba dive and how to use salvage gear like the portable air compressor that blasts away sand on the seafloor so you can see if treasure is hidden there. I fished when I wanted, which was every day. Back in Key West, I ran kind of wild. I started smoking and drinking and I met a girl. I would have wound up totally dissolute if I hadn't always had a passion for reading.

There were plenty of books on board both *The Doubloon* and the houseboat, especially history and poetry because Uncle Gerry read a lot of that. I probably learned more during that summer than I ever did during any other period in my life. There were even documents about the *Santa Lucia* that my father had a researcher get for him at the Archives of the Indies, a library in Seville that houses literally millions of documents pertaining to the Spanish trading ships that sailed the world.

The documents confirmed that the ship had indeed carried a rich cargo. There were 240,000 newly minted pieces of eight for circulation in Spain, 871 silver bars each weighing about 70 pounds, and 154 gold items weighing 211.8 pounds that were registered, and probably about the same amount in contraband had been smuggled on board. They kept detailed records.

Within a short time, I was an expert on the great Spanish treasure fleets that for centuries made Spain the richest nation in the world. For 250 years, the Spaniards sent two fleets a year to the Americas. One, the Main Fleet, the *Flota de Tierra Ferma*, went to South America. The other, the New Spain Fleet, the *Flota de Nueva España*, went to Veracruz, Mexico.

The fleets sailed together, or one sailed in the spring and the other in the fall. They headed south in the direction of the Canary Islands to pick up the westward trade winds to cross the Atlantic. The *Flota de Nueva*, consisting of 16 ships including the *Santa Lucia*, headed northwest once they hit the Caribbean and passed between Cuba and the Yucatán peninsula to make it to Veracruz.

A ship like the *Santa Lucia* would have seemed huge. It was 100 feet long, had a forecastle and sterncastle that rose 35 feet above the ship's waterline, two main decks, four decks at the sterncastle, and three masts. You have to realize that this ship was about 600 tons while Columbus's ships were less than 100 tons each when he discovered America. She was also equipped with a lot of firepower because of fear of Dutch raiders.

The *Santa Lucia* was the fleet's flagship and commanded by Marqués de Cordoba. A man like Cordoba knew it would be seven months or more before he saw home again. If he made it. Galleons like his let the Spaniards exploit the New World and create an empire. By the midseventeenth century, Mexico City had a population of more than 100,000, which made it bigger than Spain's biggest cities, Toledo and Seville. To show how modern the place was, there were even inquisitions.

The *Santa Lucia* got into trouble during the voyage home. On September 11 a hurricane pounded in. Waves turned monstrous. Hurricane-force winds tore at the sails as sailors raced up the rigging to take them in. The ship pitched violently. As the crew and passengers watched in horror, the hurricane hurtled the *Santa Lucia* toward the reefs and certain death. Of the 259 people on board, two sailors and a slave lived to recount the tragedy.

So much for ancient history. Let me get back to more recent times. One of the reasons why the *Santa Lucia* wasn't found was that, until Jacques Cousteau and Émile Gagnan invented scuba gear during the Second World War, you couldn't go treasure hunting the way you can now. Divers used to go down in those old rubberized canvas suits with the screw-on helmets that weigh a ton. It was too expensive and really dangerous to go after treasure in those clumsy rigs.

Another reason why nobody had gone after the *Santa Lucia* was that nobody knew quite where to find her. A lot of men had poked around but always came up emptyhanded. About all that was known was that she went down in the Lower Keys, but beyond that not much else. That was until Nick and his map came along.

Nick was hazy when I asked him one time how he got the map. I always suspected the worst. Anyway, my father and uncle had been after different treasures, and as I already noted, they found enough to keep backers appetites' whetted and to get more money to keep going. Nick was to get 25% of whatever was discovered, so he had a stake in protecting what they found.

I guess my father figured Nick's toughness might come in as handy as his diving abilities. You see, when wrecks were located in those days, it wasn't unusual for pirates to try to muscle in. Boats were sabotaged, divers sometimes threatened one another with guns. On one occasion, a dive boat was set afire at night and two men died. Another time an air compressor was sabotaged and exploded, tearing off a diver's foot and maiming other people around him.

One day toward the end of the summer Uncle Gerry came up from a dive and let out a scream. The rest of us ran to the rail thinking he was hurt; instead, he swam over and threw something onto the deck. When we looked down, we were staring at gold doubloons. Seawater doesn't corrode gold the way it does silver. The coins glittered in the sunlight like they were magical.

Uncle Gerry carefully marked the site by tying a guideline to a buoy while the rest of us got our diving gear on. By the end of the second day, we had pulled up about 3,200 gold doubloons as well as thirty blackened bars of silver. I can't tell you the excitement of it. All of us acted crazed, even Uncle Gerry, who had never exhibited gold-fever symptoms. Now each night we were standing guard with a rifle.

■■■■ 21 ■■■■

A knock on the door interrupts my reading. I put down Charlie's story with the feeling I'd let him down. Why the hell hadn't he told me any of this, trusted me?

"Come in."

The doorknob twists but the door doesn't budge.

Resenting the intrusion, I go over and open up, realizing I'd forgotten to undo the knob lock when I came in this morning. Harold Thompkins is standing there. I was so engrossed in Charlie's narrative, I forgot he was coming over.

"I take it you found her," he says, his voice high, agitated.

"Why don't you sit down," I say brusquely. My dislike for him had turned to disgust after what his wife told me.

"Where is she?" he demands, refusing the seat.

"She's okay and just wants to be left alone." I sit down, taking the note Beverly gave me out of the desk's top drawer and handing it to him.

Furious, he scans the paper and throws it down. The tendons in his throat stand out like ropes, and the pulse on his right temple throbs. Leaning over the desk, he's barely controlling his anger.

"Tell me where she is, goddamn it!"

"We have an agreement, son. If she doesn't want you to know where she is, I won't tell you. And she doesn't."

"Look, you bastard, tell me where my wife is or you're not getting another red cent."

Such a threat is bad enough. Then he makes an awful mistake. His right hand shoots out and grabs me by the throat.

"Tell me!" he yells.

Rising, I pry off his hand and yank him halfway across the desk. I take the offending hand and jam his fingers in the still-open drawer and smash it shut with my hip while simultaneously slamming his head down on top of the desk. The cartilage in his nose makes a sickening crunch as it fails to dent the wood.

Thompkins screams and thrashes with his free arm. The papers from Charlie's story scatter everywhere. He must be punished for that too.

Momentarily easing up on the drawer, I bang it shut a second time while he screams again. Using his hair to elevate his head, I'm dismayed by the amount of blood on the desk.

"Now you are going to get my fee from your wallet in cash or traveler's checks, Mr. Thompkins. Or do I have to get your ass thrown in jail for breach of contract? I guess I should warn you that most of the cops and all the judges down here are good friends of mine."

"All right," he says through his tears.

Usually, it makes me feel terrible to see a grown man cry, but Thompkins is that breed of creep I can't abide. Any guy who takes out his hate and frustrations on a woman is no man.

"I'll give you a check."

"No, you won't, son. As soon as you get out of here, you'd stop payment on it and hightail it back up north. Now do as I say, or I'll break your goddamn hand . . . maybe your neck too."

He hands me part in cash and the rest in traveler's checks. It takes a fair amount of time for him to sign them. His right hand isn't really up to the task, so he's using his left.

His parting glance is murderous. Pretending he's scoring a point, he slams the door so hard the glass rattles like a tea service in a hurricane.

If he wants to pretend he won something, that's fine with me. Deep down he knows he's a loser. He lost his wife, a fat fee to me, and his self-esteem, and he probably lost that a long time ago or he would never have damaged his wife that way.

I wipe the blood off the desk with paper towels. Gathering up Charlie's papers, I put them back in order. When I get them right, I read on, letting the tragedy that had shaped Charlie's life and death unfold once more. And wish that my friend had never died and that I was never sucked into this terrible business that has claimed too many lives already.

22

I resume Charlie's narrative:

The next day, my father sent Uncle Gerry back to make sure that our documentation was in order. The State of Florida granted salvage contracts for specific offshore areas and demanded a lot of things, such as keeping adequate maps of the holes dug.

Uncle Gerry had to tell of our strike, but he did it as quietly as possible. He informed the backers so he could get more money from them for new equipment. He also had to tell state authorities because Florida demanded that a state field agent be present when artifacts were removed from wrecks.

The agent who returned with Uncle Gerry was a sloppy, slow-moving Georgian named Gibbs Carlyle. He knew both my father and Uncle Gerry. The state wanted him with us because Florida took 25% of all treasure found.

My father, Uncle Gerry, and Nick worried all the time

that word would leak out. If that happened, all hell would break loose. Other salvagers would flock to the area and try to muscle in.

We kept on diving day and night. More and more artifacts and treasure were uncovered. There were muskets, daggers, swords, locks and keys, shards of pottery, all of which fascinated me as much as the 5,000 shords of silver, the gold bars, the gold coins stamped with the mint's symbol, and the four disks bearing royal seals and an assayer's mark certifying them as $15\frac{1}{4}$ karat gold.

One night I woke up on the salvage boat and heard angry voices. When I got on deck, my father, uncle, Nick, and Gibbs were standing around another man, who glared at them sullenly. Something made me stay in the shadows. The moon was bright so I saw everything clearly. The guy's name was Carlos Marti, a Cuban. I knew him from around Key West. He ran a salvage operation that had yet to find anything substantial.

"What were you doing out here, Carlos?" Uncle Gerry asked.

"Don't be a fool," Nick shouted. "He's spying on us!"

He began shaking Marti by the neck. "And why was he carrying this?" he asked, letting go of the coughing and gasping man. Moonlight glinted off the pistol he held up.

Nick grabbed Marti again and hit him, knocking him to the deck. He started kicking him until my father and Gibbs pulled him away. Nick shrugged them off, grabbed a rope, and started tying up Marti.

"What are we going to do with him?" my father asked.

"If we let him go, he'll come back with a goddamn army and take everything we have," Nick said.

My father looked sick. "He can't," he said over and over. "He can't."

"Nick's right," Gibbs said, looking around shrewdly.

"We've got to kill him," Nick said. "There's no other way."

A FOOL'S DEATH

"You can't," Uncle Gerry said.

"No such word as *can't*," Gibbs said, leaning back against the cabin. "But you've got a gov'ment official on board, and I sure as hell don't want to get killed too."

My father and Uncle Gerry looked even sicker. But not Nick. The bastard looked up and gave a short barking laugh. "How much you want, Gibbs?"

"Five percent."

"What makes you worth that much?" Nick asked.

"I keep my mouth shut about whatever you decide to do to Mr. Marti here. And I more than make that percentage up to you by underreporting what you find."

"That sounds fair," my father said.

I couldn't believe what I was hearing. I wanted to get away, but I couldn't. It was like I was frozen.

Nick looked at my father. "I become a full partner for killing the son of a bitch . . . unless you want to do it."

My father looked sicker and there was a long silence. "Okay," he finally muttered.

I spoke up from the shadows. "You can't. You're talking about murder."

Everyone turned and stared at me. "Son, just forget about tonight," Gibbs said. "You're gonna be a rich young man as a result of what happens out here. This man was about to steal from you."

I went to my father. "It's not worth it. For Christ's sake, you're talking about killing someone."

He put his hand on my shoulder. "I can't let him take it away from us, Charlie. Not after all this time."

I pulled away from under his arm as I watched Nick yank Marti to his feet. The doomed man stood there and looked at all of them and me too. His normally dark face appeared white in the moonlight and his voice was hoarse, half-strangled as he spoke. "I curse every one of you. Somehow I will see you all dead! You and your families!"

"Get Marti out of here, Nick," Gibbs said.

A FOOL'S DEATH

Nick threw Marti in his dinghy and a minute later was puttering away. My father looked at me pleadingly.

"You've got to understand, Charlie. He'd have ruined everything."

"All I know is that you're murdering a man. You and Uncle Gerry and Gibbs and Nick. You've gotten so goddamn crazy over gold that you don't see straight anymore."

I went down in the hold and flung myself on a cot. About fifteen minutes later, I heard the crack of a pistol shot. It severed whatever bonds my father and uncle and I ever had.

The next day I had my uncle take me back to Key West. Neither of us spoke a word. I cleared out, stopped long enough to say good-bye to my girl, and then hitchhiked back to Philadelphia. Once there I didn't tell anybody why I was home early. I must have projected something awful because nobody asked why.

Within another couple of months, my father, uncle, and Nick were rich men. My parents were reunited. When my mother went down to Florida, I wouldn't go. When my father and mother moved to a big house on Philadelphia's Main Line, I stayed with my grandmother. Later my mother became pregnant with my brother, Brian.

Now that I think about it, my father and I were more alike than I believed. He had married twice before he met my mother, although I was his first son. He still kept in touch with his ex-wives and gave each of them a share in his fortune. That always struck me as fair to do for any woman who has put up with a man for any part of her life. I did the same thing for my ex-wives because of the family money, though I didn't use the money myself or even tell my wives about it.

Anyway, six months after our strike a friend in Key West wrote me that Gibbs quit his job with the state and appeared to have a lot of unaccounted-for money. There was a lot of speculation about why, most of it accurate, but nothing was ever proven. The same friend and I kept in touch. Two years later, she told me that Nick died a strange death. He drowned in his own vomit in a whorehouse. A foolish way to go.

After I had joined the Navy my friend wrote that Gibbs died. I had told her about Marti's curse and she was worried. Yes, Gibbs too went like a fool. He was lying in bed listening to the radio. His water bed sprang a leak and he was electrocuted. I knew it wasn't a coincidence. Then came Uncle Gerry's death. He died by drowning in his bathtub, and then a map showed up with a peculiar epitaph for him.

Carlos Marti hadn't died that night. He was very much alive and very much wanted to exact that curse he uttered before Nick took him off *The Doubloon*. And he wanted me dead too.

Years ago, I spent six months trying to find him. I hired a private investigator, who could only learn that Marti had lived for a spell in New Mexico and had some family around Albuquerque. All I found was the nickname Mesquite Charlie, which somebody hung on me because there were two other Charlies I ran with out there.

Since I couldn't find Marti, I didn't want him to find me. I went to the last place he'd figure I'd go. The scene of the crime. Even Marti, I thought, wouldn't look for me here. I came down and built a life for myself. I never talked about my past. I was afraid word of where I was would somehow get back to Marti.

Slipping in down here undetected wasn't as difficult as it might seem. By the time I returned here, I was a lot older, the people I knew had moved on, and the treasure we had found was overshadowed by others that were much bigger.

My father died by falling into an indoor piranha pool he kept on his estate. That too, of course, was ruled an accidental death. I knew the killer was much closer and that he would soon stalk me. What's foolish about my death is that I came to realize that Andalusia was right. Any man doing what Marti was doing would have killed us all to take our gold.

So now I wonder if I'm next. That's not a pleasant thing to contemplate. If you're reading this, then he will have gotten me too.

I should have told you all this years ago, but hell, you might have thought I was nuts. So much now for pride. Right? Maybe you could have helped, maybe somehow gotten to him before he got me. He must be totally crazed by now. If you do find him, keep him from hurting anyone else. There were only the five of us on that boat, and now we're all dead. It gives me the creeps to write that, but what else can I do?

I need your help because there's still my brother. Strange, isn't it. He's a brother I barely know. I don't have anything in common with him except blood and a murderer. I hope you can help him.

Finished with Charlie's tale, I sit back with a feeling of great sadness and near helplessness as I absorb what I just read. One message comes through loud and clear. While it may seem horrible to say so, Charlie was luckier than me. He didn't know Marti would go after the wives.

■■■■ 23 ■■■■

THE washed-out blue haze that hovers over the island in the early hours is compliments of City Electric. By the water's edge, in particular, it can play tricks with your vision, changing reality, making you see things that aren't there. Sometimes that's not all bad.

Today it gives sort of a ghostly cast to *The Lady Gloria*, which is tied up at the docks and gently rocks to the sway of the sea. She's sixty feet long and painted white with gay yellow and red stripes. Like most of the shrimp boats working out of here, she looks cheerful with her huge dark green nets opened out to dry like circus rigging.

Her name is new and reflects a major change in Big Bill Rush's life. Big Bill's the captain, and until two weeks ago *The Lady Peggy* was painted on the hull.

Renaming a boat is not a chore undertaken lightly by seafaring types. But the Peggy of such former distinction came home unexpectedly one afternoon and found Big Bill in bed with a young woman named Gloria. She threatened Bill with the loss of his testicles and Gloria with the loss of her hair. A wiry little redhead, Peggy almost accomplished both before neighbors, alarmed by Bill's roars and Gloria's shrieks, pulled her off them.

Bill's shoulders are slumped and his head bowed when I find him nearby at the newer of the two Fisherman's Cafes. He has the sick look of a man who just blew a big deal, the kind you don't get a second shot at.

Physically, Bill resembles a fat old goat or a scruffy lawn gnome. His ponytail and beard are scraggly and his beer gut is bigger than I remember. He's wearing a pair of faded jeans, dirty white rubber boots, and a faded red T-shirt that states WHOEVER WINDS UP WITH THE MOST STUFF WINS.

On the fake marble counter in front of him is a large platter of ham and eggs fried in olive oil, hash browns, and Cuban bread. He isn't eating with his usual gusto. He's hardly eating at all.

"Why're you here, Mason?" he growls when I take the stool next to him.

"That any way to talk to a friend?"

"I ain't got no friend."

"You got Gloria."

He drops his knife and fork in his plate with a give-me-a-break clatter. "Have I ever. She's eighteen years old, for Christ's sake. I'll be forty-six in July. A skinny little girl who listens to rock 'n' fuckin' roll all day and thinks Vietnam is in Africa."

Baggy eyes show how little sleep he's getting. His wounded-cow expression shows how bewildered he is. "What the fuck's wrong with Peggy, Mason? We had a good thing going. We had a nice little place, you know that."

"Very nice," I agree.

"And we got a couple of great kids, right?"

"Right."

"Hell, I'd've married her one of these days. She knew that."

A fair share of people down here lead lives like sad-jokey country-western songs. Pickup trucks and fur's a-flyin'; lost loves and lots of cryin'. You expect them to tie themselves to a rusty refrigerator one day and jump off a bridge into the middle of the ocean.

"Obviously you want her back. Why'd you take her name off the boat and put the girl's on?"

Big Bill shifts uncomfortably. "Hell, Mason, I was pissed off. She almost tore my balls off with her bare hands. That's a hard thing to be cheerful about. Now, Olive Oyl thinks I'm in love with her because I put her goddamn name on the boat. She brings her friends down here and points to it, and they tell her how fuckin' wonderful it is."

His eyes dart from side to side to make sure nobody else can hear. He whispers, "Most of her friends are still in high school."

I refrain from laughing but think Peggy wouldn't. Peggy's the kind of woman who won't carry a grudge forever. I guess a girl Gloria's age was real threatening, even one who looks like a zipper if she stands sideways. Maybe Peggy will ease up on Bill if she finds out how miserable he is, especially since he realizes how big an ass he was. Eighteen. What the hell did he talk about with Gloria after they made love? What does any woman talk about with Bill?

Hell, I have to say something to get him off the dime. I want Big Bill to open up about his diving days, but he won't in this mood. All he wants to do is whine about how sorry he is for himself. "Want me to put in a word for you?" I ask.

A dim beam of hope appears in his bloodshot eyes. "You think it might do some good?"

"Can't do you any harm."

"That's sure as shit. Now what're you doing here, Mason?" He sighs loudly. "You didn't come for Olive Oyl."

"I have a couple of questions about when you were hunting treasure."

His eyes turn misty. "God that was time ago and a lot better time. You know, I used to dive a lot, and the one time I was onto something, really onto something big, I sold the rights to it for next to nothing. I blew it."

He stares at me full in the face for the first time this morning. "I'm pretty good at that."

"You remember a guy named Carlos Marti?"

"Sure, everybody knew Carlos. A crazy little Cuban. Called Switchblade. Always had a couple on him. Would whip one out before you could say Fidel Castro. I heard he gutted somebody in Havana and that's why he wound up here."

"When did you last hear anything about him?"

Big Bill tugs at his beard and stares up at the ceiling fan. "A long, long time ago. He had a salvage boat, an old wreck. Only thing that kept him going was gold fever. 'Diver's clap.' You get sicker and sicker until you're crazy. But that's the only way to find treasure."

He gives a loud sigh again. "That's why I never made a discovery. I never had the fever the way those suckers do who put aside booze and women and every other damn thing that makes life bearable and just go after the treasure."

"You know a treasure hunter named David Donne?"

"A little. From what I recall he had the fever real bad. Kept pretty much to himself and his diving. He's the kind of guy I mean. Gonna find treasure or die trying. He had a brother who wasn't so crazy. Another guy worked for him for a while, a prick name of Andalusia."

"What was wrong with Andalusia?"

Big Bill pauses to put it right. "Mean through and through and tough enough to get away with it."

"Can you tell me anything else about Marti?"

Bill wags his head. "Hell, he was like most folks who come down here. One day he was here. The next he wasn't. . . . I do recall though that he liked young kids. I mean of an age to make Olive Oyl seem ripe."

"Well, if you remember anything else, I'd appreciate your letting me know, Big Bill. Even if it's something you think might be unimportant, no matter how dumb it might sound."

"Okay, Mason. But I'm a poor judge of what's not dumb these days."

"Thanks, Big Bill."

"If you want more on Marti, talk to Dan Merkin down at the garage."

A FOOL'S DEATH

"Why?"

"As I recall it, he owned a piece of Marti's salvage boat."

"They were partners?"

"Yeah. Marti swapped Merkin a share in whatever he'd find if Dan kept the old boat running."

Walking out onto the street, I notice a tall, skinny monkey of a girl wearing a black tank top and red shorts over by Big Bill's boat. A Walkman clogs her ears. She's boogying on the dock to music nobody else can hear. I vow to get hold of Peggy real soon.

24

OVER the next few days, I call in IOUs from cops, reporters, hookers, bartenders, anybody who might have a lead on Marti. I want to piece his old life together in hopes of getting an insight into his new one. The cops I call are both here and in Miami. Chances are the man has a record.

The reporters are in the same two towns, one who works for the *Miami Herald* and the other for the *Key West Citizen*. I ask for clips on David Donne's treasure strike and any clips on Marti. The *Herald* is my better bet. The *Citizen* keeps track of a lot of local stuff, such as birthdays, high school sports, the drug trials of prominent citizens, and police blotter comings and goings under headlines such as "Minor Burglaries Galore" and "Thieves, Wackos Keep Police Busy," but I'm not sure it keeps tabs on treasure hunters or killer Cubans.

The material Joe Clark sent shows up. There is Charlie's life, part of it anyway, broken down into tight little official government paragraphs. He joined the Navy and did his basic training at Pensacola. A few drunken scrapes with the shore patrol in a couple of ports in the Pacific are recounted, but nothing serious.

A FOOL'S DEATH

He did three and a half years of a four-year hitch, getting out early on a Section 8.

There's a good bit of bureaucratic mumbo jumbo about why they greased his exit, but it boils down to this: He told one of his superiors that he was afraid someone might kill him. The murder wouldn't be pretty.

My sympathy for Charlie becomes profound. I imagine him trying to articulate his fears to the service's pencil pushers. He says somebody's out to murder him in a weird way, and they look for a form for foolish murders. When they can't find it, they send him to a doctor, who listens to a young sailor trying to explain that somebody has a marker for his life, and the doctor's sure he's nuts.

There isn't much else, just a bit about his move to Albuquerque, because he used his GI medical benefits while there. This part's without commentary. Just that he billed the government for Willows Memorial Hospital.

Altogether, Big Brother doesn't have a hell of a lot on Charlie. The government's reaction to his worry about the way he'd die is probably why he didn't tell me or even his wives about Marti. He didn't want to take the chance of being branded crazy again. That makes me feel terrible too and explains his lack of trust.

The stuff on Tommy Costello is more intriguing. Costello indeed left the NYPD under suspicion. What comes through clearly is that Mr. Costello is a slippery character. He was implicated in a credit card scam, but there wasn't quite enough proof to nail him. There were charges of his shaking down drug dealers, but no drug dealer in his right mind will give evidence against a cop.

There was also a sexual harassment charge. Seems he and another detective arrested a young woman for obstructing justice, handcuffed her, and then fondled her breasts on the way to the police station. The charge against her was dropped. The charges against Costello and his pal were dropped too, which indicates a deal was made to get the cops off the hook.

The worst charge on his record concerns his shooting three black kids who he said drew weapons when he stopped them for questioning. No weapons were ever recovered, but the review board found three notches on Costello's pistol grip. The department finally unloaded him. He turned up in Miami.

It's rumored that he opened shop with the help of the Gambino crime family from New York. These days he spends most of his time talking to witnesses against drug dealers who are under indictment. Allegedly, he's seeing if there's anything he can dig up that might help his clients. Some people might call what he does intimidation.

The newspaper stories my reporter friends get from their respective morgues are a little more peculiar in what they reveal. For one, I get a picture of Marti. He's with some other guys who stand near an old salvage boat. "Treasure Hunters" is all the headline says. The cutline identifies the second man from the right, a wiry guy who looks like a hawk, as Marti. His prominent nose is hooked and his eyes are dark and deep set. When you know a little about somebody, you read into his face what you already learned. Even though he's laughing, Marti strikes me as shifty and more than a little dangerous.

What surprises me is the man standing next to him. Big and muscular, you can tell from the picture that his eyes are strange, haunting. The cutline gives his name. Nick Andalusia.

What's unexpected in light of Charlie's narrative is the spirit the picture evokes. Andalusia has a big arm on the little man's shoulder. They're like long-lost brothers as they perform before the camera. There's a pretty young girl in the picture too, but she isn't identified in the cutline. I see what Big Bill Rush means. The girl couldn't have been more than twelve or fourteen.

My cop friends come through too. Marti has a record both here and in Miami. Here it was next to nothing. A few barroom scrapes. In two of them, he pulled a knife, and in one he stabbed a guy, but not badly enough to cause real damage. This confirms that Marti is willing to kill. Both the police reports from Key West and Miami mention a mother and a sister living in Albuquerque, just as Charlie indicated.

The Miami police blotter is interesting from another perspective. Marti was arrested in Miami for drunk and disorderly. But he was also arrested for attempted fraud. Seems he had a scam going to bilk some investors in a phony treasure hunt. The details were hard to follow. The men eventually dropped the charges, probably out of embarrassment over being conned by such trash or maybe out of fear of retaliation. What's curious is his partner in the venture. One Nick Andalusia.

Now why would Andalusia take his little buddy out in a boat and shoot him when the son of a bitch was just doing what he and Andalusia more or less tried to do? An obvious answer is that he was doing it to Andalusia so the big man did him.

Another possibility crosses my mind. What if the whole thing that Charlie witnessed was a scam? Suppose Andalusia only pretended to kill his little buddy. Why? Maybe he wanted to implicate Charlie's dad and uncle in murder and the Florida state official too. Why? Well, for one, Charlie mentioned that Andalusia got a bigger share of the pie for killing Marti, or for at least claiming he did. One fake murder could've been worth a million or so in that kind of a crap shoot.

That line of reasoning leads me to wonder if the murders were a team business. Suppose Charlie's info that Andalusia died was wrong? What if the murders aren't simply motivated by some crazy need for revenge? If it's not simply a nut, what else could it be?

I ask my cop friends for files on Andalusia. I also get back to my PI buddy in Philadelphia to see if he's learned anything. He's out, so I leave word that I'll call back later.

25

*I*T'S a mad dogs and Englishmen kind of day. The heat and humidity are ratcheted up to full tilt.

Dan Merkin's garage is just around the corner, and I can't wait to get there. My clothes cling to me like a bar lush trying to cadge a drink. Days like this even get to people such as me who think hell is really a cold place. White clouds drift overhead and huge palmetto bugs lumber across the pavement.

When I hit Merkin's office, I suck in the air-conditioning like Lawrence of Arabia who just found an oasis. Merkin himself stares at me in mock astonishment.

"You aren't going to take your jeep away from us now, are you, Mason?" Dan drawls, peering over the top of the sunglasses he always wears. "What the hell are we gonna do for scenery?"

"Irony doesn't suit you, Mr. Merkin."

He keeps it up anyway. "Hell, I thought you believed I was running a pawn shop."

I hand him a check. He takes my car keys from a pegboard where another dozen or so sets dangle, blows on them, and holds them out as if a billow of dust came up, and bows when he hands them to me.

"Dan, a while back you had a piece of a salvage boat owned by a guy named Carlos Marti."

Merkin's owlish face scrunches into a scowl. "That I did, sorry to say."

"Can you tell me a bit about Marti?"

"Why not? But it's not a pleasant memory." He sits in the chair behind his gray metal desk. "This is going back more than twenty years. Like a lot of guys who get into the treasure-hunting business, Marti did it on a shoestring. Bought an old boat with a diesel engine that needed a lot of work. He didn't have the money to maintain it, so he offered me a piece of whatever treasure he found if I kept the boat going."

Pausing, he wipes his neck with a hanky. "I did it for a while. But I found out he was stealing tools from the garage whenever he came around. I got on him about it, and he pulled a shiv."

Merkin's an easygoing guy, but I've seen him in precarious positions once or twice. He doesn't back down and gets an icy cold look that is terrible to behold.

"What did you do?"

"Went for the Louisville Slugger." He reaches behind his desk and takes out a thirty-six-inch bat. "Told him I'd take batting practice with his goddamn head if he didn't put that knife away."

"And?"

"All he did was laugh, kind of surprised like, and then wanted to be friends. He brought back most of the tools he stole, but our partnership such as it was dissolved."

"Ever hear from him again?"

"Yeah, I was kind of surprised by that too. He disappeared and then, years later, I got a call from him. Said he was at a marina on Upper Matecumbe Key."

"What was he doing up there?"

"Said he had a sixty-five-foot brigantine charter vessel. Something was wrong with the engine. Wanted me to come up and fix it. I figured he got into drugs. A boat like that would have cost a couple of hundred grand. Must have been drugs. He sure as hell never hit it with the treasure hunting."

Unless it was at the Donnes' expense. At least now I know for sure that Charlie wasn't loco when he figured Marti was alive. "You go?"

"Mason, you know me better than that. The little bastard threatened me with a knife. How could I ever help him?"

"Thanks for the information and for waiting on my check, Dan."

"That's okay, Mason. Only I may as well tell you now."

"What?"

"You're going to need new shock absorbers soon."

"Dan, death, taxes, and indebtedness to Detroit or Tokyo are life's inevitables."

■■■■ 26 ■■■■

THE jeep kicks over and sounds smoother than I ever remember, but that won't last long. I never have a vehicle that behaves itself, just invalids demanding constant treatment. That's why I had seriously considered dumping this thing and taking on Charlie's old Chevy when I thought he had left it to me. There was never any mechanical trouble with the Chevy that I can remember.

Now that I'm certain Marti is alive, I drive over to the police station and ask to see Chief Griswold. Five minutes later, I'm staring at Griswold's squint.

"Here's a picture of Marti," I say, after giving a rundown of some of what I know. "He'd be a lot older, but that nose won't have changed much. Same with those deep-set eyes. They won't have changed either."

"I'll have a set made up to give to each of my men," Griswold says. "First, I'll send this picture over to the Miami police to have one of their computer artists age him."

After that little speech, his face shuts down with the finality of a steel grate on a storefront in Little Havana. The chief, as you may have gathered, isn't somebody who enjoys shooting the bull.

"Good," I say. "And thanks. The ladies feel better with your men checking on them."

He doesn't bother looking up or otherwise acknowledging the gratitude. Hell, I don't care. I'm not looking for a bedside manner, but something a lot more. I want a man who, like me, is interested in keeping the wives alive. Griswold is.

Back at the office, I come across a manila envelope that's from the cop shop in Miami. I have a good idea what it contains as I rip it open. I'm right. There's a picture of Nick Andalusia along with his fingerprints, which is something I asked one of my cop friends to get. Now I have blotters on both Marti and Andalusia.

I call Joe Clark again. "Joe, I'm sorry to make such a pain in the ass of myself, but I'd appreciate your help at least one more time on this case."

"Okay, Mason," he says, sounding a trifle sick of my requests.

"I'm sending you a couple of Miami police blotters. I'd appreciate any possible FBI stuff on them. And once again, I'm sorry about badgering you so much. Their social security numbers are on them, so you can run them down as well."

"Don't worry about it, Mason. I'll put them through as soon as I get them."

Guys such as Marti and Andalusia are tough to find when they want to disappear. They use phony names to get social security numbers and other documents to get credit cards, driver's licenses, what have you. Hell, a clever crook can erect a fake life around him by getting new ID and setting up sixteen different corporations, none of which have his name on them.

Even though I don't have much hope, I try traditional channels as well. I call a friend at motor vehicles in Tallahassee. There's the off chance either Marti or Andalusia is still in Florida and has a driver's license. Also boats are registered with the department too. If Marti is still tooling around Florida waters in a yacht, his boat might be registered with the state.

Lastly, I call a computer service that for a fee will give you a motor vehicle rundown from other states. I have them check out New Mexico for Marti. Andalusia's record doesn't list prior addresses or relatives.

There's one source I haven't worked on yet, but I might as well go to him. As I say, Key West is a live-and-let-live place. Just about anybody can blend in down here, and just about anybody does. That doesn't mean you have to like them all. Fat Dom falls into that category. Even so, I turn to him for help once in a while, but I'm not proud of myself when I do.

■■■■ 27 ■■■■

SINCE a couple of murders occur here annually, Petronia has a reputation as a mean street. It's the gauntlet of the island's mostly black neighborhood, which lies just west of Whitehead Street.

The shabby hopelessness of poverty litters the landscape. Hardly noticed narrow lanes jammed with run-down houses slink off the main drag. A lot of the stores are boarded up. The only obviously going concerns are the bars. There's always somebody hustling pool on the brightly lit porch of Glen's Soul City, and you can get a cheap drunk on at Blue Moon Lounge, although I'm not sure how welcome you'd be.

No matter the time of day, people are on the street, on their porches, or peering suspiciously through curtains at strangers. A lot of the residents are old folks who long ago uprooted the ornate cast-iron benches from once fancy lawns and move them from one side of the street to the other, depending on the shade. Everybody down here makes do in life as they can.

Fat Dom Carlson lives in one of the run-down clapboard houses on Petronia. His neighbors ignore him, and he likes the invisibility. There are a lot of rumors about him, and I'm sure everybody around here knows the ones I know and a lot more. He's mob connected, which in this neighborhood and a lot of others makes him an untouchable. I'm always uncomfortable when I see him. Not because of his mobster ties but because of the business he's in.

I rap on the door of a dilapidated old house. He opens it a minute later, wide enough so that I take in the entirety of his enormous bulk. Fat Dom looks like a seedy elephant or a fifty-year-old fat man in the circus. He wears a gigantic Hawaiian shirt that can't reach to button and gray shorts that are specially made. Flesh ripples down him like melted wax on an outsize bowling ball.

"Mr. Collins, to what do I owe this honor?"

"I'm hoping you can help me out."

"Why should I?" he asks pleasantly, adding, "Come in. Come in."

Inside, his house is surprising, like something out of *Better Homes and Gardens*. The ground floor is one big room. The rear wall is patio doors that look out onto a garden and a small pool with goldfish. The walls are white stucco, the floor red Spanish tiles, and the furniture a mix of light oak modern, dark Spanish Mission, and black leather. Lighting is recessed and the paintings on the wall include a Picasso.

The focus of the big room though is the kitchen. It's raised on a platform like an altar, and the stainless steel everything glitters in the sunlight. There are two big stoves. Two refrigerators. An enormous oak-topped worktable. Racks of spices and rows of knives. Copper-bottomed pots and pans polished to a dazzle dangle from hooks in the ceiling along with strings of garlic and other herbs. Something is cooking and it smells delicious.

After seeing this cathedral to cuisine, a guy I know said to Fat Dom, "Cooking must be your passion." "No," he answered. "Eating is."

Leading me into the living room section, he sinks down on an enormous black leather sofa. I take a chair opposite him.

"There's no reason in the world why you should help me, but maybe one day there will be."

"Very good point, Mason. One you always make. Yes, the

world is made up of reciprocity, isn't it? So let's see if I can assist you."

"I'm trying to track down a guy named Carlos Marti. He lived here about twenty-five years ago."

"And he liked young stuff, didn't he?"

"That's right. Girls twelve or fourteen."

"Twenty-five years ago. I would've only been in business a short time then. Refresh my memory about Mr. Marti."

"He had a salvage boat. Cuban. Little, deep-set eyes, a hawk-like nose."

A trace of something I can't quite get flashes across Fat Dom's filmy eyes. "Yes," he says. "I remember your Mr. Marti. An unpleasant little bastard as I recall."

"So you did business with him."

"Mason, let me just say that I helped him meet his needs. People get so moralistic about what I do, but I simply cater to a public with offbeat tastes that must be met."

"What was he interested in?" I ask, ignoring the philosophy.

"Some photos and then a, uh, young girl. I helped him with both. As you said, he was interested in the budding stage. Twelve, thirteen, or so."

"Nice."

"Don't be so moralistic, Mason. Some of these runaways aren't all little victims. When they leave home, their parents are glad to see them go. Some are much crueler and more devious than just about any adult."

"Have you heard from him since then?"

"Of course, but that's normal. My business depends upon repeats. After all, such tastes aren't met easily."

Though I can't stand judgmental people, I find myself in that frame of mind whenever I'm here. I almost say how disgusted I am. Instead, I stay within the confines of pragmatism. That's how badly I want information. Such compromises grind away at my soul, which by now is mostly a pile of dust.

"Could you give me his last addresses?"

"Mason, every time you ask me for a favor, the favor becomes two or three." He heaves himself to his feet. "You act as if one of my missions in life is to earn your living."

As he crosses the room, I wonder if he will ever get nailed. The postal authorities are always trying to get him for sending kiddie porn through the mail. But how he does it nobody knows. He must have couriers who send it from Miami or somewhere. None of it goes through the Key West post office.

Fat Dom makes me edgy. By helping me, he acts as if I'm somehow complicit in what he does. Though he takes pains to hide his operation from outsiders, with me he doesn't. It's as though he has something on me, and I guess, by my having any kind of a working relationship with him, he does.

He walks to a wall and presses a button. A huge modern painting that must be twelve feet long and from floor to ceiling slides to one side, exposing rows of white metal filing cabinets and a computer console.

From being here before, I know the file drawers contain photos going back to when Fat Dom first went into business. Fat Dom turns on the computer. His pudgy fingers dance across the keys. He turns on the switch for the printer. A second later, the printer's chugging away.

When the printer stops, Fat Dom tears off a sheet of paper and hands it to me. There are dates, names of cities, post office box numbers, and a variety of names.

"Marti's aliases?" I ask, inwardly groaning. It means turning to Joe Clark for more help.

"Yes. Due to the repressiveness of our government, my clients not only are afraid to publicize their penchant for the sexually different but don't want their real names attached to their tastes."

"Thanks, Fat Dom."

"Mason, just knowing the level of your indebtedness to me is comforting."

I sort of wonder about that again. What will it mean if he ever calls me on my promises? I feel a little the way old Dr. Faustus must've when he was dealing with Mephistopheles. What pound of flesh will he exact?

A FOOL'S DEATH

For the moment, though, he extends hospitality. "I'm cooking paella as a little afternoon snack. You are welcome to join me if you have the time."

Reluctantly, I get up to go. What additional hold would he have on me if I ate with him? "Thanks, but no thanks. I've got to see if I can prevent Mr. Marti from harming someone."

A flicker of concern appears in Fat Dom's brown eyes. "Not . . . not a young girl . . ."

"No. A young man and people who used to be young girls."

I could be wrong, but I think Fat Dom's relieved by what I just said as he accompanies me to the front door. Maybe he isn't so bad after all. A lot of people get caught up in work that's harmful to others, but they try to put the best face on it. People rationalize away just about anything to keep from confronting what they do. In that regard, Fat Dom's not much different from the rest of us.

28

FAT Dom's printout lists Marti's last postal drop as only three years ago. The city is Galveston. That figures. Another Gulf Coast town. Another place where a tough little bastard who knows something about boats might gravitate, another place to land another hustle. Long ago, he probably went through whatever dough he picked up from the Donne deal with Andalusia.

While working up the nerve to call Joe Clark again, I call the PI helping me in Philly. "Matt," I say when I finally get him on the line. "What have you got for me?"

"A lot of clippings from the *Philadelphia Inquirer*, the *Main Line Times*, and from the *Philadelphia Bulletin*, which carried articles on the Donnes before the paper folded. I put the family company incorporation papers in too."

"Good, Matt. Anything unusual about the family?"

"I didn't take a close look at the clips. The only strange thing that hit me is the dumb ways the Donnes die."

"I'd appreciate it if you'd Express Mail the material down to me."

"You've got it."

"Don't forget to enclose your bill."

"I already have, Mason."

With great reluctance, I call Joe Clark. "For Christ's sake," he mutters when he hears my voice. "You're as bad as the president. He calls for one thing. Then he wants another. Then something else. Pretty soon, I'm checking out enough stuff to choke a horse."

"Joe, I am not the president. What *I* need is important. This isn't a bullshit case. It's murder. I'm trying to prevent other people from getting murdered."

Joe's real quick. "You mean Mesquite Charlie's killer is after someone else?"

"Not just someone else, but three women and a young man. He already killed one of Charlie's ex-wives too."

"What do you need?"

I explain about Marti and his taste for porn and rattle off the info Fat Dom gave me. "Thanks again," I say defensively.

"Sorry I got on you. If I can help in a life-and-death situation, I'll always do it. Besides, you know how Connie and I feel about what you did for us."

The rest of the day drifts by slowly. Nothing pans out. I cast out a lot of leads but don't have any nibbles, let alone bites. Just as I'm about to leave the office, Mike Sanders calls.

"Mason, the chief says your picture of Carlos Marti is ready. Want me to drop it off?"

"No thanks, Mike, I'll come by. Tell Griswold I've got another for him to do the same with." I grab a mug shot of Nick Andalusia and head for the door.

At the cop shop, Mike comes up to me. He holds out a stack of pictures of Carlos Marti with the face aged twenty-five years. It's eerie. Sort of like looking at an actor or actress in a lot of makeup to look old, yet knowing that's what they'll actually wind up like. The hair's almost white. Lines are etched deeper in the face. The kind of blurring of the facial structure that age brings on is there too. Sooner or later, if we're lucky, we all become our grandparents.

"The chief rushed your picture over to Miami and had a lot of copies flown right back. You've got him worried."

"Glad to hear it."

"How many copies do you want? Plenty were made up. The chief wants us to pass them out at all the hotels, motels, and restaurants."

I need at least four. One for each of the wives and one for me to show around too. "As many as you think you can spare."

Mike gives me a dozen and promises more if I need them. I hand him the Andalusia photo. "Tell Griswold I need the same workup on this guy."

"Will do."

"And tell him I said thanks."

■ ■ ■ ■ 29 ■ ■ ■ ■

NIGHT, the time we're most vulnerable, is coming on as I mount the steps to my apartment. For the first time in eons darkness makes me uneasy. Marlene was killed at night. Charlie must've been too.

When I open the apartment door, I encounter a now familiar sight. The wives are gathered around the living room, talking in almost murmurs. We all exchange greetings. I'm glad to see them. In a way, I think about them the way you do real little kids. As long as they're within touching distance, I know they're all right.

"Tomorrow's the funeral," Amanda Kay reminds me as I sit down.

Their red eyes and slightly puffy faces give away that they've all been crying. Most likely they've been talking about Marlene. Each of them, of course, feels the pain of loss coupled with intense anger at the killer. And they feel guilt and fear. Each knows she's lucky the killer didn't call on her first.

The women order in Chinese food. With the prospect of what we all have to face in the morning, there isn't much talking while we eat. Toward the end of the meal, I pass around the pictures of Marti.

"Who's this?" Virginia demands as I pass the photos.

"Carlos Marti, the guy who threatened everybody on the salvage boat when Charlie's father hit it big."

"What a mean-looking old guy," Amanda Kay says.

"He may not look just like this, but it should be close enough," I say, explaining about the Miami police artist aging Marti's mug shot. I tell them a bit more about Charlie thinking Marti wasn't dead and about Dan Merkin and Fat Dom hearing from him years later.

"What did Dan and this Fat Dom have to do with Marti?" Betty asks.

Quickly, I relate about Dan's fixing Marti's salvage boat and about what Fat Dom told me. I don't go into details, just that the fat man kept photos and records going way back and that's how I got a bit of a fix on Marti.

"Jesus, what a creep that Fat Dom is," Virginia says.

"I didn't even know anyone like that was on this island," Betty said. "It's horrible to think someone like him is your neighbor."

"Not yours," I say. "Just the poor folks down on Petronia."

"You didn't say he was black," Amanda Kay says.

"He's not. He just lives down there."

"Let's change the topic," Betty says with a quiver of disgust.

For the next few hours, our talk is desultory. We all drink more than we should, but that's what happens when you verge on putting the young and vital in their graves. When Amanda Kay and I drive the others home, the wives are all sobbing again.

Virginia's first, and we all walk her inside. She has her pistol drawn and I have mine. I go through each of the rooms, turning on one light after another and opening closets, checking under beds. Outside again, I'm glad to see she put her double lights on in the front window. The cops will look for that when they check on her later.

At Betty's, Amanda Kay and I are right behind her as she opens the front door of the shop. All three of us head up the narrow steps to the apartment above and tensely wait while she unlocks that door too. There are only two rooms up there. A living room and a bedroom. There's a tiny kitchen like a closet. Even so, I'm careful as I check around.

When I come out of the bedroom, Betty's holding up a key ring. "Here's an extra set of keys, Mason. I'm afraid to go down when you leave. Will you please lock up?"

"Of course," I say, wishing I'd thought of it myself.

"I should have asked both you and Virginia this," Amanda Kay said. "Do you want to stay with us at Mason's?"

"No thanks. I'm like Virginia. I don't mind being on my own. But I don't feel comfortable until I've locked myself in up here. During the day, I'm not afraid. But the night noises bother me."

We drive home in silence. I think how easily the dark conceals people who want to be hidden. How unseen danger can lurk around and you know it's there. Amanda Kay must have similar thoughts. She can't snuggle up next to me. The seats in the jeep don't let you do that, but she places her hand on my thigh, her fingers digging into the flesh. I look over to interpret her mood. There's nothing sensual about the pressure. I doubt if she's even conscious of it. The look on her face tells me it's fear.

The next morning we all stand at the sun-baked Key West cemetery. The air is hot and still. The voice of the reverend saying prayers over Marlene's coffin is mesmerizing, like the drone of a bee.

The turnout's big. Her mother and father and some other relatives are down from New England. There are a lot of sport-boat captains and deckhands who had worked with her, as well as the many friends she made here from all walks of life. The wives and I are a little off to one side, none of us quite sure how Amanda Kay, Virginia, and Betty fit into the gathering.

In a way, the funeral provides a bit of formality we all need to make the deaths seem real. There was no funeral for Charlie. He wasn't a religious man and didn't want a fuss made when he was gone. He wanted to be cremated, so I guess the hand and foot will go to the mortician's oven when the coroner releases them. For the wives and me, this gathering at the cemetery is a way of dealing with grief for both Charlie and Marlene.

On the lookout for anyone resembling either Marti or Andalusia, I scan the crowd. I know most of the people. The expression on most of their faces is disbelief. I feel that way myself. I still expect to see Marlene down by the waterfront, smiling brightly and wearing a pair of cutoff jeans in a way that made you forget your problems.

I study faces I don't know. It's highly unlikely that the killer will come, but there's that craziness about the deaths that makes me think the killer is capable even of showing up here. For a weird moment, I think of Count von Cosel and how he dug up Elena's grave in a nutty attempt to bring her back to life. Suddenly, I realize I'm exhuming Charlie's past, and the results are even more gruesome than what happened to poor Elena Hoyos. Or at least more tragic.

30

*F*OR the next couple of weeks, I do donkey work. Joe Clark comes through for me, and I follow up his leads. Marti spent time not just in Galveston but in New Orleans, San Diego, and Fort Lauderdale, plus a lot of places that don't show up. Aliases include Jose Consuelo, Tomes Lama, and Juan Martin and maybe a lot more too. Document searches of the names in those towns and in Louisiana, Texas, and California, though, don't turn up anything. As for Andalusia, I still don't have anything to go on, except the now altered photo showing what he probably looks like today.

Wherever I go, I show their pictures around and leave copies with bartenders, waitresses, and other people who come in contact with a lot of strangers. I stick mostly to the boatyards and the bars, figuring those are the most likely places to pick up anything on such guys. The cops are flashing the photos around the motels, guesthouses, and general tourist stuff.

Huff keeps calling and I keep stalling. The packets of clippings come from Philadelphia. I wade through them whenever I find the time. A lot of the stories are repetitious, but I keep searching for something that might help.

At home, I fall into a domestic routine with Amanda Kay that seems to satisfy us both and is composed of a good measure of companionship. Each of us went through a lot of hoops over the years for other people. We don't expect a hell of a lot from one another and are constantly amazed by how much we do get.

After a while, looking for a partner is a lot like looking for a good used car. You always suspect there's a sound reason why someone let go of the one you're considering. Almost superstitiously, neither Amanda Kay nor I talk about it. When we fight, it lacks bitterness. When we make love, there's plenty of kindness. You can't ask for much more.

Virginia and Betty continue to be very much on my mind and in my presence too. I stop in on them once or twice a day, and they eat dinner with us most evenings. I wish I could lock them in a high tower and stand guard at the door until the killer is found.

One afternoon, I stop off to see Peggy Shaffer at the Turtle Kraals, where she works as a waitress. With her fluffy red-gold hair and pointy small face, she looks like a fox. Not long after talking to Bill Rush, I told her how sorry he was about the mess he made out of their lives. After a bit of a fuss, she admitted she still cared a little for him, but thoughts of Gloria drove her to distraction.

The Kraals is at Land's End Village, a scraggly boatyard where the commercial appeal is broadened by an oyster bar, a tourist shop, and the Kraals restaurant. *Kraal* is an Afrikaans word meaning holding pen and harkens back to the days when Key West was the nation's major turtle processor. Huge pens were filled with big green sea turtles, which can grow as old as Methuselah and weigh up to six hundred pounds or so.

"Hello, Peg."

She glances around. It's almost three o'clock. Right behind me, a party of four show up, the dregs of the lunch crowd. "Let me seat these people and I'll be with you."

A FOOL'S DEATH

"Okay, I'll grab a beer at the bar."

A few minutes later, she takes the stool next to me and curls out her lower lip, blowing a wisp of hair out of her eyes so it sticks to her damp forehead.

"How's Big Bill?" I ask.

"Oh, I'll let the slob come home," she says nonchalantly. "I wasn't going to as long as that goofy girl was around, but she went off to Miami with some kid with acne who plays drums in a band."

I look at her out of the corner of my eye. "I'll bet Bill was real broken up."

She grins. "The son of a bitch celebrated for two days and then showed up on my doorstep and proposed."

"What'd you do?"

"Told him to come back and do it when he was sober if he meant it."

"And . . ."

Peggy actually blushes, but her voice becomes very matter-of-fact to cover up what she's feeling. "The kids told me he put my name back on the boat before he came back and asked me again. We're getting married next Saturday. You and Amanda Kay will receive an invitation to the church and the reception, which is back at our place."

"It's about time somebody made an honest woman out of you, Peggy."

Blushing again, she pokes me in the ribs with her elbow. "Here I am mouthing off about Bill and me. I wanted to tell you a customer recognized one of those pictures you gave me to show folks who come in."

I suck in my breath. This might be the break I'm waiting for. She digs into the pocket of her black nylon apron and takes out a little white notepad.

"Here it is. Harvey Mallard. He's got a boat moored over at Garrison Bight. Said he'll be there another couple of days anyway."

She tears off the slip of paper. "I hope you can read my writing. His boat's the *Purple Mermaid*."

"Thanks, Peg."

"Watch yourself, Mason. This guy's as jittery as a bridegroom and out-and-out weird."

For Peggy to think somebody's strange, let alone comment on it, the guy must be something else again. "What do you mean?"

Hustling away, she calls out, "You'll see."

■■■■ 31 ■■■■

I drive the jeep out to Garrison Bight, which is just off Palm Avenue and right by the big Naval Air Station Annex. I go along the dock, passing boats I know, including Charlie's deep-sea charter *The Sand Dollar*. I guess the other boat captains are divvying up his and Marlene's customers.

A bit farther along is Peter Matthews's graceful sailboat that was made with an all-teak hull. Usually, he parks it down at the Yacht Club. Eventually, I find Mallard's boat. A fifty-seven-foot deckhouse cruiser, it's a beauty that's like the old presidential yacht and was probably crafted in the late 1920s. It has a couple of staterooms, crew quarters, and other niceties and must have set the owner back a tidy fortune.

I yell, but nobody's around. I climb aboard anyway on the off chance that I wasn't heard. What with air conditioners running, refrigerators humming, and stereo systems blasting, boats today are as noisy as any house or apartment. After banging on the cabin door, I'm rewarded. It's half-opened by a skinny, dark-haired guy wearing a bathing suit.

He looks as if he lost a crazy advertising contest. His left arm and right leg are completely tattooed. The leg resembles a tube of Colgate toothpaste. The left arm is a pretty fair replica of a toothbrush with his fingers as the bristles when it's down at his side. It's not. The bristles grasp a German Luger, which is pointed at my gut. And he's shaking like a leaf.

"Who are you?" he demands.

Staring him in the eyes, I slowly look down at the gun and then back into his eyes. His shaking makes me nervous.

"I'm with the Key West Welcome Wagon, son. Now, why don't you put that pistol away or you won't get the goodies the Ladies' Auxiliary makes up for new neighbors."

"I said, 'Who are you?' wiseass."

He raises the gun so it's six inches from my face. His arm is quivering like a tuning fork.

The door opens outward, designed that way, I suppose, to give a little more space inside the cabin. I kick the door shut on his hand and smash into it with my shoulder. The gun falls and skitters across the deck. The wristbone crunches and a scream squeezes out of his mouth. Snatching up the gun, I carefully open the door. Mr. Tattoo is bent over holding his injured arm. His face is sweaty and white. He looks as if he might get sick.

"Are you Mallard?"

Wincing and whimpering, he splutters, "What if I am?"

I shove him inside and push him into a seat. I try to look solicitous. "Your wrist might be broken."

"I'm sure it is," he snuffles.

"Now we could get to a doctor right away or we could waste a lot of time. If you aren't civil, I'm going to abuse you with this pistol. By the time you do see a doctor you'll be in truly terrible shape. Understand?"

"Yes!" he cries out.

Bending over, he's holding that wrist as delicately as a newborn. Slowly, he extends his fingers and makes a weak fist. The wrist isn't broken. Even so, I doubt if he'll give me more trouble.

"Oh, oh," he moans with agony deeper than any physical pain.

"What's the matter?"

A FOOL'S DEATH

"My boss is going to kill me."

"What for?"

"For you getting my gun. For letting you come on board. For whatever the hell he wants."

"If you don't tell him, I won't," I promise.

"You won't?" he asked, his eyes taking on new life.

"Hell, no."

I look around and spot the bar. Going over, I pour a couple of fingers of bourbon in two glasses and hand him one. "Drink up. It'll do us both some good."

He throws it down in one swallow. "Thanks," he says almost happily.

"Now, are you Mallard?"

"Yes."

"A waitress at the Kraal says you might have a lead on a man I'm looking for."

I put the gun on a table and withdraw Marti's picture from my pocket. Nothing registers in Mallard's eyes. When I show him Andalusia's photo, he tries to look cool but a twitch of recognition's there.

"Why do you want these guys?"

"It's a long story. How do you know Andalusia?"

"Who?"

I tap Andalusia's picture with the gun.

Mallard's fearful again. He holds his head with the toothbrush arm and looks like he's about to cry. "I should never have told that waitress I knew him," he complains. "All right. All right. He's my boss. He owns this boat. But his name isn't Andalusia."

"What is it?"

Despite being hurt, he smiles. "Carl Durango. You must have heard of him. He wants me to check out anyone who might ask about him, but when you came, I simply became too frightened."

No wonder he's uptight. Durango runs a fair-sized cocaine business in south Florida. He goes by the nickname Snowman. Federal, state, and local cops have tried to nail him for years, but he's never where he's supposed to be when a drug deal is going down. And when he is, the deal isn't. Obviously, the guy has good snitches high up in law enforcement."

"What do you do for him?"

"This is the first thing, and probably the last. He hired me to bring the boat down from Miami. He said he'll show up in a few days."

"Where can I reach him?"

"You can't."

"Why not?"

"No one can. He reaches you. Like he calls me up and tells me to bring the boat down. If something goes wrong, there's a phone number to call. He may or may not get back."

"What's the number?"

He rattles one off. "It's just an answering service in Miami."

I store away the number, intending to call. I doubt if Andalusia or Durango or whatever he goes by today will get back to me. Why should he see some PI who's trying to check out his past? But I have to give it a shot.

"When he hits town, let him know I want to see him." I put one of my business cards next to the gun on the table.

As I'm leaving, his voice calls after me, kind of anxious. "Aren't you going to ask me?"

"What?"

"Why I got these tattoos."

Pausing, I turn and see the pathetic expression on his face. Those stupid tattoos. I feel a little bad for momentarily forgetting my curiosity. But, in truth, I already have him figured out. He's a lonely little guy who got them so people would ask about them. "I meant to ask, but that gun made me so nervous I forgot to."

"Sorry about the gun, but working for Durango makes me afraid. I've never done anything illegal before, if bringing a boat down is considered illegal. But I guess just working for the man must be illegal."

"Your tattoos."

"Right. I got them because no one else has anything like them. People are always curious about them."

A FOOL'S DEATH

That's all there is to it.

Heading down the pier, I see the back of a redhead entering Peter Matthews's boat. It looks like Amanda Kay. I don't get a good look, so I can't be sure. But I know it is. Why isn't she at school? I almost run up to her, but I don't. The hollowness of jealousy and disappointment comes over me. For a moment, I feel as if I should go over and fight for her or make some outrageous scene. But hell, all that would do would be to make me look like a bigger fool than I already am. I simply turn away, as if that will make me forget that I just saw her. To try to blot out my crumby thoughts, I turn my mind back to the case.

I'm wary about closing in on Andalusia. Maybe he and Marti are still in business together. Maybe that business still has something to do with Charlie. If so, why do they want the wives dead?

Goddamn it! What's Amanda Kay doing on Matthews's boat?

■■■■ 32 ■■■■

*L*IKE on a lot of nights of late, I'm tossing and turning. With a start, I wake up. Amanda Kay isn't lying next to me!

Frantic, I jump out of bed and enter the living room just as she comes through the front door. From the way her eyes open wide, she's as startled as me. She looks away and heads for the kitchen without saying anything.

I rush after her, so worried I'm furious. "Where the hell have you been, goddamn it? You could've gotten yourself killed."

Grabbing her, I pull her close as the truth of my words strikes home. She pushes away.

"I just had to get out for some air," she says. "I had to. I'm feeling so confined, so claustrophobic since this whole business started, Mason. I feel hemmed in."

Nodding wearily, I don't follow her back to bed. I spend the rest of the night in the living room, sitting in my favorite chair and thinking bad thoughts until I'm watching the sun rise. I haven't done this since she came to stay. Since I had someone to share my life. That worries me almost as much as the danger she might have put herself in when she went out and left me behind.

■ ■ ■ ■ 33 ■ ■ ■ ■

I'M in the office, feeling like a failure for the millionth time since starting on Charlie's case. I try not to think about Amanda Kay. Thankfully, the phone rings. Will Griswold's on the line.

"Mason, can you get down to Fat Dom's?"

"When?"

"Now."

"Why?"

"Somebody killed him."

As I walk down Petronia ten minutes later, the street is still. You can almost feel the dozens and dozens of eyes boring down from folks who disappeared into their houses. With the exception of two patrol cars out front with their red lights flashing, the neighborhood's as empty as a bar that ran out of booze.

A cop shows me in the front door. Griswold walks over and stands in front of me, hands on hips. "What do you know about this, Mason?"

Griswold isn't asking a question. He's making an accusation. Murders always make him mad.

"Nothing, Will. Not a thing."

A FOOL'S DEATH

I'm dismayed. Not by what he says but by what's here. Fat Dom's place has taken on the look of one of his modern paintings turned macabre. Splotches of red adorn the white stucco walls, and ripples of the same color are on the tiled floor.

The big man himself obviously did the redecorating in bewilderment, disbelief, fear, and finally agony. I can imagine what happened. Fat Dom clumsily crashing into walls and crawling across the floor. Right now, he's on the kitchen floor, a butcher knife buried in his back. A hell of a way to go.

"He wrote your name on the memo pad next to his phone and put a couple of exclamation points after it," Griswold says.

At least I know why I'm here. Usually, the chief tries to keep me away from everything. Now I might be a clue. Hell, maybe even a suspect.

"He called, but I was out. He left word on my machine he wanted to see me tonight." I eyeball Griswold. "You can check the machine. I haven't erased it yet."

"You know why he called you?"

"It may've had something to do with the Donne murders. He knew Marti. Did business with him a long time ago and kept doing business with him over the years."

"What else?"

Griswold's a good cop. He always wants as much information as possible, and he's suspicious of everybody. I've seen him grill rabbis, priests, and ministers as though they had just kidnapped his daughter.

"I owed him. He may have wanted me to do him a favor."

"Christ, I'd hate to see that favor."

"Me too, Will. Me too."

At the moment, I'd do a favor for Satan rather than have just about anybody wind up like garbage on the floor. Even Fat Dom deserved better. Probably.

"You know why anybody wanted him dead?" I ask.

He lets out an exasperated sigh. "Get serious, Mason." Griswold steps aside to let a police photographer get around him.

The question was pretty dumb. There must be hundreds of

people who wanted Fat Dom in his grave. Crazy customers. Used-up kids. Parents who saw a picture of their child in the kinds of collections Fat Dom sold. Maybe somebody he double-crossed. Who knows? When you choose a life on the dark side, your chances of dying of natural causes decrease exponentially.

"No sign of a break-in. He must've let the killer in himself." Griswold's talking more to himself than to me.

"Neighbors see anything?"

As the words climb out of my mouth, I realize that's another dumb question. Folks around here trust cops about as much as they take cruises on the Riviera.

"Ever try to get blood from a stone?"

"I assume the knife was one of his carving knives."

"That's right."

"Surely no prints."

"That's right."

"Anything stolen?"

"Place was ransacked, but doesn't appear to be."

"Think it was a professional hit?" I ask. "The mob getting back at Fat Dom for some infraction or another?"

"They're not this dirty."

His replies are even a bit more abrupt than usual, which for Griswold signals that he's holding back. In a way I figure it lets me off the hook. Now I don't feel too bad about being slow in telling him who Nick Andalusia is or that he's due here any day.

Still, it strikes me funny that Fat Dom died just as Marti's old partner and possible still partner is heading back to town. Maybe Mr. Marti is either with him or preceded him a bit. Or maybe they're both already here.

■■■■ 34 ■■■■

As the day shuts down, Amanda Kay calls. "I'll be a little late getting in tonight."

Her tone of voice makes my stomach knot up and leaves a metallic taste in my mouth. A faraway voice that's sliding away from me.

"Okay, honey. See you when you get there."

On the way home, I stop at the Full Moon where I fall into conversation with whoever comes and goes and stay longer and drink more than I should.

Like in most bars, people babble on about the state of the world. I babble back, feeling sorry for myself over losing the woman in my life. It makes me afraid. Who am I losing her to? Hell, I know the answer. A very charming guy.

When I finally bid everyone good-night, the falseness of booze has me in its grip. I'm best friends with people I wouldn't ordinarily have much to say to. Everybody thinks I'm a great guy. Tomorrow, we'll have trouble recognizing one another.

I go on automatic pilot to get home, wondering if I should take a ride out to Matthews's boat. What would I do if I got there? Act like a bigger jerk and take a swing at him?

Two blocks from the bar, a car pulls alongside of me and comes to a halt. "Hey, buddy," one of the guys inside calls out. "Can you tell us how to get to . . ." The address is lost in the night air.

As I approach the car, the rear door opens. A big guy gets out and offers an invitation. "Get in."

Though I'm sorely tempted to beg off, I comply because of what's in his hand. Glinting in the moonlight is the blue-black barrel of a vaguely familiar German Luger.

Silently, we speed off as I lament my fuzzy state of mind. There are two of them in the back with me and two more in the front. All are as beefy as ex-boxers. I'm wedged in like a fat lady's hips in a girdle. My bookends' fingers are decorated with heavy gold rings, the kind that fill in the space between joints.

I lean forward just to move my arms and to try to hatch a brilliant plan for what to do next. "Mind telling me what this is all about?" I ask.

Obviously, none of them find me charming. They don't bother answering. I slip into silence too, still trying to figure out what to do. A few minutes later, the car slows as the driver pulls onto the big old field off White Street and across from the Naval Air Annex. The only people who might be out here this time of night are occasional hippies or young people who sleep in their vans or cars. Tonight the field looks empty.

Since I have a pretty good idea of what they're about, I act fast. I smash my right elbow into the windpipe of the one on my right and grab the balls of the one on my left, squeezing for all I'm worth while he lets out an awful scream. The car erupts in pandemonium.

"Get the son of a bitch," yells the driver.

The guy on the passenger side turns around, swinging his fist like a jackhammer that strikes the guy on my right more often than me. I grab the driver by the throat as he brings the car to a stop. A split second later, I feel the cold steel of the Luger jammed against my temple.

"Cool it," says a panting voice.

I desist.

"Out of the car."

Climbing out, I know what's coming but not why. So I ask the obvious. "Who are you boys working for?"

"Mr. Durango doesn't like you asking questions about him."

Of course.

Two of them grab my arms and hold me. The two others take off their rings and I give a silent prayer of gratitude. They start working methodically, professionally. I'm glad they are pros. My getting the jump on them in the car didn't get them too pissed off. Amateurs might be so mad they'd cripple me or worse.

The first blow breaks my nose. The next few are to the kidneys. After that I lose count. As the blows rain down, I tell myself I'll get used to the thudding pain exploding in different parts of my body. In the few seconds between getting hit, dread of the next punch builds up and evaporates as a fist crashes into my ribs or gut. Eventually I black out.

When I come to, every inch of my body hurts. Each time I tentatively move, a new part of me screams out in agony. I vomit, not caring that booze and bile dribble down the front of me. Somehow, I get to my feet and determine that, except for my nose, no bones are broken. I don't seem to suffer any truly terrible damage. But a beating like that leaves more than physical pain. It does something to your spirit. Right now, I just want to crawl away and hide.

Eventually, I make it home and try not to make too much noise when I enter. Given the hour, Amanda Kay must be asleep. In the bathroom, I strip off my vomit-and-blood-stained shirt and pants. The face staring back at me from the mirror is swollen. The nose is in the wrong place. The eyes are slits. Vomit is caked on my jaw. The whole effect is like some child's lumpy clay man. Trembling, I feel icy cold even though the night is warm and the humidity high.

The bathroom door opens. Amanda Kay lets out a gasp. Her

right hand clutches her robe around her throat as she stares. "Oh, my God, Mason." That's all she says as her eyes well up with tears.

Without another word, she leads me to the bedroom and helps me lie down. A minute later, she lifts my head and gives me a stiff drink of bourbon. I hold her hand, grateful she's the kind of woman who's sensible enough not to ask right now what happened. Tears of pain and rage trickle down my face. If I ever need tenderness, it's now. The last thing I remember is her caring look as she lightly places cold compresses on my face and carefully washes the dirt away from the bruises on my tired, battered body.

■■■■ 35 ■■■■

THE man is never alone.

I keep Andalusia under surveillance. Several days of monitoring his activities result in a pattern of sorts. He takes his meals on the boat, and he's never by himself. The four heavies who worked out on me plus little Mallard are usually around either en masse or two or three at a time. Other than that there is no real pattern to his movements.

When I'm not watching Andalusia, Mike Sanders is. I occasionally hire Mike on his off hours to tail somebody for me. He's getting good at it. More than for the money, he does it for the experience. He's smart and realizes the more he can do the better off he is.

I tell Mike that Andalusia's also the drug lord Durango. For his own protection, I want him to know just what he's up against. That, of course, makes the assignment that much juicier to him. Naturally, he wants to know if I've informed Griswold. I assure him I'm just about to do so. And I will at some point. But I don't want to jeopardize anything. There's no telling what the police chief will do when he learns who's on his island.

The police rendering of Andalusia is recognizable but off

the mark. Now he's tall with an iron gray mustache that's cut a lot shorter than in the newspaper pictures and mug shot. The most startling physical change is that he isn't brawny anymore. He looks haggard. His face is thin, almost sunken. He lost a lot of weight and it's recent, judging by the way most of his clothes hang on him. He looks like an old bull who ran out of steam.

As I noted, Andalusia's activities are pretty much unpredictable. One day he's driven up as far as Plantation Key, stopping off at various marinas on Plantation, Windley, Upper Matecumbe, Lower Matecumbe, and Long keys. Maybe he's setting up drug runs. Another day he's driven out to the airport and just sits there for a couple of hours before returning to the boat. Another day he takes out the boat, but not far, and I can monitor what he's doing through field glasses. All I see taking place out on the water is him and a couple of the heavies fishing.

There's no sign of Marti, which makes me more than a little uneasy. I expect the bastard to show his face around Andalusia. Now I worry that Andalusia might disappear, and I won't have a clue to where Marti is or why he or both of them are killing the Donnes. I figure I have to do something drastic. To do that I have to catch Andalusia alone. If that isn't possible, I'll have to act anyway.

While tracking Andalusia, I'm slowly mending, both in mind and body, and even better, my relationship with Amanda Kay is getting back on track. Physically, I feel human again. A doctor rearranged my nose. Most of the swelling left my face, so that I look fairly normal. I've also taken to carrying a Colt .45, which I wear in an ankle holster.

One night, three heavies and Mallard leave the boat. The one who stays on board sits in the stern drinking beer and watching TV. Andalusia's out of sight. Fortunately, the break comes just as Mike and I are about to change shifts. We work out a little plan, a simple one with Mike acting as a decoy. Still in uniform, he goes up to the boat to lure the creep on board into a vulnerable position.

"Say," Mike calls out when he gets near the boat.

At first, the heavy doesn't hear because he's watching a baseball game. The volume of his TV is so high you could hear the game in Havana.

"You!" Mike booms.

The guy's head snaps up. When he sees the uniform, he puts down his beer and tries to act like an ordinary citizen.

"Help you, Officer?"

Mike stands there and says something, but the guy can only catch a couple of words. Finally, he gets up from his seat and leans over the stern. "What's that, Officer?"

As he bends down, I step out of the shadows with my gun drawn, reach up, bunch up his shirt, and yank him over the tail of the boat. Sprawling on the pier on all fours, he finds a gun jammed in his face.

"Remember me?" I ask.

Panicky eyes scream that he does. "On your feet," I say softly.

He complies. I search him quickly before taking him into the shadows. When we were almost to the jeep, he tries an old trick. Dropping to his knees, he hopes I'll stumble over him since I'm right behind. In one of those rare moments of foresight, I anticipate the move and stand my ground.

As his hand snakes out toward my ankle, I smash down on it with the heel of my shoe and whip the pistol barrel across his mouth. Teeth crunch sickeningly. When the gun next collides with his temple, he goes out cold. I cuff his hands behind him, shove a hanky in his mouth, and load him into the rear of the jeep where I lash his feet to his hands.

"Nothing personal," I say when the slob starts coming to. The comment isn't quite truthful.

I creep aboard the *Purple Mermaid* a lot quieter than I have to because the TV set's on. When I open the door to the cabin, I see the back of Andalusia's head. He's sitting in a swivel chair, staring out at the water, a headset plugged into his ears. The pungent scent of marijuana fills the cabin. Coming up behind him, I yank off the earphones. Angrily, he spins around and finds himself staring into the barrel of my gun. There's no fear in either his eyes or his voice.

"Who the fuck are you?"

"Mason Collins, Mr. Andalusia. I've had difficulty reaching you."

He takes a drag on the joint between the thumb and index finger of his right hand. "Oh, yeah. The asshole who was flashing a picture of me around here." He shakes his head. "It's real stupid of you to come here. What happened before will happen again, only worse."

"And you could wind up dead if it does."

Andalusia lets out a bitter barking laugh. "Now that's funny. That's real funny."

I look at his sallow, drawn skin, the deep circles around his eyes, and the joint in his hand. I'm staring at a dying man. "Cancer?"

"You're a smart guy, Collins. Yeah, it's cancer."

"How much longer do you have?"

"Couple of months."

"The grass help?"

"A lot. Funny, isn't it. A doctor told me to smoke it to help with the pain. Me of all people." That laugh barks again.

"Maybe there is a God after all."

"Don't be a wiseass, Collins." He laughs a little more. "Now what the hell are you doing here?"

"How do I reach Carlos Marti?"

Andalusia looks at me oddly. "Switchblade? Christ, I haven't heard about him for years. What the hell do you want with him?"

"To find out why he's acting out that vendetta against the Donnes."

He looks at me even more strangely. "Back up, Collins, you're not making any sense. What the hell are you talking about?"

I stare at him coldly. "The night you allegedly killed Marti, he threatened David Donne and his brother, Gerald, and his son, Charlie. Over the years, he's carried it out, and now he's after

Charlie Donne's ex-wives and younger brother. Maybe you're in on it too."

"You're real good for laughs, Collins." Barking again, Andalusia holds up his joint. "Christ Almighty! How much of this shit have you been smoking? The night I allegedly killed Switchblade, huh? Tell me more."

"Don't bullshit me, Andalusia. You know what I'm talking about."

"Honest to God, I don't. Take the word of a dying man. What the hell are you talking about?"

What strikes me as odd is that he looks perplexed. Maybe he smoked his brains out. So I play along and rehash Charlie's story, taking him back to the diving days, the big discovery, Marti spying on them, the alleged murder. Every once in a while, he lets out an appreciative chuckle or gives that goddamn unnerving laughter. I end up with showing his and Marti's picture around in an attempt to find them.

"That's pretty wild," he says. "You say you got all that from a long letter Charlie Donne wrote you in case he died like a fuck-up?"

"That's it. What's your version?"

He stares hard at me for a full minute. "Why not?" he finally mutters, then takes a last drag from the joint and pinches it out. "Yeah, I knew David Donne. I worked for him a bit that summer and had a small stake in the dive boat. That part's right. But we had a falling-out before he hit it big."

Sitting back, he collects his thoughts. "What pissed me off was that it was just a little bit after I left that goddamn salvage boat that he made his big strike. I never had no map. I never got cut in for a major percentage of the treasure. I saw his kid, but until you reminded me of his name, I'd forgotten it and him too. As for my killing Switchblade, well, maybe I should have, but for other reasons than you gave me."

He shoots me a black look. "All that stuff you just said about me is bullshit. Pure bullshit."

A FOOL'S DEATH

My head feels about as hammered as it did the night Andalusia's boys got hold of me. What bothers me is that I consider myself a pretty fair judge of character. Andalusia's up-front about what he is. A tough son of a bitch. If the percentages are right, he'd lie, cheat, steal, and cut your heart out and eat it. Yet, right now, I have the uneasy feeling he's telling the truth.

What does he have to gain unless he's the one killing off the Donnes? Why would he when he could hire somebody to do it for him? Moreover, he strikes me as the kind of guy who doesn't have the patience to wait years and years to kill somebody he wants dead. He'd just pick up a gun and blow his intended victim's head off and go after the next one a minute later with about as much remorse as if he'd stepped on a roach.

"Is Marti capable of murder?"

Andalusia laughs again. "Are you capable of breathing, Collins?"

Getting up, he goes to the bar and puts ice in a couple of glasses. "You look like you need a drink. What'll you have?"

"Bourbon." A terrible thought crosses my mind. Charlie's Section 8. What if he were crazy? Like the wives, how much did I really know about him? Angrily, I shove aside such thoughts. Remorse sweeps over me for betraying a friend.

Andalusia hands me my drink. "Congratulations," he says, raising his glass. "You made me think about something other than dying for the first time in months."

Sitting down carefully, he gives a grunt of pain. One thing I'm sure about. He isn't lying about dying or being in agony.

"One thing you said makes sense. This kind of squirrelly death thing is like Switchblade. Right before we split up, he killed a guy. Took him by surprise when the guy left a hotel. Marti had seen him register and knifed him later. I asked him why. It turned out the guy had insulted him years ago. Switchblade never forgot."

Taking a swallow of his drink, Andalusia's tired eyes lock on mine. "You made me remember something else."

"What?"

A FOOL'S DEATH

"Switchblade had a hard-on for David Donne and his brother. I don't know why, but he hated them."

"Is he squirrelly enough to knock off the whole Donne family?"

That barking laugh comes again, mixed with a strain of pain. "Switchblade is as crazy as they come, Collins. I wouldn't put anything past him."

"So what you're saying is that I'm looking for the right guy but for the wrong reason?"

"Sounds it. What I don't understand is why the kid came up with that wild tale about me."

"How'd Marti screw you?"

Andalusia glowers. "Just as we started making good money running dope, he stole my share. I heard he bought an old cruiser with it."

"Do you have any idea where I might find him?"

The laugh comes out one more time.

"What's so funny now?"

"If I did, you wouldn't have to go looking for him." Anger clouds his face. "Nobody would!"

Once again, I believe him. We're both quiet for a minute.

"If you do find him, you can be sure of one thing."

"What's that?"

"Some real young girl will be with him."

I finish off the drink, put the glass down, and get up to go. "So I've heard."

As I head toward the door, Andalusia calls after me. "Come back anytime, Collins. I'll be around the island another week or so. And don't worry about the leg breakers coming after you again."

"Thanks," I say dryly.

A minute later, I'm on the dock, trying to sort out the conversation. My head aches.

"Everything all right?" Mike asks.

"Yes and no. But we don't have to bother tailing Andalusia anymore."

At the jeep I untie the heavy and take the cuffs off him. The idea of avenging myself is pointless. Andalusia will do more to him for screwing up than I could think of doing. All the while I wonder about the versions of what happened down here twenty-five years ago. Charlie's and Andalusia's. Who's right? What's real? Who's playing games?

■ ■ ■ ■ 36 ■ ■ ■ ■

I'M eating lunch at El Loro Verde, a little Mex joint right next to a hard-drinking bar named the Green Parrot. This is as close as I get to the Parrot during the day. It's too easy to get wrapped up in a game of pool and then another and not emerge until dark.

Halfway through a pair of burritos, I move over as Georgie Two Foot sidles up next to me. He's not wearing his dancing duds but a straw cowboy hat and khaki work clothes that probably make him look like his father, who ran a sugarcane plantation in Cuba until he fled with his family to the U.S. after Castro came to power. He whispers so low I can't hear.

"Speak up, Georgie."

His soft brown eyes dart back and forth, even though nobody around is trying to eavesdrop or gives a damn about us. Sometimes my being a private eye makes Georgie act simpleminded. He comes on mysterious as hell when he sees me in public and knows something he thinks I want to know. It drives me nuts. Now, without saying anything, he gives me a look heavy with meaning and jerks his head toward the door.

Annoyed, I ram the other burrito into my mouth and wash it down with the last of my beer, leave money on the counter, and follow him outside. I wipe my mouth with the paper napkin I take out of the waistband of my trousers.

"This better be good, Georgie."

He walks over to his Ford pickup truck, which is so ancient and battered it makes Charlie's Chevy look spanking new. He finally turns around. "You are looking for a Señor Marti?" he asks softly, still glancing around furtively.

"You know goddamn well I am. Everybody on the island does."

"A friend knows where he is."

"And just where is this friend?"

"Tonight, I will take you to him."

Georgie isn't here out of the goodness of his heart. What'll he hammer me for? "How much?"

"Fifty dollars."

"You goddamn bandit."

"Half now."

I pull out my wallet. At this moment, I have a total of seventy dollars to my name. Reluctantly, I fork over two tens and a five. Georgie isn't always the most trustworthy of men. "Don't stand me up, you dancing fool, or I'll have Griswold shake down your shack." He worries about Griswold. Georgie sells moonshine *compuesto*, a Cuban drink whose ingredients include anisette and rock candy. It packs a wallop.

"I'll pick you up outside your office at eight-thirty," he says.

As he climbs into the old truck, I'm about to suggest that we go in the jeep. "How far we going?" I ask.

"Upper Matecumbe Key."

Hell, let him drive. I don't want to spend the gas money.

Edgy and anxious the rest of the day, I'm hoping that Georgie's contact is for real. Another possibility crosses my mind. Carlos Marti is a common name. Maybe the guy we're going to see doesn't know the right one. But Georgie's not stupid. He's my best tipster in the Cuban community.

Sure enough, the truck rumbles to a stop in front of my office building at eight forty-five or so, which is punctual for him. I never consider Georgie late until at least an hour has gone by.

He has a bottle of *compuesto* going, which he passes over, but I decline. I want all my wits about me tonight.

In a little bit, we leave Key West behind and putter up the coastal highway. The moon shining off the sea is our only light. If the old truck could move faster, I'd worry about Georgie's drinking and driving. But if he can stay reasonably in the northbound lane, we'll be okay. It's Friday night and the only traffic is going the other way. Mostly it's pickup trucks filled with guys and girls revved up to bust loose in the Key West bars.

"What is this guy?" I ask.

"A *partido*."

That's Latino for an owner of fighting roosters. Cockfights are supposed to be illegal, but then a lot of things are supposed to be. Down here you scratch around a little and you can usually find what you're looking for, including high-stakes gambling on cockfights. In Key West, the fights used to be held on Amelia Street right next to the Cuban social club. Now they're mostly held on the other keys.

Cubans in particular take the sport seriously. The owners hire *galleros*, or trainers, and pay them to get the birds in fighting shape. The roosters are bred around the Keys and in Puerto Rico much the way racehorses are. Winners are big studs. Bloodlines are important.

Georgie rambles on about the cockfight business, which he has been exposed to since he was a kid. "Before the revolution, my father would get fighting cocks in Havana for maybe thirty or forty dollars," Georgie says in a tone bordering on awe. "Today you could not get one for ten times that price."

He just telegraphed that he's drunk. When he's sober, Georgie professes to hate Castro and equates Fidel's takeover of the island with Stalinism. When he's drunk, he nostalgically refers to "the revolution" or "before the revolution," just the way dedicated Castroites do.

After we hit Upper Matecumbe, we drive on a bit before Georgie

A FOOL'S DEATH

turns onto a narrow road that cuts through such lush foliage that I didn't even see the turnoff. All goes black as even the moonlight is blocked by the flora. We further slow down as we push through dense palms and bushes for a spell before we hear the rumbling of an occasional motorcycle, car doors slamming, and voices talking. All at once we are in a clearing that's jammed with cars, bikes, and pickup trucks. We park and go over to a twenty-foot-high, corrugated-steel building.

The place is cavernous. Tiers of crowded benches encircle the big sawdust ring where the fights take place. The arena is jam-packed, hectic, smoky, and noisy. The crowd is mostly Latino males who are feeling no pain from rum and home brew; greasy, tattooed bikers with their women; and expensively draped couples, black and white, who look as if they have money to burn. Chances are the latter are financing their lifestyles through the drug trade. The atmosphere creates the frenzy that blood sports always bring out. Tempers flare. Booze and drugs fan the flames.

The betting is feverish. Besieged bookies, holding decks of playing cards, stand by the edge of the ring. As the crowd yells, the bookies hold up the decks of cards. Bettors fork over money and the bookie rips a card in half, keeping half and giving you half. If you win, you match up your half with the one he holds.

We squeeze into seats just as the cocks are brought into the ring. A hush falls over the arena.

The birds, one red and golden and the other almost pure black, are lean and mean. Most of their feathers are plucked, except for some around their necks and wings. They look scrawny, but don't be fooled. Their weapons are their beaks and sharp spurs, deadly metal talons that are fitted onto their feet.

The birds are held by men who move closer and closer until the birds are almost beak to beak, straining viciously to get at each other. Suddenly, the men drop the birds to the ground. The crowd lets out a wild roar.

Propelled by the hysteria in the air, the birds charge. They leap and tumble over each other in a mini-riot. The crowd goes nuts. People jump up and down, screaming, waving their arms, and generally having a good time. The building shakes and thunders like a giant oil drum somebody's beating on. Bloodcurdling yells urge the birds to peck their rivals to death: *"Pica! Pica!"*

A vein rips open on one bird. Shrieks go up: *"La vena! La vena!"*

The roosters look like they're in a blender. Swirling, sawdust flying, they lock together in a tumbling ball, attacking like mad things. The black one flies in the air, suspended for a couple of seconds, spurs jutting like switchblades before pouncing on the red rooster's neck. Red screeches. His neck rips open. Blood showers the sawdust.

Red valiantly tries to get to his feet. Blackie moves in for the kill, beak hammering. The first of the wild fights ends with one rooster a mangled loser.

Halfway into the second match, a man comes up and shoves into the seat next to me. Fascinated by the spectacle, I don't bother looking at him. Everybody's pushing and shoving to get a better look at the feathered gladiators.

"Are you looking for Carlos Marti?" he whispers in my ear in heavily accented English.

Turning, I face a stocky Cuban with the wide, serious brown face of a Kodiak bear. He's in his fifties and wears thick-lensed, horn-rimmed glasses. Like a lot of Cubans his age, he's meticulously dressed in a starched white shirt, tie, and brown slacks.

"I am."

"Come with me, please."

Rising, he pushes through the crowd toward the exit. Georgie stays where he is, but I follow right behind. We pry and shove our way through the wall of glassy-eyed people, who grow more feverish as the violence builds up and up again. I feel the heat of blood on my back as we near the door. Passions run high. A fight starts somewhere in the center of the crowd. Near the exit and oblivious to everyone, a biker couple are locked in a torrid embrace and a young Latino couple are in a hip-grinding number.

Outside, the air feels cool. I look around quickly, waiting to see if anyone comes through the door after us. Nobody does.

The Cuban looks at me expectantly. "We are alone, Señor Collins."

"Just making sure."

Pulling cigarettes from his shirt pocket, he holds out the pack while putting one in his mouth.

"No thanks."

"Why do you want to see Señor Marti?"

He doesn't bother offering his name, and I don't ask. He's setting the ground rules.

"I'd like to see if we're talking about the same guy," I say, but from his watchful expression I'm sure we are. "He had a salvage boat in Key West about twenty-five years ago and got into the drug business after that."

Letting out a stream of smoke, he replies warily. "Sí, sí. This is the same man. Now I ask again. Why do you want to see him?"

"I think he killed a friend of mine," I blurt out angrily. "A couple of friends actually. I want to see that he doesn't hurt anybody else."

He looks at me with dismay. "Yes, of course. You must have carried this burden with you a long time now. This need for vengeance."

Maybe I should have kept my mouth shut in front of this guy, but it's too late now. "Not so long. They were both killed within the past month. And I don't want vengeance as much as I want the killings stopped. Other people are on his crazy hit list. I just want him put away before he gets them too."

His look becomes more curious. "I am sorry. My English is not always good. How long ago were these friends of yours killed?"

"Within the past several weeks."

"Yes, that is what I thought you said." He seems lost in thought. For a moment, I think he's going to say something else about the time frame, but he doesn't. "I will let you meet Señor Marti."

"When?"

"Soon, Señor Collins. Soon."

A FOOL'S DEATH

Taking out one of my business cards, I put my home number on the back. "Real soon, I hope."

He takes the card and starts walking away. "Say," I call after him. "Mind my asking your connection to him?"

He gets a troubled look. "Yes, I mind."

I dismiss the notion of following him to his car and getting his license plate number. I don't want to risk getting caught and blowing the whole deal. The guy appears sober and responsible. I don't think he has a scam going. For one, he didn't squeeze me for any dough. Yet.

As I head back inside, I brush against a drunken biker. That's all it takes. Spinning around, he smashes a right hook into my left shoulder. I go flying into the doors, manage to turn around, and a fist crunches into my chest. Incredible pain explodes where I'm hit. My body's still black-and-blue from where the pros worked me over. The pain makes me madder.

I sidestep a kick. Coming from down low and with all my might, I drive a fist into his gut. He lets out an "Ooomph!" and doubles over. Holding his head down with both hands, I knee him in the face. His head snaps back and his legs shoot out into mine. Both of us tumble to the ground in a sweaty, heaving heap.

A roar of laughter makes me look up. Snake stands there laughing like a fool. Bending down, he grabs my arms and drags me to my feet. He yanks up my sparring partner too.

"Don't start anything else, Leroy," Snake warns the biker, who is doubled over but looking at me mean again. Snake's words barely came out, he's laughing so hard.

"What the hell's so funny?" I growl.

"You're too old for this shit, Mason," he says, brushing me off.

"You want to find out?" I roar, trying not to sound as winded as I am. Pride is my stupid side.

He drags Leroy away and a herd of Padres follow. A few minutes later, they're roaring their way out of the parking lot when Snake stops his bike in front of me for a moment. "There's something else about that guy who was askin' about Charlie. I'll tell you the next time I see you."

A FOOL'S DEATH

Before I have the sense to ask what, he blasts away in a shower of cinders. The Padres disappear, polluting the night air with earsplitting rumbles. Like those in heavy-metal bands, bikers must be deaf by the time they're thirty.

Back inside, I struggle to my seat. Judging by Georgie's goofy, glazed look and incoherent screams, it's obvious he's hit the *compuesto* pretty hard.

I bet on the next couple of bouts, but I can't concentrate on the bloody chickens. My ribs are aching, and I'm thinking of the Cuban. When will he put me onto Marti? I also wonder what the circumstances will be like. One-on-one? I doubt it. More likely, Marti will have men hidden everywhere with guns pointed at my vital parts. So what can I do when I come face-to-face with the killer? No answer comes to mind.

Georgie's shouts come less frequently. His brown bottle is finally empty. Finally, he slides sideways. His mouth is wide open when his head hits the bench. I heft him over my shoulder. Using Georgie as a battering ram, I get through the crowd.

Outside, the night seems hotter. Georgie weighs a ton by the time I throw him into the cab. Searching his pockets for the truck keys, I find them and drive us home. All the while, I'm anxious as hell, hoping the Cuban calls soon and worried about the women.

Back in Key West, leaving Georgie to sleep it off in his truck, I get in the jeep and drive past Virginia's. Two lights are in the window. While I'm stopped outside, a patrol car comes up. A voice calls out, "What are you doing there, mister?"

Before I can answer, a blinding flashlight beam hits me full face. "Oh, it's you, Mason."

I now recognize Tim Marples's voice. He's one of the young cops who live below me.

"Like you guys, I'm checking on the ladies. I take it there're no problems."

"None at all, Mason. None at all."

I drive home feeling a little better. All three wives are staying at Virginia's tonight. I asked Amanda Kay to go there since I didn't know what time I'd be getting home. She asked Betty over too. I feel a little better knowing they are all together. Virginia has her weapons and Amanda Kay took along my .38. She didn't want to, but I insisted.

At the apartment, the old restlessness comes on, the not wanting to go to sleep because there's nobody there to share the bed. When you're alone, it's easy enough to sleep or eat too much or too little and definitely to drink too much. Some of us need other people to help us regulate our lives. At least I seem to.

■■■■ 37 ■■■■

A big yellow-and-red-striped tent takes up a good portion of Big Bill and Peggy's backyard. Under the tent, tables are laden with enough food and booze to maintain an army. There's also an ice swan. Peggy insisted Bill get one for the reception. She read about them in a brides' magazine.

The wedding went off without a hitch. A couple of days ago, they decided to skip a church ceremony. Instead, a preacher married them on the deck of the newly renamed *The Miss Peggy*. Peggy turned out in a long white dress and a veil, which she wore proudly. She looked pretty and happy. Bill looked like a lawn gnome in a morning suit. Amanda Kay was late meeting me, so she and I got to the service after it started.

This promises to be the biggest reception of the year. Half the island is here. In one corner of the yard is a stage where the band plays loud and sometimes well when it isn't being interrupted by drunken boat captains who hog the microphone as they toast the bride and groom. After getting up there and thanking everybody, Peggy and Bill make the rounds to see everyone personally.

A FOOL'S DEATH

When they come up to Amanda Kay and me, there are big hugs and kisses all around. "I just want to say thanks, Mason," Bill says, grabbing my hand and pumping it. "You got Peggy to give me another chance and I won't forget it."

"It wasn't me, Bill."

He looks a bit fuzzy. "Then who was it?"

"You. You're the one who got your life back in order."

"Yeah, but thanks for what you did, Mason. You softened the old girl up for me."

" 'Old girl'?" Peggy says in mock horror. "Christ, you'd better do better than that if you don't want this 'old girl' to hand you divorce papers tomorrow morning."

We all laugh and they head off to talk to other people. A slow number comes on.

"Let's dance," Amanda Kay says.

She's wearing a pale green dress that's great for her hair and coloring, making her look even prettier than usual. She puts her head on my shoulder.

"Lucky, aren't they?" she says.

"Yes, but I feel lucky right now too."

"So do I, Mason. I just wish things could go on like this forever. People having a good time. No cares. This is the way life is supposed to be. If I ever get rich, I'll buy a yacht and float around the world having a carefree time with you at my side."

She hugs me tight and speaks softly through her tears. "I just wish no harm would ever come to anyone, Mason. That the sun would always shine and that . . ." She lapses into quiet.

I know what she's thinking. I hold her as hard as I can but feel powerless at the same time. The murderer is around somewhere. She doesn't want him to get her. We all know I can't stop him from going about his grisly business.

Like a changing tide, Amanda Kay's mood lifts. She wants to keep dancing, but I beg off. She dances with some younger guys and with some women, while I catch up with some folks

A FOOL'S DEATH

I haven't seen for a while. At one point, a dark-haired, good-looking woman comes up and taps me on the shoulder. She's wearing a red and white polka-dot dress and high heels and looks like a model for evening wear at some elegant place in the Caribbean.

"Mason Collins, you probably don't remember me," she says.

"Sure I do, Beverly. How are you?"

"Good. I just wanted to thank you for not telling Harold where I was and to tell you everything is going okay for me."

"If you have any more trouble with him, let me know," I reply. "How'd you get here?"

She points across the crowd to a guy I know slightly, another boat captain who knows Big Bill. "He's my date, but I wanted to invite you out to see the show again."

Life is funny. When you're without a woman, you can't find one. When you have one, others are stepping over themselves to find you.

"Someday I will," I promise, just wanting to be obliging.

"Someday you'll what?" Amanda Kay asks, slipping her arm through mine.

Before I can introduce the women, Beverly gives me a mischievous look. "Hope to run into you again, Mason." She melts into the crowd.

"Who was that?" Amanda Kay demands. She puts her hands on her hips and glares after Beverly.

"The soon-to-be ex-wife of an ex-client. She is not a romantic interest of mine. I only have one of those, and that happens to be you."

"Good," she says, standing on her toes and kissing me.

The afternoon continues on a pleasant note. By nightfall we've drunk enough and eaten enough to feel as if maybe God doesn't hate the human race after all. As the moon rises in the sky, I once again realize how lucky I am to be with Amanda Kay. Like a lot of other people, we're lying on blankets on the ground. There's a slight breeze and the humidity has lifted. I'm feeling that contented laziness you get when things are just right. Suddenly, my name is called out over the band's microphone.

"Mason Collins! Mason Collins. Please go to the front of the house."

"What could that be?" Amanda Kay asks.

"Damned if I know," I say, hauling myself to my feet.

A few minutes later, as I come around the front of the house, I get a sinking sensation when I see who summoned me. My limbs turn leaden. My walk slows.

Will Griswold is leaning against the side of a squad car. Instinctively, I feel sad, frustrated, and guilty for not being more than I am. The whole day becomes a bad joke, a way of lulling Amanda Kay and me into thinking that maybe all was right with the world for a change. Griswold's face tells me everything's lousy.

"Didn't want to come back to get you and disturb the party," he says.

"Yeah, that wouldn't've been right."

"I'd like you to come with me."

"I've got Amanda Kay with me. I take it you don't want her along."

"Rather not. You see, it's Virginia." He rubs his weary eyes. "She's dead."

I knew he was going to say the word. I just hadn't known if the name would be Virginia or Betty.

Awkwardly, he looks at his feet. "I'll have two of my men take Amanda Kay back to your place and stay with her until you get back."

I walk to the backyard as if in a trance. Kneeling next to Amanda Kay, I hold her to me and start rocking her like a baby. A shudder shoots through her.

"It's happened again, hasn't it?" she says.

She pulls back from me, eyes blazing. "He's done it again, hasn't he?" Suddenly, she yells, "Hasn't he!"

A hush falls over the crowd. People gather around.

"What's wrong?" somebody asks.

"What's happened?" asks somebody else. Questions and murmurs ripple through the crowd.

"Yes," I say, reaching out for her, but she pulls away again.

"Who?" she asks hoarsely. "Who this time?"

I have to answer, but at first I can't. I clear my throat. "Virginia. Griswold just told me. He wants me to go with him. Two officers will take you back when you want to leave."

"*Ooooooooaaah* . . ." A howl of agony and despair erupts from her. She hugs herself and wails in a piercing, terrible way. That dissolves into tears and crying, the kind of crying that makes you think the person will never stop. When I try to hold her, she fights me, scratching and punching.

Peggy runs up and kneels next to Amanda Kay. She speaks softly to her, as if gentling a horse. "There, there, girl. There, there."

Just as suddenly as she started up, Amanda Kay collapses like a rag doll. Her crying stops too.

"I don't want to die, Mason. Please don't let me die."

"I won't, honey," I reply. "I won't."

All I know is that I'd do anything for her, die for her if need be, but I'm a fraud. Dying for her would be easy. I don't think I can keep her alive.

Rising, Peggy goes over to Big Bill. She's crying and he holds her tight. There's a grass stain on her wedding dress from where she was kneeling. For some reason, that smudge brings all the misery of the past few weeks down on me. My legs buckle. I catch myself and will myself to keep going on, keep moving like a dray horse going through life. If I don't keep trying, everything will fall apart.

A few minutes later, I help Amanda Kay into the back of the cop car. I'm glad Tim Marples is one of the officers who will be with her. He's a good cop. I trust him right now as much as I can trust anybody with Amanda Kay. As they drive away, her sobs ring in my ears. I feel guilty for not being with her, but I'd feel guiltier if I didn't go with Griswold. I have to get on with what I'm doing.

"Where's Betty?" I ask as I climb into Griswold's car.

Banging the steering wheel with the palm of his hand, he speeds up the street, tires screeching. "Can't find her!"

■ ■ ■ ■ **38** ■ ■ ■ ■

THE two lights are still on in her window, but it doesn't mean a damned thing.

Virginia looks peaceful. She's sitting upright in the old-fashioned metal tub, the kind with lion's-claw feet. Her eyes are closed as if she's asleep. Her dark hair is dry and her arms are outstretched, gripping the sides of the tub. Her flesh looks supple and alive. A red silk bathrobe, casually draped across the top of a white wicker hamper, waits for her. Her shotgun lies on the floor by the tub. You expect her to wake up and tell you to get the hell out.

The water is room temperature. She may have been here for a number of hours.

Sickeningly, I think Betty might be in a similar state.

As I leave the bathroom, my legs wobble again. I manage to get to a bed in the room next door and sit down, hoping the light-headedness passes soon. But it worsens with her presence around me.

Her white T-shirt, navy shorts streaked with what looks like paint or caulking, and the pale blue underwear that she kicked out of just before taking a bath are scattered on the floor. The aromas of her life are in little bottles of perfume on the vanity. Pictures of family and friends, including a large photo of Charlie, hang on the walls.

Virginia herself is now only a woman trapped in photographs, a signature on paintings, a fading memory for those who knew her. Soon we'll feel bad that there isn't more of her with us. Nothing makes sense, this kind of death least of all.

I'm sick of myself. How could I have let this happen again? I should have followed that goddamn Cuban, beaten him until he told me where Marti is. But I acted rationally in the face of crazy murders. I let him walk away like a guy debating about whether to tell me about a good used car, instead of a murderer, a psycho who thinks he has a license to kill my friends.

"You okay?"

There's more than a trace of concern in Griswold's face. He looks older than he did at Pepe's when I told him Charlie and Marlene were killed. I'm sure if I could see my own face for real, I'd see wrinkles of weariness, bitterness, and frustration that weren't there long ago either.

"Give me a few more minutes."

He heads downstairs. I hear him talking to some of his men who are dusting for prints, checking to see how the killer gained access to the house, and doing all the other lousy things cops do when confronting the business of murder.

I go back into the bathroom, and careful not to disturb anything, I kneel next to the tub. "I'm sorry, Virginia. God, I'm sorry."

Tears of sorrow, frustration, and rage roll down my cheeks. Another wonderful woman, one filled with the energy of life, is gone. And what about Betty? How could I have let this happen again?

"I'm just not up to the job Charlie left me," I say out loud. "He should have entrusted you wives to someone else."

Struggling to my feet, I wipe my eyes and head downstairs just as a crash of thunder breaks the sky and rain roars down. I think of all the people scurrying around at Bill and Peg's reception, jamming together under the tent, or racing to cars and trucks as the storm tears everything to shreds.

In my mind's eye, I see Peggy in her wedding dress with the grass stain in the front, the rain mercilessly pounding her so that her dress is ruined, the way her day is ruined. Years back, she went out with Charlie for a while. I breathe a sigh of relief that she never married him. She has Bill to look out for her, not me.

Griswold is in the kitchen, checking out the windows. "I can't figure it," he says. "There's no sign of a break-in. It's like the killer hid in here waiting for her, but I don't know how the hell he got in."

Mike Sanders drifts over, holding a caulking tube. "This was by a window off the second-floor porch, Chief. A pane is newly puttied. The killer might've broken the pane to enter and then fixed it so nobody'd notice."

Griswold scratches his head and looks at Mike as if he never saw him before. "Could be, boy. Could be."

I can tell he's impressed both by Mike's powers of observation and his reasoning, especially since Griswold himself was stumped as to how the killer got in. Better yet, Mike knows he's impressed. I don't remark on the caulking on Virginia's shorts, which indicates she did the window job herself. She always did all her own repairs. Maybe they'll figure that out when her clothes are examined, if they are. Let Mike have a moment of glory.

"The regular coroner's back," Griswold says. "I asked him to do the autopsy, instead of farming it out."

"Good," I say. Neither of us wants to mention our lack of confidence in poor Joe Wilson.

"You got any leads on this Marti prick?"

"I don't know where he is," I reply truthfully.

Griswold picks up right away on the discrepancy between what he asked and what I answered, but he doesn't pursue it. He knows he wouldn't get anywhere.

Nodding across the room at Mike Sanders, Griswold says, "He

told me about this Andalusia being Durango. From the way he's acting, he knows I have him under surveillance. He's not doing a damned thing. Near as I can figure it, he's waiting. Who or what for, I have no idea."

I'd never heard Griswold volunteer so much before. A sure sign he's upset.

What he says makes sense. Andalusia must be waiting for Marti, which must be why he gave me the stuff about Charlie's story being way off base. Maybe they have another drug run cooking, a way of marking time until he dies. Maybe he's waiting for Marti to be finished with his fun and games when all the wives are dead. All I know is that I have to get to the Cuban fast. Time is running away from me while I'm standing still.

After a bit all the cops, except Griswold, leave. "Now I've got to find Betty Donne," he says.

I was waiting for him to mention her again since we left the reception. We share the same thought. Missing. Presumed dead.

"Know where she might be?" he asks.

He's trying to sound nonchalant as if that lessens the horror spreading around us. I respond in kind. Keep it cool, keep it rational, so you don't go crazy and accomplish nothing. "Where have you tried?"

"The gallery, the apartment above it, her and Charlie's house. What concerns me is that her car's still there and her things are around."

"Amanda Kay said you asked her to tell you if she was going out of town. I assume you did that with Betty and Virginia."

"Yep."

"I don't think Betty has too many friends down here. She's only lived here six months or so."

"Tried a couple of her customers but got nowhere," Griswold says. "Checked the airport and the car rental too just in case she headed out of town but forgot to tell me."

"How about Peter Matthews?" I ask. "I know she was doing business with him. He lives on a boat and commutes on it to Miami."

A FOOL'S DEATH

Though I try not to, I think of Amanda Kay out on his boat. But once I do, one jealousy-inducing scenario leads to another. Hell, after I saw Amanda Kay out there, I had warned both her and Betty to steer clear of the area because of Andalusia. What really bothers me is that Amanda Kay claimed she hadn't been around there when I asked her about it. I didn't press the matter, but her response made me even more depressed. At the time I wasn't sure whether I was more afraid of Marti or Matthews.

"Where's he keep his boat?"

"The Yacht Club out at Garrison Bight."

"I'll head out there now."

"You want company?" Maybe my wanting to go along is simply perverse.

We drive in silence while the storm lets up. Along the way, we pass the field where Andalusia's heavies worked me over. How peaceful it is at the moment. A bright moon peeks through fast-disappearing storm clouds that resemble strange, odd-shaped birds. Wet grass glistens in the moonlight.

How quickly everything can change. Violence and death tear in and out of our lives, transforming them forever when we least suspect it. Then it's over. Only we've got to try to pick up the pieces.

I don't like the idea of barging in on Matthews, but what choice do we have? At least I tell myself that. I don't have to ask myself what Amanda Kay can see in him. Matthews is divorced and has the accoutrements of a guy with money. There's the live-on boat, the classy clothes, a dark green Jaguar convertible, and its clone parked at a marina in Miami. He's good-looking, and, of course, he's charming.

There's a possible flaw in this perfection. "Anything to the rumors about him being on the financial edge?"

"Yup," Griswold says. "He's lost a lot of money in the market. To generate commissions, he churned some of his clients' accounts and they're pressing charges."

At the Yacht Club, we walk out to the dock. It's about ten

o'clock. Since the storm slunk by, stars are coming out. Matthews's boat is sleek and graceful as it rocks gently in the water. Lights are on in the cabin of *The Money Pit*, the whimsical kind of name only a guy who deals in high finance all day is likely to appreciate more than the rest of us. Because of his troubles, the name now has the ring of irony.

Nobody's on deck as we climb aboard. Griswold knocks on the cabin door. Moments later, an outside light comes on, illuminating the deck and casting a soft glow on the water. Matthews opens the door. When he sees Griswold, he looks as if he's going to have a heart attack. He quickly recovers, but there's more than a trace of fear about him.

"Why, Chief! What are you doing out here this time of night?"

"Like to talk to you for a minute, Mr. Matthews," Griswold says.

"Come in. Come in. And how are you, Mason?"

"Not so good, but thanks for asking." I get the feeling he's glad I'm along. The chief isn't likely to bring me along on an arrest.

We go down into the cabin, and Matthews indicates that we should take seats. The boat isn't spacious, but everything is tasteful and comfortable. The furnishings, such as the swivel chairs we sit on, are the kind you might see in a picture of a ritzy penthouse apartment. Everything is to scale for the boat. One wall is lined with books. Paintings are on the other walls. A couple of modern brass and iron sculptures are mounted in corners. The varnished teak and polished brass glisten.

"What can I get you to drink?" Matthews asks, acting as though we're invited guests.

"Bourbon straight up," I say. Thinking of both Virginia and Betty, I add, "Make it a double."

Griswold checks his watch and realizes he's working another sixteen-hour day. "Scotch and a little water."

Matthews goes to a bar that opens out of a wall panel. A minute later, he's back with our drinks. His hand is unsteady, and he has the flush of somebody hitting the sauce hard. He too is drinking undiluted bourbon, only his glass holds twice the generous portion mine does.

A FOOL'S DEATH

"I don't want to alarm you, Mr. Matthews," Griswold says.

At the word *alarm*, Matthews's eyes widen and he shrinks back a bit. "What . . . what's wrong?"

"We're looking for Betty Donne."

Matthews is still frozen up. His eyes don't give away the relief I expect to see. I guess Griswold's showing up put a meaner fright in him than I thought.

"Do you mind if I ask why?"

"I want to give her more police protection," Griswold says. "Virginia Donne died earlier today. It may have been murder."

"Oh, God!" Matthews says with genuine distress and shock. His chin sinks down to his chest.

"God, how horrible!" he whispers after a minute. There is true horror in his voice this time around as the news works its way through the booze that's been insulating his life lately.

He pulls himself together and sits up straight. "This is terrible. Betty mentioned to me that she and Charlie Donne's former wives might be in some kind of danger, but I . . . I just didn't . . . I mean, I guess I didn't believe it. Even after Charlie and one of his wives were found dead, I simply believed it was a dreadful coincidence."

Turning to me, he says, "Marty Huff was out on my boat last week and said you are working with him on this business. Even then I didn't get how serious this is."

"Huff's a friend?" I ask.

"I've been his broker for years."

I wonder if Huff has been taken for a ride by Matthews. Be a shame if true. Huff is an ethical man, even if he is something of a little prig, such as always asking for secrecy on a case even though that's damn near impossible. And he doesn't have many friends. He'd be hurt more deeply than just financially if it comes out Matthews double-crossed him.

Matthews quickly drains the rest of his glass and gets up to fix another. In his shoes, I would too.

"Any idea where Mrs. Donne might be?"

"God, no! I buy some art off her, but I'm not a close friend.

A FOOL'S DEATH

I was at her gallery a week or so ago to see about a piece of sculpture, but I wound up not buying it."

Griswold and I finish our drinks and bid Matthews good-night. We walk up the dock toward the car. "Nervous as a jackrabbit," Griswold says.

"I don't blame him."

"Me neither."

"His case come under your jurisdiction?"

"No. Feds in Miami."

"What are you going to do now?" I ask.

"I'd like to go back to Betty's gallery and go through her desk calendar to see if there's any indication where she might have gone. But the place is locked up. We had to use a ladder to peek into the windows upstairs. My lock guy is off the island today."

"Let's go. She gave me a spare set of keys."

Fifteen minutes later, I turn the key in the gallery door. We put on the lights. Griswold immediately goes to her desk and checks on her calendar. There's a notation for today's date. Exasperated, he hands it to me.

I look at it. "Sorry, I can't make it out either."

Nothing seems out of the ordinary. I go upstairs and poke around, but not thoroughly. I'm not about to search through any of her things. I quietly shut the door behind me.

"Nothing, huh?" Griswold grunts when I come back down.

"No. Maybe she's all right."

"What makes you say that?"

"The killer didn't take pains to hide his other victims. Anything but. Why break his pattern now?"

"We're dealing with a crazy," Griswold says matter-of-factly. "They don't always adhere to the patterns that you private investigators seem to think they do."

I feel sicker. Of course, he's right. An edge of panic comes on again, and I quickly search my mind. Where could Betty be? She didn't mention going anywhere special. A chilling thought hits me. The killer hid her body. But why?

I try to get a grip on myself and think positive. It's useless.

The day has been too long, too sad, and too discouraging. "What can we do?" I ask.

"Wait," Griswold replied. "Nothing else to do."

"You wait."

Staring at me as if he's about to say something, Griswold apparently changes his mind and remains quiet. He's in one of those cold, quiet rages that hit him when murder's on the agenda. He looks as if he wants to kick something or somebody. Suddenly, all his tiredness washes over him. Wearily, he goes to the squad car, looking as bushed as I feel. We ride in silence. There's nothing left to say. When he drops me off, he yawns and stretches and drives away without a word.

Walking up the apartment stairs, I'm in turmoil, contemplating what I should have done before. When I enter, Tim and Jerrard King, another officer, are playing pinochle.

"Amanda Kay sleeping?" I ask.

"Yeah," Tim replies. "It's been rough on her."

I creep into the bedroom and take my .38 and ankle holster. Amanda Kay is curled up childlike on the bed, sleep smoothing out her features again. The tenseness, fear, and, yes, hatred that were there earlier are erased. I'm glad she's sleeping but wonder how she can. My skin is taut and itchy, and it feels as though my nerves are coming through my flesh. I wonder if I'll ever sleep again. Suddenly, she shudders and almost awakens. God, how I wish none of this had happened.

Slipping out, I enter the living room again. The boys are getting ready to go. "Sorry, but would you mind staying a while longer?"

Tim looks at the gun. "Okay with me, how 'bout you, Jer?"

King stares at me for a moment and turns his eyes down to the floor. "It's okay with me too, Mason."

"You won't let anybody in, will you?"

"You're under stress, so I won't get mad," Tim says with a smile.

I leave without even apologizing for asking the dumbly obvious.

■ ■ ■ ■ 39 ■ ■ ■ ■

*I*N the jeep, I turn the engine over and check the .38. It's loaded. I strap it on my right ankle and pull the pants leg over it. The drive out to Georgie Two Foot's is easy. This time of night there's nothing on the road except some drunks on bicycles. Key West must be one of the few places in the nation where people will bicycle to a bar, get loaded, and weave their way home at six miles an hour on a two-wheeler.

Georgie lives in an ugly 1950s motel-hotel in the Cuban pocket off White Street. The style is that flat, cinder-block structure that looks like a couple of shoe boxes piled on top of one another and is appreciated by people with souls of mud. The walls are whitewashed. Chipped red paint is on the metal stairs and walkway outside the second-floor rooms.

I park in the street and climb the outside stairs to Georgie's room. I don't like the mood I'm in.

"Georgie!" I yell, fiercely rattling his door.

A light snaps on. A moment later, his head peeks from behind a torn shade. There's a click and rattle as door locks are undone.

A FOOL'S DEATH

Suddenly, Georgie stands there in his underwear, a sleepy scowl on his face.

"What is wrong with you, Mason? You'll wake up the whole damned neighborhood."

"Your pal. The hombre we went to see on Upper Matecumbe. I've got to get to him. Tonight!"

Georgie looks worried. "He said he would contact you. He will. He will."

"I can't wait. I shouldn't have waited Friday. Now how do I get to him?"

"Please, Mason. This isn't right."

My right hand shoots out and grabs Georgie by the throat. "A lot of things in life aren't right."

Wild fright flashes across his face. I let go, wondering what the hell I'm doing. Here I am, taking my anger and frustration out on this poor guy who did nothing wrong. All he did was pass me along to someone. I'm the one who blew it. Now I need a favor, and I'm dumping all over him.

"Sorry, Georgie."

"That's okay," he says, but he's breathing deeply. He takes a step backward, ready to duck. I scared him real bad.

"Come in," he says, opening the door wider and quickly shutting it once I'm inside.

I flop onto a chair covered in green vinyl. "I've got to get to the guy, Georgie. There's been another killing. Another one of Charlie's wives. Maybe two of them."

Georgie wrings his hands. "Wait here. I will make a phone call."

There's no phone in his room. He has to go out to a pay phone. He pulls on a pair of chinos and a cowboy shirt. Vanity gets the better of him, and he looks in a mirror while carefully combing back what's left of his hair. Finally, he makes his exit.

Looking around, I get more depressed. The room is the kind that poor bachelors live in all over the country. A couple of shabby stuffed vinyl chairs with sagging seats. A sofa that pulls into a bed. A little chipped Formica table with two matching chairs. A hot plate. Two lamps. A bureau and several five-and-dime-store pictures on the walls, one of a sailboat and the other of a fluffy pussycat with human eyes. The rug is a brown, braided thing that looks as if it's fashioned from worn-out ropes.

A little while later, Georgie comes back. He looks solemn. "He says you can come to him."

"Who is he?"

"His name is Julio. I will give you his address. Just ask for Julio."

Sitting at one of the kitchen table chairs, he writes the address on a piece of paper that he tears off a notepad. He hands me the paper, crosses the room, and opens the door. "There is nothing more I can do, Mason. Good luck."

"Sorry again, Georgie. I'll try to make it up to you."

I climb into the jeep, which is parked under the streetlight in front of the motel-hotel, and check the note. The directions are clear. The address is on Key Largo, a good shot away. I hope the jeep won't give me any trouble; everything from the carburetor's going to hell again to four flat tires enters my mind. Funny how anxiety focuses on the inconsequential. My real concerns, of course, are what happened to Betty and whether I'll get Marti before he gets Amanda Kay.

The drive is monotonous and the jeep doesn't fly. The long stretches of water play weird tricks with light and shadows. Other than water, there's little else to see except road and bridges. Forty-two bridges link the Keys, and some are miles and miles long.

Tonight, there's a strangeness about the drive, a disorienting eeriness. The time of night has a lot to do with it. I'm feeling alone in the world, while most people are snug at home. I envy them. As the miles slide by, tension grows and pushes out the loneliness. Excitement builds at the prospect of finding Carlos Marti.

Hours later, I pull up at the end of a dirt road. To the right is an old, two-story, Bahamas-style house with a wraparound porch. The house is set behind a large, overgrown yard. As I get out, an old woman comes out on the porch. She's tiny. Even though I can't make out her features in the dark, I feel her disapproval. A moment later, a man emerges and gently touches her arm. Talking to her, he directs her back inside. He's the guy from the cockfight. Julio. Leaning down, I slide my pistol out of the holster.

Coming down from the porch, he crosses the lawn and opens the gate in the old, worn picket fence that surrounds the place. "Georgie said it was very important that I see you."

"It is."

"My mother isn't sleeping well. Do you mind if we talk here?"

"There's not much to say. You know why I'm here."

"Yes. Carlos Marti. You still wish to speak to him."

"Not speak to him. Take him in."

He looks at me strangely again. "For those murders you talked about?"

"Those and one, maybe two more. You see, Mr. Marti's been busy. He killed another friend of mine just hours ago. And if I don't kill him, I'm going to take him in."

I point the .38 at Julio. "I don't like doing this, but I don't see what choice I have."

"That will not be necessary, Señor Collins."

"If you don't mind, I'll just keep it pointed where it is."

"As you wish," he says. "Come with me."

We go through the gate and down a pathway. The grass is moist with night dew and hasn't been cut for a while. The smell of hibiscus settles around us like a sensuous mist. In the moonlight, I make out what must be a little cottage that's almost hidden in the foliage. It's back a good bit from the main house. From the road or maybe even halfway across the yard, you'd never see it, even in daylight.

At the door, my guide raps.

"Who's there?" a voice calls out in Spanish.

"Julio."

A FOOL'S DEATH

The door opens and a man stands in the darkened room. I can't see what he looks like, but I instinctively point the gun at him. Julio goes inside and I trail along.

The man starts yelling in Spanish, probably because Julio brought someone with him.

"A man who has some questions," Julio says in English. "Do not worry. He is not with the police, and he is not with the man you want to avoid."

There's another rapid-fire exchange in Spanish. Julio says something that shuts the other one up and then turns on a light. Carlos Marti stands in front of me. I'm so startled I almost pull the trigger. There's no mistaking him, although he must be close to seventy years old. Unlike Andalusia, he looks exactly like the picture the Miami cops doctored up.

"Do I know you?" he snarls.

"No. No, you don't."

Suddenly, my head's reeling and I'm sweating as if I'm ill. I need air. There's something about Marti the police artist didn't factor in. Something I almost can't believe. There's no way he's faking. His eyes are deep-set and milky.

Slowly, I lower the .38. Jesus, Marti's blind!

Julio speaks up. "I didn't want to tell you. You wouldn't have believed me. He has been blind for the past three years, ever since he came to live here. He is my uncle. My mother is his sister. He came with a great deal of money and asked my mother if he could live with her. He wanted to hide here. He was worried about a man coming after him, someone from a business dealing."

"Andalusia," I said.

At the mention of the name, Marti panics. His head bobs around like a clown head on a spring, and he spits out more Spanish at Julio. Marti's terror doesn't let up much even though Julio's obviously trying to reassure him.

Finally, Julio turns to me. "He thinks this man Andalusia has sent you."

"You double-crossed him years back, and Andalusia's not the type to forgive and forget. Is he, Marti?"

A FOOL'S DEATH

Marti turns my way. "No, and neither am I!"

"I'd bet on that too. A real tough guy, weren't you, Mr. Marti? Real tough."

"Tough enough!" The words snarl out of the miserable old creep.

Having lost my bearings, I'm overwhelmed by depression as I scratch Marti off the killer list. The goddamn trip is a waste. I chased a phantom. Sitting heavily in a chair, I hold my head. What am I going to do? I'm no closer to nabbing the killer than I was a week ago.

"Do you wish to leave now, Señor Collins?" Julio asks.

I nod but catch myself. Maybe I can salvage something from this wild-goose chase. I want to hear Marti's version of what happened twenty-five years ago. If he'll talk, I wonder who he'll back up. Charlie or Andalusia?

■ ■ ■ ■ 40 ■ ■ ■ ■

*Y*ES. *The Doubloon* and the Donnes. I remember those bastards."

Marti's sitting in a stuffed chair. Those unseeing eyes stare eerily toward the ceiling fan. With the creakiness of someone who doesn't talk enough to people, he's reminiscing about his Key West days.

"The Donne brothers. Fools. How they found that treasure, I don't know. Dumb fucking luck! I know what they were like. I worked for them when they first came down. I taught them how to seek treasure. I told them about the Archives of the Indies in Spain where information about treasure ships is stored. They knew nothing!"

He cocks his head disdainfully and generally in my direction. The contemptuous expression on his hawklike face turns fierce. "*Nada!* Nothing! I helped them find a salvage boat. A boat to live on. A seaplane. Equipment. It was me! I got them divers. I showed them how to read the maps."

As he loses himself in bitter memories, his face contorts into an evil mask. "When they found the treasure, do you think they were willing to acknowledge their debt to me?"

A FOOL'S DEATH

His lips curl into a sneer. His face becomes a mask of hatred. "No! They act as if Carlos Marti does not exist!"

His hate seems to make the ions in the atmosphere crackle. He squirms, wanting to lash out, but is hindered by his blindness. His cruelty is obvious in his half-angry, half-mocking snarl.

"Did you kill them?" I ask.

Sitting back insolently, he tilts his head toward me again. "Kill them?"

The way he says it makes it sound like a perfectly reasonable question. "Perhaps I should have, but I did not. But I did get some little revenge. Yes, I did that."

He breaks into a gale of laughter.

"There's a lot of supposition that you killed the Donne brothers. Something to do with an altercation on *The Doubloon* when you came snooping around the boat one night just when they discovered the treasure."

He moves his head suspiciously from side to side, as if waiting to fall into a trap. "What are you talking about, señor? What's this craziness?" He stands, yelling. "What are you trying to get on me!" Turning toward Julio, he rattles on in Spanish. Julio replies in the same machine-gun-type bursts.

Julio speaks quietly to me. "He thinks that the man he is afraid of sent you. I have told him that is not true. I am correct, am I not?"

"You're right," I reply wearily.

"What the hell's going on?" Marti demands in English.

Like Andalusia, he sounds sincere in his ignorance. Can both these goddamn villains be right? Was Charlie wrong? Had he thought something happened that hadn't? Was his letter some kind of crazy joke? Or maybe just crazy?

"Did you know David Donne's son, Charlie?"

Marti's expression becomes crafty, secretive. "Yes, I knew him. As much a fool as his father. Yes, I knew him."

The laughter returns, a malevolent cackle. He keeps it up so long, he sounds as if he's having a convulsion.

"What are you talking about?"

A FOOL'S DEATH

He gasps for breath from laughing so hard. "My present to the Donnes." His laughter becomes almost uncontrollable again.

"Make sense," I say, irritated by his craziness.

He breathes deeply before he can talk. "My gift to the damned. Yes, damned!"

I'm suddenly tired of this piece of nastiness and his bullshit. "I don't know what the hell you're talking about, Marti. I don't think you do either."

"Damned! That is what I mean, señor. Damned! Now get out!"

Julio gives me an exasperated look and motions me to leave. Nodding, I get to my feet. He says something in Spanish to Marti as we leave. At the doorway, I pause and whisper a parting shot at the miserable son of a bitch, one I know will get him. "Andalusia's closer than you think."

His yells are still audible as Julio and I walk up the path.

"I'm sorry you did not get what you wanted," Julio says. "As you can tell, my uncle is not right in the head these days. But I wanted you to know that he is not your killer."

He stops at the gate. "It might have been better for us if he was. He would have been taken away from here. He is not a good person, not someone fit to be around my mother."

"I wish he'd been the killer too," I say, feeling tired and defeated.

I'm more worried than ever. Charlie fingered the wrong man, and I wasted a lot of time. The killer's still loose out there, hidden in the night. Who's killing the wives and why? The old question digs deep into my heart and mind. When I think of what might have happened to Betty, I'm sick all over again. The mere thought of harm coming to Amanda Kay makes me shudder. I'm heavy with so much dread that I can't even lift a phone to find out if Betty turned up or to make sure Amanda Kay's still safe.

On the drive back, I push the jeep to its limits. But when I finally get to my apartment, I sit outside for a good ten minutes before working up the nerve to enter, afraid of what I'll find.

▪ ▪ ▪ ▪ 41 ▪ ▪ ▪ ▪

STEPPING into the apartment, I stop. My mouth opens and nothing comes out. Betty and Amanda Kay and the pair of cops are sitting around a table drinking coffee. I collapse in a chair and continue staring, while they all stare back.

Amanda Kay pipes up. "I was so frightened, honey. When I woke up, you were missing and everyone was out looking for Betty." She wipes her eyes. "Where have you been all night?"

"All over the damn Keys looking for the killer," I answer. Staring at Betty, I add, "Lady, I am *very* glad to see you."

She flushes. "I'm sorry I caused so much trouble. A client came into town and I drove up to Miami with him, had a late dinner, and flew back. I forgot all about promising Chief Griswold I'd tell him if I left town, but frankly I didn't even consider a quick trip to Miami leaving town."

Her voice becomes more subdued. "Mason, perhaps Amanda Kay and I should go away, but won't the killer just come after us? Is there any place safe we could go? What can we do?"

Amanda Kay gives me the same trusting look. After all that's happened, how could they still have any faith in me? I wasn't able to help Charlie or Marlene or Virginia. Maybe I should just tell them what a useless creature I am. But what's the point? Honesty would just scare them all the more, so I act like I'm capable of doing something other than standing by while people die. I decide all I can do is try to keep them both as close to me as possible.

"This apartment is the safest place in town," I reply, trying to sound confident. "Betty, you're going to have to move in with us. I'll talk to Griswold about having men assigned to you as much as he can. But I think you'll feel safer here. I know I will."

The last part's true. I never want them out of my sight.

"Whatever you think best," Betty replies.

She's so trusting, I want to throw up.

■ ■ ■ ■ 42 ■ ■ ■ ■

THE Philadelphia newspaper clips about the Donnes remind me of the fable about the purse of plenty. The more you take out, the more there seems to be. The more damned clips I read, the more loom on the desk.

Whenever I get a chance, I sift through them, hoping to spot something I may not know, something I may have overlooked, anything at all that strikes my fancy. It's a good thing I do.

Going through one pile, I pause. A chill ices through me when I come across a story about Brian Donne. He was arrested a few years back for threatening to kill some guy. There's more. He actually tried to murder a young woman. What disturbs me more than anything else is the way he nearly killed her. The story says he tried to drown her. The victim said Donne was going to kill her and make it look like an accident. Hurriedly, I skim the rest of the stories to find out what else happened. I can't find a follow-up.

Where did young Donne go after he left the island? If he left. I start thinking I noticed something odd about him, but I'm kidding myself. I took him at face value, much the way we all took his older brother. I realize I didn't learn anything about him while he was here, except that he was the rich young brother who was worried about being knocked off.

Maybe he wasn't worried at all.

I call my PI friend in the City of Brotherly Love again. "Matt, it's Mason."

"I still haven't gotten paid," he says ungraciously.

"You will. You will. My client's giving me another retainer tomorrow," I lie. "I'll send you a check first thing. Meanwhile, I'd like your help a bit more with the Donnes."

"What do you need?"

"The newspaper clippings you sent mention young Donne being in a jam a few years ago for threatening to kill a woman. Could you find out what happened? Also, see if he has a history of this sort of thing."

"Okay, Mason. But send that check."

"Don't worry about it, Matt. Did I ever not?"

"No, but they build tall buildings faster than you pay bills."

I make a mental note to do my expenses again for Huff. "In the mail tomorrow."

"Sure," he says, and hangs up.

Next, I do something that I don't want to do but feel I have to get out of the way. I pick up the phone and dial 505-555-1212, information for New Mexico.

"What city, please?" the operator asked.

"Albuquerque."

"Go ahead."

"I'd like the number for Willows Memorial Hospital."

Once I get the number, I dial the hospital. "Whom do you wish to speak to?" the switchboard operator asks.

"Can you tell me what kind of a hospital this is?" I ask, wincing a bit because I'm pretty sure I know.

"We are a psychiatric hospital."

Unfortunately, my hunch is right. "Give me the director, miss."

"Dr. Foster's office," his secretary answers.

"Dr. Foster, please."

A FOOL'S DEATH

"May I tell him what this is about?"

I'm about to say "This may be a matter of life and death," but I figure that's the standard line the truly disturbed use. Instead, I say, "I'm calling in reference to a man who was a patient. This is Police Chief Will Griswold in Key West, Florida."

A moment later, Foster comes on the line. "Yes, Chief Griswold, how can I help you?"

The doc sounds a bit unhinged. I imagine heads of psychiatric hospitals sit around holding their breaths with fear that former patients are out raping, pillaging, and worse and that somebody's going to sue their hospitals for letting them go.

"You had a patient named Charles Donne. D-O-double N-E." I give the dates Charlie was there according to the backgrounder Joe Clark sent. I hear Foster ask his secretary to get Charlie's file.

"Yes, Captain?" he asks, giving me a new title as high anxiety settles into his voice.

"Dr. Foster, Mr. Donne was killed in Florida recently. We're trying to find anything in his background that might help. Can you tell me why he was at Willows Memorial?"

Foster sighs with relief. One of his ex-patients is only dead and hasn't done serious damage to some sector of the nation.

"I have his report right here. Let me see. He admitted himself. This was some time ago. Let me see. He was treated by Dr. Paul Grover. Why, you're in luck, Commander Griswold!"

"Why's that?" How does he get the name Griswold right but keep changing the chief's title? Is he trying to make me feel good? Is he just forgetful? Or am I trying to read the mighty into the meaningless because I'm talking to a shrink?

What's more obvious is that Foster wants to weasel out of talking about Charlie's case or probably any other. "I wasn't even here when Mr. Donne was a patient. Dr. Grover is now head of the psychiatric unit at Mercy Hospital in Coconut Grove. He will be able to tell you much more about Mr. Donne than I or anyone currently on the staff could."

"Thanks a lot, Doctor." For a moment, I debate about growling some obscenity into the line just to make him feel good.

■ ■ ■ ■ **43** ■ ■ ■ ■

A Chinese curse goes, "May you have two wives." I manage to top that: "May you try to keep two women who live under the same roof from getting killed or killing each other."

At first, Amanda Kay and Betty get along pretty well given the circumstances. Better yet, they both get along with me. At least as much as possible. But it doesn't last long. One problem is me. I fret over them so much that I succeed in escalating everybody's anxiety. I try to catch myself, but it doesn't do much good. I hire Mike Sanders to watch them when I'm not around, but that doesn't help the edginess.

After a week, the women take to complaining about feeling like living in a goldfish bowl. As the days continue to peel away, they bitch about other stuff too. Like everything.

Our experiment in communal living becomes not so hot in most ways. With Betty around, Amanda Kay's and my love life goes to hell. I wind up moving onto the living room sofa and letting them have the bedroom. Plus, we're staying indoors too damned much in a climate that's designed for not spending a hell of a lot of time at home. And we're all used to a good bit of freedom and a lot of alone time, which doesn't help matters either. Not surprisingly, we all get more than a little snappish.

One night I come home and both women are sitting in the living room, glaring at one another. "It's your turn," Betty says petulantly.

"No, it's yours, goddamn it!" Amanda Kay yells.

"What the hell's going on?" I ask politely.

"None of your goddamn business, Mason," Amanda Kay says.

"It's her turn to get dinner," Betty says.

"It's your turn," Amanda Kay shoots back.

I get a beer, come back, sit down, and drink half the bottle while they rev up for a brawl. The accusations show the shabby level to which their relationship has deteriorated. "Getting dinner" consists of one of us deciding what kind of takeout to have and calling for it to be delivered.

"You're always trying to get out of your fair share of doing anything around here," Amanda Kay says.

"Me?" says Betty. "You're so damned lazy it makes me sick."

"*Bullllshiiiit!*" I suddenly roar.

The women look at me as if I'm something that just fell from the sky. "Let's go out to dinner," I say.

"Isn't that dangerous?" Betty asks.

"The son of a bitch'll have to kill all three of us at once, and there's nothing to indicate he's willing to take such a gamble. Better than us killing each other here."

"You're right," Amanda Kay says. "I'd rather take my chances with a crazy killer than spend another minute in this goddamn apartment."

"Me too," Betty says.

Amanda Kay gives her a funny look, as if she's amazed Betty agrees with her about anything. Suddenly, they both burst out laughing. I'm relieved. I didn't feel like sitting through a meal with them sniping at each other, looking to take offense at every little thing.

A half hour later, we enter Bagatelle, a pretty restaurant on Duval that's in an old Victorian house. There're porches and rooms for dining both upstairs and downstairs. The Bag's expensive, but none of us gives a damn. We just broke out of jail for a bit and know we have to go back.

"This is a wonderful idea, Mason," Betty says.

"Sure is," Amanda Kay says. Turning to Betty, she adds, "Sorry I was such a bitch. This business is wearing me down."

"Same here," Betty says. "It's wearing all of us down."

We have drinks, and I order wine when we place our meal order. The food here is good, and we all begin to unwind.

A little while later, Precious enters with some friends and heads over to our table. He's wearing a white silk evening dress. I introduce him. "Amanda Kay and Betty, this is Precious Adams. He knows more about the history of this island than God does."

"Don't blaspheme, Mason," he says primly, reminding me as usual that he's religious. To the women he says, "I'm so sorry for what you've been through. It's terrible, simply dreadful."

After talking to them a bit more, he turns back to me. "I was going to call you, Mason. I did a bit of checking on your coin. There's a possibility, a strong possibility, that whoever got it didn't get it directly from a treasure ship."

"What do you mean?"

"A friend who is a dealer in Miami Beach sold two of them about a month ago. They match the description of the one you showed me down to a T. If you want, you can send it to him and have him see if it's one he sold."

How weird, I think. "I'm going over to Miami tomorrow," I say. "Give me his address."

He opens his wallet and extracts a card. "Here's his business card. I'll tell him you're coming."

"Thanks, Precious."

"Anytime. Good-night, all. Have a fabulous meal."

For the next hour, we all agree the dinner sure as hell tastes a lot better than anything we would've had back at the apartment. Finishing up, we head across the street to the Bull and Whistle for a nightcap and just to unravel our freedom a bit more. There's

A FOOL'S DEATH

a bar on the second floor as well as the first, and the place can get kind of raucous. Once in a while, that's not all bad. We take a table, and Betty gets up to pump a buck into the jukebox.

Amanda Kay puts her hand on my thigh under the table and I groan. "Don't do that if you don't want me to have a fit," I say.

"Maybe I'll sneak in to see you on the sofa tonight," she whispers.

Betty comes back, smiling. "God, it feels almost like we're normal," she says as she sits down.

Unfortunately, a drunk is right behind her. He's a beefy, shaggy-dog type with a lot of hair and a red face and wearing a sweat-stained khaki shirt and pants. Leaning over the table, he leers. "Remember me? How's about you coming out to the car?"

Betty ignores him, but he keeps it up. Gross quantities of booze turn people into pigs. An unfortunate alchemy. I try to be understanding.

"The lady doesn't know you, son. Now you head back to the bar, and I'll have the waitress get you another drink."

He looks at me and laughs. "Lady, shit, this 'lady's' got the hottest little ass in Florida. She took on me and three of my buddies last year and was begging for more."

"Now you've insulted the lady and made me mad. I suggest you give her an apology and clear out."

He turns to Amanda Kay. "If you're as much of a 'lady' as your friend here, you come along too and we'll see if the goddamn fleet's in."

Leaning over, he tries to grab her. I reach up and jam my index and middle fingers down under his collarbone right below his neck. He gasps for breath and stumbles backward, grasping at his throat. I get up and put a hammerlock on his right arm and escort him outside. It occurs to me to make him apologize, but an apology from a drunk doesn't mean a damn thing. Once outside, I give his arm a little extra twist so he won't feel like trying anything else and let him go. He's so tanked up, he won't feel anything until tomorrow.

"Go sleep it off or you'll get hurt real bad," I say.

"She's more than you can handle," he slurs, rubbing his arm as he staggers off into the night.

The incident puts a damper on the night. The women take it hard. Betty sinks into a sad silence, while Amanda Kay's bottled-up rage has her snapping at everything and everyone, especially me. We stay for one more drink to see if our spirits lift, but they don't.

"Let's go," Amanda Kay finally says. "It's no use staying and pretending everything's all right."

"I'm sorry," Betty says.

Furious, Amanda Kay turns to her. "Don't apologize. Until women learn that they have nothing to do with the brutish way men behave, we won't get anything right."

She storms out, while Betty and I bring up the rear. On the ride home, none of us speak. Amanda Kay glares at me before she goes to bed. Needless to say, she doesn't pay me a visit on the couch. Women are often indiscriminate in their blame for all the hurt men have inflicted on them. But then I guess in one way or another all men contribute to that kind of rage.

■■■ 44 ■■■

When I wake up the next morning, Amanda Kay is gone already as usual. That means we don't have a chance to say whatever should be said to clear the air between us.

Betty normally leaves early too, but I hear the shower going. She's getting a late start as she sometimes does when she has an appointment before going into the gallery. Since I'm going into Miami later, I'm not hitting the office this morning. I'm to see Dr. Paul Grover at Mercy Hospital and the coin dealer Precious mentioned.

I enter the bedroom to retrieve the gold coin. But it's not in the bureau drawer where I thought I put it. I start rummaging through other drawers. I know it's here somewhere. I'm rooting around when Betty interrupts me.

"Mason, what are you doing?"

I turn and swallow. She's only wearing a damp towel. She tries to act nonchalant, which must be to hide her embarrassment. She comes and stands beside me.

"I'm looking for the gold coin I found near where Charlie was discovered," I say. "I seem to have misplaced it."

"Let me help."

She opens the drawer next to the one I'm looking through. "You might want to check with Amanda Kay. I think I saw her open this drawer after we got back last night, but I'm not positive."

Without looking at me, she says, "I should have thanked you for getting rid of that horrible man last night. I'm sorry I didn't."

"That's okay."

"Mason, I just get so frightened now." She begins trembling.

Instinctively, I hold her to me, and once again I feel the heat of her body. She puts her arms around me too.

Suddenly, the towel slips to the floor and we're both trembling. I'm not sure how it happens, but it does. We start kissing and I forget everything else. There isn't even enough time to be self-conscious. Moments later, we're on the bed, urgently biting, licking, and kissing until our bodies lock in a passionate tangle.

We make love again and again with an abandon that seldom happens. There's a desperation about us, as if this were the only way to keep death at bay.

Exhausted, we become separate people again. "God, I'm sorry, Mason," Betty says, looking at me imploringly. "Everything has gotten so out of hand since Charlie died. I just don't know what's happening or even what I'm doing. It's . . . I don't know . . ."

She strokes my face and I pull her to me. It's as if we're both on fire, incapable of holding back. Once again, we lose ourselves in the only natural oblivion known to man.

An hour and a half later, on the plane ride to Miami, I'm confused. What will happen now between Amanda Kay and me? How will this alter our relationship? Will it end it? She wouldn't understand. How could she? How can I go on living under one roof with both of them? Where else can any of us go?

Something else bothers me a lot. Why did Amanda Kay take the coin and not tell me?

■ ■ ■ ■ **45** ■ ■ ■ ■

THE psychiatric unit of Mercy Hospital is in a modernistic glass and beige-brick wing of an older complex of buildings. As in all newer big buildings, the windows don't open. When the air-conditioning goes down the way it has on a sweltering day like today, it's murder inside.

I take the elevator to the fourth floor where Dr. Grover keeps his office. My appointment is for one o'clock. I arrive at twelve-fifty. For exactly ten minutes, I sweat in a gray chair covered with some itchy material like carpet, then a heavyset guy wearing a blue seersucker suit comes up and sticks out his hand. His beard and hair are graying and he wears glasses.

"You must be Mason Collins," he says. "I'm pleased to meet you. I'm Paul Grover."

He surprises me on several scores. First, he's on time. Second, he doesn't put *Dr.* in front of his name when introducing himself. Third, he's pleasant. And lastly because of the next thing he says.

"That trip from Key West is hell on a day like this. Why don't we go out and get a beer?"

"Sounds like the perfect prescription, Doc."

A FOOL'S DEATH

"Wait a minute. I'll get Charlie's file. I had Willows Memorial Express Mail it out to me."

Fifteen minutes later, we're sitting in an air-conditioned cocktail lounge about a mile or so from the hospital. We're sucking on our beers and talking about fishing.

"I caught a couple of groupers and a barracuda last weekend," Grover says.

"Come down to the Keys and I'll make sure you do better than that."

"I'd like that."

"I hate to drag up business," I say. "But you know why I'm here, or you're at least reasonably sure why I'm here."

"After the newspaper stories, I expected someone to call. Funny, I thought it would be the police. When so much time elapsed, I assumed the case was closed."

He takes another pull on his beer. "Ironic. His death was just like the one he was always afraid of."

"Where's the irony?"

Grover looks thoughtful. "Charlie was delusional. He thought someone was going to kill him in some strange way around water. And that's the way he died."

"Now, Doc, let's get our terms straight so that we're sure we both mean the same thing. I always thought *delusional* meant that someone thought something was real but it wasn't. Are you using it that way?"

"Yes. Charlie was diagnosed as being paranoid. There was no basis in fact for his belief that he would be murdered." He smiles sympathetically. "Now what can you tell me?"

I go through the weird business about Charlie's leaving me the story about Andalusia, Marti, and the salvage boat stuff and his going to Albuquerque and moving back to Key West. I also mention his uncle's and dad's deaths and his thinking Marti came back from the dead. I throw in about Marti's not being capable of the killings. And I end up with the wives being killed and the visit from the Donne kid and maybe his being capable of murder too.

"What do you think, Doc?" I ask when I'm done.

"The business about the letter to you. Are you sure Charlie wrote it? It's possible but unusual."

"Hell, Doc. I don't know anything for sure anymore. Maybe he didn't. It's typed, but it sounds like him."

Grover takes off his glasses and wipes them before putting them back on. After adjusting them, he opens the folder he brought along.

"I haven't had much chance to study Charlie's file, but when I saw his picture in the paper and read about the way he died, his case came back to me."

He flips through pages of notes and scans files. "Charlie had essentially what we call a paranoid personality disorder."

"Remember I'm a layman, Doc."

"The main feature of such people is an unwarranted tendency, usually starting in early adulthood, to interpret other people's actions as deliberately threatening or demeaning. Usually, they think they're going to be harmed or exploited. They often don't trust friends and associates, so they hold information back from them."

I think of Charlie's not telling even his wives or me about his past and how he feared he was going to die in an odd way. That sure as hell didn't smack of trust. I shift uncomfortably. Much the same thing can be said about me and a lot of other people I know. Maybe Key West is just a colony of paranoids.

"In new situations, people who are suffering from this disorder often read threatening meanings into remarks or events that aren't threatening at all," Grover goes on. "They are often reluctant to confide in others out of fear that what they say will be turned against them.

"Charlie was like many people with this disorder in that he was hypervigilant and took precautions against the perceived threat. In Charlie's case, he came to Albuquerque looking for a man he thought was going to kill him. Apparently, enough people told him he was crazy that he thought for a little while that might be the case. That's when he wound up in my care.

"Unlike most paranoid people, Charlie wasn't into making

mountains out of molehills, and he wasn't tense and ready to counterattack perceived threats. Often such people get into a lot of lawsuits. No, Charlie was unique in that his disorder focused on the threat of being killed in an odd way."

Leaning back, Grover signals the waitress to bring two more beers. "Fortunately, Charlie wasn't hostile, stubborn, and defensive the way so many paranoids are. And he wasn't like so many of them who get a romantic fixation on someone and then start worrying that the object of their desire is in danger."

"I know the type," I say. "Some people who want to hire me are like that. Usually it's a guy who's in love with some woman who doesn't know he's alive. He thinks she's in some kind of danger and wants me to help 'rescue' her from whatever dragon he has in mind."

"And they only come to you after the police have told them to get lost."

"You got it, Doc. But back to Charlie. How did you help him?"

"To be truthful, Mason, I don't think I did."

"Doc, you keep telling the truth like this and you'll get the Diogenes prize for honesty that's been going begging lo these thousands of years."

Grover laughs. "You didn't let me finish. I think I could have helped him if he stayed longer. But it took me a long time to get out of him what I did, to develop his trust. Most paranoid people are very stubborn about talking about what's bothering them. In these patients, silence can be a primitive defense against anxiety-provoking and guilt-related needs for condemnation and punishment."

"So you mean that the paranoia itself could have been brought on by some guilt thing in Charlie? Something he wanted to blot out?"

Grover takes another swallow of beer before answering. On a day like this, no matter how much you drink you sweat it right out.

"That may have been it. I never got to the bottom of it."

"All his fears were groundless?"

"I have to say yes. There were often elements of truth woven into the fantasy, but Charlie was paranoid."

"One more question, Doc. What kind of a killer might I be dealing with?"

Grover thinks about that one for a bit. Propping his elbows on the table, he hunches his face into his upturned hands.

"This is purely speculative, of course. But from what you said, the murderer may be someone who knew about Charlie's paranoia and played on it. Your original supposition that the killer was someone from Charlie's past may still be accurate. In a way, Charlie seems to have created his killer out of his paranoia."

I ponder that hard while the talk turns to fishing again, which we both find a hell of a lot more pleasant. The doc's a good man. When we part, I know I'll see him again not that far off. We'll both be lashed to fishing chairs on the kind of game boat Charlie had.

I get up to go, but Grover stops me by putting his hand on my shoulder. There's genuine concern in his eyes.

"Being a paranoid doesn't mean that Charlie wasn't a nice man and that he wasn't a good friend or that there's anything wrong with you or the people who grew close to him." He smiles. "You should know that."

The words are comforting. After hearing a blast of bad about a friend, I sort of wonder if maybe there's something wrong with me for having that friend.

"Thanks, Doc."

"If there's anything else, Mason, let me know."

"We'll get our fishing schedules in sync."

"Charlie would appreciate that."

"Very perceptive, as your colleagues are prone to saying."

We both laugh, but I don't feel the least bit happy. I think, "Poor old Charlie." Hell, poor everybody.

■ ■ ■ ■ 46 ■ ■ ■ ■

*O*MEGA Rare Coin Gallery is a fancy setup in the high-priced hotel strip on Miami Beach. Classical music wafts from unseen speakers. The teal blue carpet's plush. Modern art hangs on the walls, and the salespeople have that snootiness found among hucksters in high-priced jewelry stores.

Walking as if he has an ice cube up his ass and rubbing his hands like Uriah Heep, a skinny praying-mantis-type salesman comes over. He examines my jeans and work shirt and debates whether I'm here to fix the plumbing or if I'm an eccentric billionaire. "Can I help you, sir?"

"Tell Mr. Richard Barstow that Mason Collins wants to see him on the recommendation of Precious Adams."

At the mention of Barstow's name, he becomes craven, obviously opting for the billionaire. "Of course, sir."

I barely have time to look at a case of glittering silver coins when Uriah's back. "Follow me, sir."

We cross the spacious showroom and take an elevator to the third floor. The decor is sand-colored walls, potted palms, and Navaho rugs and furniture that go by what I believe is called desert motif. The whole effect is classy and soothing and smells of money.

Uriah stays outside the office, but he indicates I should enter. "Please have a seat. Mr. Barstow will be with you in a minute."

The office is airy and has a good view of the ocean. This too is expensively and tastefully furnished with mahogany bookcases, tables, and desk and tan leather chairs. The bookcases are filled with books and magazines about coins.

"Mr. Collins, how are you?"

A silver-haired man in his late fifties comes forward and pumps my hand in a hearty way. His pink, bulldog face is stamped with prosperity. He wears a black silk suit and a white silk shirt and a paisley Italian tie that probably cost as much as a surfboard. He looks like a TV preacher but exudes even more optimism.

"I'm fine, Mr. Barstow. How are you?"

"Wonderful, just wonderful. It's such a lovely day! We certainly are fortunate to live in this part of the world, aren't we?"

"Some of us, Mr. Barstow." I think of the starving Haitians and the desperate poor folks flooding into the state from the other forty-nine in hopes of catching work in a shrinking job pool.

"Precious called," he says without hearing my answer. "I believe I sold the coin you have in your possession. The way he described it to me made it sound like one of them, and there aren't that many around that I know of. How is Precious anyway?"

"Why, the same as ever."

"I wish he'd come to work for me. He's one of the best, you know. I even offered to finance an operation for him in Key West, but he always tells me he'll think about it and then never does anything about it."

"He's pretty well ensconced down there. Maybe he just doesn't want anything more."

"You're probably right." Barstow's pampered face bears a perplexed expression. "Hard to believe, isn't it?"

I don't bother answering. Barstow wouldn't listen anyway. He's already opening a book on coins on the coffee table and talking.

"Let me see your coin, because I believe this is the one we are talking about." He jams his finger at the lower right-hand corner of the left page.

"I didn't bring it."

He looks up, his face creased with disappointment. "Well, perhaps you can judge from the picture if it's the same."

I stare at the photo his index finger taps. The picture of the gold coin is to size and shows all the details. "It sure as hell looks the same."

"I thought so!" he says triumphantly. "It's a rare day in May when Dick Barstow is wrong about a coin." He gives me a shrewd look. "Since Precious sent you, I won't ask how the coin came into your possession."

He slams the book shut. "What else can I do for you, Mr. Collins? Are you interested in adding to your collection?"

"No, but I'd like to know who bought the coin."

"So would I. He bought two and I was hoping he would become a regular customer. I would like to contact him and see if there's anything else we could do for him. That's only good business, isn't it, sir?"

He doesn't wait for a reply. "Yes. Yes, it is good business. But that's the only way to be successful. Follow up sales when you can!"

"Why can't you get him?"

"He refused to leave his name. A shame, but that's the way it was. A cash transaction, Mr. Collins. A lot of collectors are that way."

"Why's that?"

"They don't want anyone to know their names or addresses so as not to alert thieves. When that kind of customer comes to trust you, and they do come to trust Dick Barstow, then they will entrust their entire collections with you. But you must earn that trust, Mr. Collins. Earn it!"

I think about Precious and the Massey business. Barstow's right about thieves lurking around looking for such booty. But he still hasn't given me anything to go on with this case.

"Can you tell me anything about the buyer?"

Barstow stares at the wall for a second, his right hand held near his ear as if he's listening to a seashell. "Well, he was young for a collector. Early or mid twenties. He was less than average height and had black hair."

A sick feeling wells up in my gut. The description sounds remarkably like Brian Donne. Who else could it be?

"Did he look a little like a squirrel?"

For a moment, Barstow looks perplexed. Then he smiles. "Why, yes. Yes, he did."

"Mr. Barstow, when did he make this transaction?"

He buzzes for his secretary. An elegant woman about forty years old enters. "June, could you get us the purchase date for the last sale of doubloons?" Barstow asks.

"Anything else you can recall?" I ask when she leaves.

He cocks his head closer to that invisible seashell. "He wanted to make sure that the coins were from a Spanish treasure ship in the early 1620s. That's why I thought they might be the same when Precious mentioned the one you possess."

His secretary comes back and tells us the date that the coins were bought. My stomach sinks a little further. It was several weeks before Charlie died.

Giving me the kind of smile that lets me know he has already spent too much of his valuable time on this business, Barstow says, "I'm sorry, but I'm not particularly observant about people other than their interest in coins. An occupational hazard, I imagine."

"Thanks for your trouble, Mr. Barstow. If I ever need any coins, I'll know where to come."

"Give my regards to Precious. One of the best, that man. One of the best!"

On the way out, I wonder what the hell young Donne is doing. Why would he have to buy a coin like that? His family must still have hundreds of them from their big salvage score.

■ ■ ■ ■ 47 ■ ■ ■ ■

*B*ACK at my office, I start to see the wives as the Athenian maidens who were packed off every year to the isle of Crete as a blood sacrifice to the half-man, half-bull creature called the Minotaur. The girls were placed in a maze. Whoever was unfortunate enough to get put in there could never find her way out. The Minotaur was sure to get her.

Only in this case, the face of the Minotaur keeps changing. Now he's Brian Donne.

Why would Donne want the ladies dead?

The provisions of the will is the easiest answer. With Charlie and the wives gone, Brian stands to get the entire fortune. He must have known about his brother's paranoia. To have set up this whole thing, he'd have done a fair amount of research. I recall what Snake said about Tommy Costello.

I call Matt in Philly again. "Matt, it's Mason."

"You conveniently forgot to send my check."

As he speaks, I realize there was something I forgot to do this morning, probably plenty of things. "Sorry. I'll send it right along."

"This afternoon I shipped a couple of follow-up stories on Brian Donne's trying to kill that girl. What else do you want?"

"See if you can get a picture of him and Express Mail it down here. The cops or somebody are bound to have one."

"I'm way ahead of you, Mason. I threw his photo in too."

I want Amanda Kay and Betty to know what Donne looks like. His anonymity allows him to get close to them just about anywhere.

But where in hell is he? The only starting point is the rental limo he and Mongo used. So many things drop out of my head these days that it's worrisome, but for some reason, that license plate on the vehicle is still there: 370XX2. I call the computer vehicle-search outfit I use and give them the plate number. Within two hours, I find out the limo belongs to one of the big rental agencies with offices in Miami.

Now comes the tricky part. How to get the record? Somebody who works for the company could pull it, of course, but I don't have contacts inside the company. There's yet another way. I pick up the phone and dial.

"Hello," Joe Clark says on the first ring.

"It's me, Mason."

"Surprise, surprise."

I explain about the rental agency, give him the license number and the date Donne visited me. What I'm proposing sounds to me a bit in the gray area of the law if it's in there at all. I mean, I want him to dip into a company's records, which by all rights ought to be confidential. But he doesn't remark on it, and I don't either.

"So you want to know if the person who rented the limousine still has it, if not, if he's rented another car, and if he left a local address?"

"Any address, Joe."

"Okay."

Hanging up, I worry about all the stuff to which the government can gain access. Can anyone have secrets these days? Maybe only Charlie.

The afternoon bends over into evening and I'm ready to go home. Our options for dinner are narrowed down because of last night. We could stay home and have a not great time or go out and have a not great time. And what about what happened this morning? I try not to think about it, but it chips away at my mind. I'm a couple of blocks from the office when I run into Margie Collins. "How's the funeral business, Sis?"

"More peaceful than I hear your life is lately."

"You're right on that score."

"Here's a bit of information about Fat Dom's death you may not know. The word on Petronia Street is that a policeman killed him, but the killer didn't wear the kind of uniform our police or state troopers wear."

What the hell is this all about? A cop who got screwed on a payoff? One who didn't like the merchandise? One who found out the fat man got his hands on his kid? A cop hired to do a hit? Fat Dom's enemies must have covered the spectrum.

"Thanks for the tip, but I don't have anything to do with that murder. I'll pass it along to Griswold."

"Well, some people mentioned that you were with the police when they found his body. I thought maybe you were investigating his death."

"My plate is full right now," I say. "I couldn't and wouldn't want to take on another murder case."

She smiles sympathetically and touches my arm. "I know how terrible it must be for you with Charlie, Marlene, and Virginia all dying on you. My heart bleeds for those other two women Charlie married."

"Thanks for your thoughts, Margie, and thanks again for the tip. In a way it makes me feel a bit relieved."

"I'm glad, Mason. I've got to run. I'll say a prayer for you."

She hurries down the street, a strong, graceful woman who is kept on the run with her job and tending to the needs of her husband and five kids. You see all these articles nowadays about career women remarkably juggling exhausting lives as they race from job to family. Not to take anything away from them, but it's what poor black women have always done, but few people consider them important enough to comment upon.

What she said does make me feel better. On Petronia, that's not idle gossip. Somebody saw or heard something. They won't tell the cops, but they know. At least now I'm sure he wasn't killed because of what he wanted to see me about. Pretty sure.

When I reach the apartment, I'm the first one home. There's a note on the coffee table that I must've missed this morning. It's a reminder that Amanda Kay's at a PTA meeting tonight. She told me about the meeting a few days ago, but like everything else, I forgot. I grab a beer and sit down with the newspaper. Betty comes home a few minutes later. She smiles tentatively and takes a deep breath.

"Mason, can we pretend that this morning didn't happen? I wouldn't hurt Amanda Kay for the world, so this can't go any further."

"You stole my very words. Betty, you're a very attractive woman who has been through a harrowing time and you've stood up under it remarkably well. If I didn't feel for Amanda Kay what I do, I'd be groveling at your feet. I'm the one who was in the wrong, not you."

Her face reddens and she appears, well, virginal. "That's very gallant of you." In a voice that's almost a whisper, she adds, "I've felt so alone lately that . . . that . . ."

The rest trails off. Determinedly, she wipes her eyes. "You can be very sweet in your own gruff way, Mason. Very sweet."

I actually blush. Long ago, I gave up on trying to figure out women. When I'm trying to impress one, I can't. When I'm fumbling around like a fool, I attract them like bees to honey.

She calls for Mexican food. While we eat, I'm grateful the air is clear between us. The limits are well-defined on our relationship. Neither of us wants to cross them again. After a bit of awkwardness, our conversation finds a rhythm again. We talk about this and that. Then I ask her something that has bothered me since Doc Grover said Charlie's long letter to me might be a phony.

"How did you find the envelope that Charlie left for me, Betty?"

"I didn't actually find it."

"Who did?"

"Amanda Kay. She came over to help me go through Charlie's things. I guess she felt I wasn't up to doing it by myself."

This bit of news is disconcerting. I think again about Amanda Kay and the missing gold coin. What's going on? Ugly thoughts press my mind, but I shove them away.

Betty smiles ruefully. "Amanda Kay was probably right. The full impact of Charlie's death didn't hit me until a couple of days after he died, but I was trying to go on like it was business as usual."

"Was anybody around the house then who shouldn't have been?"

Her brow furrows. "Mason, I honestly can't say. There were so many people around. The police, newspeople, insurance agents, even someone asking me what I was going to do with Charlie's boat . . . I knew a few of them slightly. Many I didn't know at all. I'm sorry I can't be more precise than that."

"How about a guy in his midtwenties? Dark hair. A thin face and on the short side? Looks like a squirrel."

"I don't know. Maybe. I . . . I . . . just can't remember."

"Hey, don't worry about it."

"You're thinking the killer might have come around, aren't you?"

"It's a possibility, but anything's a possibility."

Shortly after dinner, Betty got ready to turn in. "I'll give you some alone time with Amanda Kay," she says with a trace of wistfulness. "God knows, you both need it."

For a second, I think about that slob in the bar and am filled with rage, a delayed reaction, the male version of the kind Amanda Kay felt last night. If he was within striking distance at this moment, he'd be a cripple when he picked himself up off the floor. The burn of anger doesn't go away for a long time after Betty goes to bed.

A FOOL'S DEATH

When Amanda Kay finally gets home, she curls up on the sofa next to me and puts her head on my shoulder. I can't help it but the image of her on Matthews's boat comes to mind and I go tense on her.

"Say, did you come across my old gold coin by any chance?" I ask.

"You mean the one Precious was talking about?"

"Uh-huh."

"No. Why?" she asks, annoyance creeping into her voice as she sits up and edges away from me.

"Forget it." I pull her closer, not wanting to wreck the moment, but wondering if I already haven't. I'm still thinking about Matthews and me and Betty and the coin and why it disappeared after Precious mentioned it at dinner last night. And I'm thinking of how it was Amanda Kay, not Betty, who found the manila envelope of possibly phony stuff from Charlie. What a weird coincidence. If it was.

"Sorry I was such a harpy last night," she says. "Sometimes I get that way when a guy acts like such a bastard. It's easy to believe all men hate women when you see something like that."

"Not all," I say, trying to make light of it but not succeeding very well.

"What's the matter?" she asks, looking at me oddly and moving away again.

"I'm just feeling a bit jumpy. That's all."

"Good-night," she says coolly.

She gets up and heads to the bedroom before I can stop her. I'm not sure I was even going to try.

48

THE packet of stuff comes from Philadelphia, and Joe Clark's car rental information arrives from D.C. Both were by overnight mail. The Philadelphia newspaper stories say the girl dropped the charges against Donne. There was an out-of-court settlement, which was believed to be quite big, but the girl and her lawyer as well as Donne's lawyers refused to comment.

The photo Matt sent isn't useful. The picture's about three years old. Donne was in his long-hair and full-beard stage. With all that hair, it's impossible to recognize the young man he is today.

The limo info is another matter. The Mercedes was rented by one Vincent DiNardi, whoever the hell he is. His home address and phone number aren't listed, but they are for his work: T.A.C. Corp. in Miami. I'll have to visit Mr. DiNardi to try to bleed out of him Donne's whereabouts. First, I call to find out when he'll be in.

"T.A.C.," the operator answers.

"Mr. DiNardi, please."

"Sorry, sir. Mr. DiNardi isn't in right now."

"When do you expect him?"

"I'm not sure, sir. Perhaps Tommy Costello can help you."

Tommy Costello? Hell, how many Tommy Costellos can there be in Miami?

"Miss, this may sound kind of foolish, but maybe you'll humor me. What kind of a company is this?"

"Why, a detective agency, of course."

"Thank you. Will Mr. Costello be in all day?"

"Yes. Would you like to talk to him?"

"No. I'll call back."

I cradle the receiver, wondering what the hell's going on. Costello? He rooted around in Charlie's life. But why? What game was the man playing? It looks as if young Donne hired him to play on his side.

Suddenly, I remember Snake's saying after the cockfight that he has something to tell me. Since I've decided to go to Miami to pay Costello a visit, maybe I can see Snake on the way. I call the garage in Key Largo where the Padres usually congregate.

"Yeah!" a voice on the other end of the line challenges.

"Get me Snake!" I roar back.

The receiver is dropped on a desk or the floor or somewhere so it clatters with ear-puncturing little blasts. A minute later, Snake's eerie hiss skitters across the line.

"Whose asking for Snake?"

"It's Mason, Snake. You have something to tell me."

"Right, Mason. Right."

"I'm heading up your way. Want to meet at Alabama Jack's?"

"Will do, bro," he says, and hangs up after we set a time to meet.

Since coming across Costello somehow again being mixed up in this business, I feel as if I'm on shakier ground than ever. I check my .38, put the holster around my leg, grab a pair of handcuffs, and leave word at Amanda Kay's school that I'll be late. I call Betty at the gallery and tell her too. Betty sounds friendly. That's a lot warmer than Amanda Kay did.

When I reach Alabama Jack's, the place has as much activity as a grade school on a hot July day. The bartender emerges periodically from somewhere. He obviously has better things to do. Actually, I like it sleepy like this. Looking over the water, my mind roams freely.

I drove a rental car up from Key West. A lot of tourists like the idea of driving down, but the prospect of facing the monotony of the road on the way back results in their ditching cars down there. I worked out a deal to drive the car for free and use it for the day.

All day I keep thinking the same thoughts. The Squirrel turned to Costello to learn as much about Charlie as possible, so that when he went after him and his wives he more or less knew what he was up against. He got to know what each of the ex-wives did, their habits, et cetera. When he moved in on them, he felt he was in the driver's seat.

Still, why did he come to me? To remove himself from suspicion? I'd race around after shadows when the killer was right in front of me. Clever.

Snake shows up fifteen minutes after me. The usual road toads are in tow, reeking of grease, gas, and oil. As they indulge in Cro-Magnon snorting, grunting, and generally uncivilized behavior, it's hard to believe that they were ever babies. Snake takes the barstool next to mine and gives me a playful punch on the shoulder.

"Leroy wants another couple of rounds with you," he hisses.

"Tell him to get in line."

"You got him pretty good. He had to go home lying on the backseat of somebody's car. Somebody else rode his cycle home. For Leroy that was like having somebody take his dick home for him."

I'm about to speculate on what Freud might have to say about such a statement but decline. Snake might take offense. "So what do you remember about Tommy Costello's visit with you?"

"I asked him who he was working for. He nodded toward some guy who was sitting nearby."

"What was he like?"

"One of those blandly perfect moneyed guys who could've been a movie actor or own a string of polo ponies. Dark complexion.

Tailored clothes. Put him in a Hathaway shirt ad and you wouldn't go far wrong."

What he says is interesting from a perceptual standpoint. The grooming and money parts sound like Donne. But the Squirrel isn't my idea of a matinee idol. Maybe our tastes in movies differ. I wish I had a photo of Donne.

I could've asked Snake about this over the phone, but I've found that in person I can pump him and often get additional information. "Anything else you can think of about the man?" I ask.

"Well, he was jittery and seemed mad that Costello pointed him out. Kept checking his watch and looking around as if somebody might see him."

"How old a guy are we talking about?" I ask.

"Late forties. Maybe fifty."

"You sure?"

"Hell, I might be off a few years one way or the other."

Damn! It's not Donne. So much for my jigsaw puzzle falling into place. "Who the hell is he?" I wonder out loud.

"There's one person who knows," Snake says.

"Costello," I say.

"You got it."

"Thanks, Snake." I toss some money on the bar. "Bartender, give the Padres a round on me." Hell, it's Huff's money. Let it buy me some more goodwill. I always need more than my fair share.

"I saw about Charlie's wives dying," Snake says. "What are there, two more to go?"

"I wish you wouldn't put it that way."

"Sorry, Mason. But you're up against some pretty heavy shit. If you need any muscle, let me know. You know how much I appreciate your finding my kid sister."

I clasp his arm as I get up to go. "I hope it doesn't come down to that."

▪ ▪ ▪ ▪ 49 ▪ ▪ ▪ ▪

T.A.C. detective agency is in a once-nice building that now blends into its seedy surroundings without straining. That makes me feel good. I didn't like the idea that Costello might be doing a lot better than me. Still, the mob throws work his way, which must be lucrative. Maybe he's just cheap.

Driving from Jack's, I considered my options. I could take the direct route by simply approaching him as one PI seeking a bit of help from another. But from what I'd heard about Costello and read about him in Joe Clark's report, I don't think that would do much good. My second option is to go up to his office and get a good look at him. He doesn't know me, so I can pretend to be looking for someone else. Once I know what he looks like, I can wait for him outside, tail him, and come upon him when it's convenient.

The building directory gives an indication of the transient nature of the tenants. The glass covering the black panel with the little white letters to form tenants' names is cracked and taped. Half the spaces are empty. The listings that are there were put in crooked. T.A.C. is on the fourth floor.

A FOOL'S DEATH

After an interminably slow ride for such a short distance, the rickety elevator unloads me on four. The corridor is long and of a grimy white marble. Office doors are off to each side.

As my footsteps echo along the corridor, I realize how many doors I pass and how small the offices are. The woman who answered T.A.C.'s phone must be with a phone service. That coupled with the fact that this DiNardi fellow works here means Costello is doing better than me. Not much, but some. But then again, maybe dealing with the mob is like dealing with Snake. It's prudent not to bill at your regular rate.

Before knocking, I hesitate, taken aback by a familiar voice coming from inside.

"Look, Tommy, I can't do the surveillance thing this weekend. I told you rehearsals were scheduled."

"Vinnie, I'm gonna have to find somebody more reliable if you keep this shit up. These fucking rehearsals are fucking up my business."

I know that voice too.

"Look, I'll see what I can do."

"Yeah, you do that."

I perform some quick mental gymnastics. I'm positive about the voices, but they aren't using the names attached to them when I met them. Suddenly, the game is weirder. There are only the two of them in the room. Tommy and Vinnie. Mongo and Brian.

"I'll call you tomorrow," Vinnie-Brian says.

I hurry back to the exit by the elevator and go through the stairwell door just as Vinnie-Brian comes out of the office. I hotfoot down the stairs, not too worried that he'll beat me to the lobby. The elevator's as slow as if it's pulled up and down by a couple of one-armed dwarfs imprisoned in the basement.

Outside the building, I bend down to tie my shoelace, one of the oldest tricks in the book. A couple of minutes later, Vinnie-Brian walks right by me. I give him a half a block and kick in behind him. He goes to a big indoor parking garage a block away. I close the gap between us. As he puts his key in his car door lock, my .45 tickles his ribs.

Vinnie-Brian turns. The expression on his squirrelly face is one of classic horror when he sees me and the gun. No one else is around, which he frantically notes as well.

"Collins!" he says hoarsely.

"Vinnie-Brian, give me the keys to the car."

He hands them over. I open the door and shove him in front. I pull the door lock release and climb into the back. "Now, whoever the hell you are, tell me what I walked into."

He sits in a sullen silence. I take a handful of his hair and bend his head back over the front seat so I'm staring down into his eyes. "I don't care what I have to do to you to find out what I want to know. Three friends of mine were killed, and you're neck deep in it, son. As far as I can judge, you've been an active participant in murder. And *that* doesn't sit too kindly with jurors these days."

"Look," he gasps. "Costello's the guy you want. I work for him. I swear to God, I don't know anything about anybody involved in any murders."

"But you're here right now, son, and he isn't. And if you want to keep the cartilage the way it is in your nose and your teeth in your face and your fingernails intact, then start talking."

His pop eyes open even a smidgen wider.

"Okay. Okay, for Christ's sake. Just cool it!"

"Get going, son. We don't have all day."

"I got into this about ten days before I saw you down in Key West. Costello was working for somebody and pulled me into it. He thought it was perfect for me being as how I'm an actor. I only do this private eye bullshit to keep the lights on."

The way he says *actor* indicates a pride in his craft. Maybe he has a future. He sure as hell fooled me.

"Costello had me buy some rare coins off a swank coin dealer out on the Beach. I turned them over to him and then got one back when we headed down to see you. He coached me on this whole elaborate number we did on you."

"What the hell did you think you were doing?"

He doesn't answer right away. I yank his hair back a bit more.

"Damn," he screeches. "I . . . I read about Donne being killed and figured somebody had some kind of scam. Maybe there was double indemnity on an insurance policy or something if the guy was killed in some weird way. Costello gets a lot of sleazy clients."

"How did the coin I found get out by Charlie Donne's body?"

"Hell if I know."

I let go of his hair. Slowly, he raises his head, looking in the rearview mirror with frightened eyes to see if I object.

"I hope you're not acting now, son, or I'll come back for you. If I do, I promise there won't be enough of you left to ever set foot on a stage again."

"I'm not lying, Collins. I swear it."

"What time is Costello leaving the office . . . ?" I'm about to call him Brian but catch myself.

"He usually goes home about five."

"Where's that?"

"He's got a place on Key Biscayne."

"How does he afford that when he works out of a dung heap?"

"He cuts costs by not paying much in overhead . . . or salaries," DiNardi says ruefully. "As I said, a lot of his clients are sleaze bags. They feel comfortable in a place like that."

"Give me his home address."

DiNardi takes an address book from inside his jacket and flips through it. He passes it back opened to the page with the info on Costello.

"Just don't tell him where you got it, okay?"

"Don't worry," I say, ripping the page out. "And you know what will happen, don't you, if you tell him I'm coming?"

"Okay. Okay. I won't say anything. But I'm not part of any murder."

He glances into the rearview mirror again, hoping that he has a look of sincerity in his eyes. "I'm way out of my depth on this thing. I know it was bullshit the way we set you up, but I didn't want to think about it."

"What's the best way to get Costello?"

"He's a health nut. At six-thirty every night he jogs from his apartment about five miles along the beach. He hates to break the routine for anything."

I toss the car keys on the seat next to him, climb out, and watch him drive away. The unpredictable nature of life's twists and turns makes my head spin. I feel as if I'm locked in a hall of mirrors where nothing and no one I see is what or who they should be.

50

COSTELLO lives in an expensive, high-rise condo that's on an oasis of green lawn, palm trees, and ocean views like you see in ads depicting the good life. I half expect to see willowy, beautiful women in gossamer dresses standing on balconies and staring at sunsets while guys who skydive when they aren't whitewater rafting while reading good books bring them booze in Waterford goblets.

Instead, the people streaming out are mostly rich old folks revved up for their evening superwalks. In their funny little shorts and straw hats and with their dried-apple faces, they look like children from a planet where everybody starts out old and gets younger by expending terrific amounts of energy. Arms pumping like pistons, they march fiercely up and down the sidewalks, determined to aerobics death away.

At 6:32 Costello comes through the front door. A sculpted physique means a lot of bodybuilding at a gym. He wears blue shorts and a black muscleman T-shirt and has a white towel around his neck. A steady lope takes him in the direction of the state park that leads to the beach.

Climbing into the rental car, I let him get a good distance ahead and drive up to where he disappears along a path to the beach. I figure he'll come back by the same route. When he does, I'll be waiting.

The park is well maintained but not well used this time of the evening. Palm trees and bougainvillea are carefully tended. There are picnic tables and parking areas. Out on the beach, occasional solitary joggers appear off in the distance, but otherwise desolation is rampant.

To do his five miles at that pace will take about thirty-five minutes. As he disappears in the distance, I look around, scouting a location. I settle on a spot that seems right. The surface is flat and a good ten yards away from the foliage, but still well screened from the roadway but not the beach.

The wait doesn't do me much good. I think about the kind of guy Costello is. His blowing away the kids. His fondling the girl. His work for the mob. His churning up Charlie's past. I think about the deaths, and how he must've had a hand in them, even if it was an indirect hand. Funny how you can loathe someone you don't even know or even really want to know.

I do some knee bends and push-ups and stretch out cramped muscles. I'm loose by the time he's a tiny figure coming back across the sand. Removing my sunglasses, I put them in my shirt pocket. I take off my shirt and put it on the ground by a little fence along with the holster from my leg and the handcuffs. I slip out of my shoes. I work better barefoot in the sand.

I stand there waiting, staring at him. After a while, he's staring back. About fifty feet away, he recognizes me. He doesn't slow his pace but flexes his arms, getting ready. He knows what's coming. Ten feet away, he stops.

"What are you doing here, Collins?"

"I came for you."

He laughs a little. "That's what I thought you'd say."

We move forward at the same time, chins tucked into chests, fists raised. Feinting and jabbing, we feel out one another. We close in. His left fist grazes my temple. I give him a short right hook to the gut, which he mostly deflects as he backs away. He knows what he's doing, and that beefcake body is as hard as it is strong.

I roll my right shoulder and feint to my left. He takes the bait. He strikes out, leaving an opening to his face. I smash him in the left eye, sending him back a foot or two. He grunts but doesn't lose his balance. Closing in, he uses his extra weight to his advantage and lands a couple of powerful body blows.

Sweating and heaving, we trade punches toe-to-toe. I vow to take up jogging again myself. I'm getting winded too fast. But a minute later, I realize he's good but not that good. Those bulked-up muscles make him tight, unable to get full extension on his arms.

I move in and out, picking off bits and pieces of him and working on the eye I hit first. A shot to his jaw snaps his head back. His arms fly open. I pound his gut and pour fists into his face.

He's mad and lunges. I sidestep and hit him in the face again with a right hook. A cut opens over the right eye. Another punch pulverizes his nose. His breathing is raspy. Blood's flowing over the one eye. A lot of people don't realize boxing is like the thrusting and parrying of fencing. The end results are often similar.

Another shot to the jaw sends him stumbling backward and he lands on one knee. When I move in, I see his hand flick upward. The sand seems to be in slow motion, whirling softly, timelessly toward my face, before it wipes out my vision. Eyes stinging, I lower my head, try to protect myself with my arms, and bull toward where he's coming from. We crash together. I'm battered left and right as we stumble to our knees. I grab a fistful of sand and fling it.

"Damn!" he screams.

From his groping, I know I hit my mark. We cling, trying to get a grip on sweaty, gritty bodies. Gasping hoarsely, we smash blindly. As in the cockfight Georgie Two Foot and I went to, there will be only one winner here too.

Clutching me in a bear hug, he knees me in the gut again and

A FOOL'S DEATH

again, and I start losing it. Suddenly, I think of Charlie, Marlene, and Virginia. Rage roars up. I grab his hair and pull his head down with all my might while I butt upward. His jaw crashes into my scalp. I do it again and again and again until my teeth rattle.

Suddenly, he goes limp. As he sags to the ground, I tumble to my side in pain. I feel as if I landed on my head after falling five thousand feet without a parachute.

Gradually, I pull myself together and clean out my eyes. Hauling myself to my feet, I stumble to my clothes, grab the handcuffs, and make it back to where Costello still hasn't moved. Turning him on his stomach, I cuff his wrists behind him and sink down next to him to catch my breath and wait for the bastard to come awake.

He's out for a long minute or so before he stirs. "Shit! Shit! Shit!" he repeats over and over.

Twisting and flopping like a beached shark, he manages to sit upright. His breath whistles through his bashed nose and parched throat.

"I can't see a goddamn thing. Wipe the fucking sand out of my eyes."

His towel is nearby. I grab it, go over, squat next to him, and rub his eyes until he starts yelling because the sand digs into the cuts on his face.

"Stop, for Christ's sake. Stop!"

Coughing and spitting, he blinks a dozen or so times and shakes his head like an old dog. I stay right next to him, thinking all the time about Charlie, Marlene, and Virginia.

"No games, Costello. There are a couple of women's lives at stake. Now tell me."

"Tell you what?" he asks sourly.

"I don't have time to mess around with you anymore, son. Now tell me about this caper and who hired you."

"Fuck you, Collins."

I take a handful of sand and grind it into the cut over his eye.

A FOOL'S DEATH

His screams could wake the dead. Grabbing him by the hair, I yank his face close to mine.

"I don't care what it takes, Costello, and I'll enjoy every minute of it."

For the first time, fright is part of his package. His eyes open wide and he shrinks back, but I keep my hand on his hair and pull his face even closer to mine.

"Now you talk, you miserable son of a bitch, or you'll wish you'd never been born."

One more look at me convinces him he finally met the devil. He recoils from the hate and rage coming off me like heat from a blast furnace.

"Okay, for Christ's sake. Okay!"

He takes a deep breath. "I got a call about six months ago to check out a guy name of Charlie Donne down in Key West. The client wants a whole rundown. What he does for a living, hobbies, his love life, his friends, business associates, what he eats, for Christ's sake. I mean a whole rundown.

"What's a little strange is that the client doesn't want the guy's total history. I'm supposed to just pick up on him from the time he moved to Key West."

Costello pauses for a moment, spitting out sand. He wipes blood and saliva from his mouth on the little shoulder strap on his T-shirt. Most of it winds up on his shoulder.

"I get a cash retainer in the mail, so I do the job. I don't think much of it. He's a dime-a-dozen guy down here. He's got a boat with payments due. He fishes when he's not taking other people fishing. He likes to drink, and he likes broads. He's tight with a couple of guys, you most of all.

"About the only offbeat thing about Charlie Donne is that he likes to get married. He married four times and he marries in less time than most guys take to pick a number at the track. He divorces them but keeps in touch with them."

He looks at me, trying to act nice now. "You run a guy down like he's gonna be a presidential candidate and it's pretty easy money. Right? You ask a lot of questions of a lot of people and you get a lot of stuff that fleshes out the records. The guy who hires me even tells me some people to question, and he goes with me on a couple of interviews. He gets the report and I get paid."

"What else?"

"So I don't think nothin' of it until about a month ago when the same guy calls. He's got a proposition and wants to know if I'm interested. I am. He says it pays more than the last job but should take less time. Now I'm very interested."

Costello wriggles around on the sand, trying to get comfortable. "The guy comes by the office. I still don't even have a name to call him. He tells me that he wants somebody to do a favor for him. Buy some coins from a coin dealer out on the Beach. I figure he's a big-time collector or working for one and maybe doesn't want the dealer to know he's buying. Who knows? But then he says something weird. He says I can't buy the coins myself. I gotta get somebody with dark hair in his twenties to do it."

"Why?"

"He don't tell me. Anyway, I luck out. I've got this kid who works for me off and on. He fits the bill. Better yet, he's an actor, so I know he'll dig the job. The kid goes out, gets the coins, and brings them back. I get good dough."

"What else?"

"A week goes by. I get another call from the guy. He's got another job and he wants the kid who bought the coins to do it. He comes around and outlines something strange. He wants the kid to impersonate Donne's brother. Donne just died. That I know because the way Donne checks out makes him the lead freak story on the front page of every newspaper. He wants the scam done on you."

He looks at me kind of wary when he says this. "We do the job and get real good dough for that too. End of story."

"So who's the client?"

"Like I say, he don't give his name. He takes a cab in and out of here so I never see a license plate. He doesn't open up about who he is or what he's up to."

Even though I know, I ask, "What's he look like?"

"A classy guy. You can tell he never had to dig ditches for a living. Good clothes. Good tan. Dark hair. A Rolex. In pretty good shape. Mid to late forties."

It's the guy Snake was talking about. So who is he?

There's no way Costello won't find out who the client is. If the guy takes a cab, Costello will take down the number and talk to the driver later to find out where he dropped the client off. Or he'll simply follow the cab. No PI would work in the dark like that, especially somebody like Costello, who routinely works for shifty clients. You have to know what you're getting into.

"What's his name, Costello?"

"Who?"

I flick the cut over his eye with a fingernail and pick up some sand and make as if to rub it into the wound while he shies away. "The client . . ."

"Okay!" he says angrily. "He came with a broad one time and I follow them back to a marina. He has a sailboat docked there in the name of Matthews. Peter Matthews."

"Matthews!"

I can hardly believe it. How the hell is Matthews mixed up in this? What does he have to do with Charlie? What does he have to do with murder?

"Yeah, he's a hotshot stockbroker who rotates between here and Key West. Had a good-looking redhead with him. I did a little checking on him."

I tense. "What did you find out?"

"That'll cost you, Collins," he says reflexively.

One look at my face and he hurries along. "For one, he has this hot thing going with the redhead. She's from Key West but I don't check on her, so I don't even know her name."

I get a sinking sensation. "What else did you pick up on him?"

"He's in some kind of bad financial shit. He's been fucking

around his accounts. There's the possibility he could go to the slammer from what I can tell."

"What was his interest in Charlie Donne? Why'd he go through all that?"

Costello looks as perplexed as I feel. "I could never figure that. I tried out a lot of different angles but couldn't come up with anything that made sense."

He looks at me as if I don't believe him. "I ain't shittin' you. I thought maybe he's one of Donne's relatives and stood to make some big dough if the guy died, but I couldn't find any link-up that way. I thought it was some kind of insurance scam or something. Maybe it is."

Maybe the link is a woman he was married to who will come into a fortune if she doesn't have to share Charlie's estate.

I haul Costello to his feet and take off the cuffs. He rubs his wrists and gingerly touches his face, which is a mess. The nose is broken. The right eye is shut and getting bluer by the minute. His chin is split and caked with dried blood. His lips are swollen. I figure he looks about as bad as I did after Andalusia's boys worked me over.

"No hard feelings, Costello," I say as he makes his way up the path in front of me.

"Yeah, right," he says sarcastically, and starts jogging back toward his building.

He can't be too bad if he still has the energy to jog, or else he just summoned it up from somewhere deep down to try to convince me he's not really hurt. About twenty yards along, he stumbles and falls over, gets to his knees, and falls out straight again. Yeah, right.

I turn around the rental car and drive to a gas station a little ways from the park. Once there, I breathe deeply before I get the nerve to call Amanda Kay. I decide not to question her yet, but I've got to warn her anyway, thinking all the while that there's no need for a warning at all.

"How did everything go?" she asks tensely.

"Okay. But I found out Peter Matthews is very involved in

this. Stay away from him. Tell Betty too. No matter what, don't go near him."

"Peter?"

"Yes, Peter. Just like the stuff about Marti being the killer, the stuff about young Donne asking for my help was a ruse, a charade, and somehow Matthews is right at the heart of it. I'll tell you about it when I get home."

Next I call the Yacht Club in Key West and get Ansel Woods, the manager. "This is Mason, Ansel. Can you tell me whether Peter Matthews is keeping *The Money Pit* in Key West tonight or taking her over to Miami?"

"Hold on."

A minute later he's on the line again. "Far as I know, he'll be here. Supposed to take her over tomorrow but be back Friday. Shall I tell him you want to see him?"

"No thanks, Ansel." I think he may already know that I'm coming.

■■■■ 51 ■■■■

WHEN my plane gets into Key West, I drive right to the Yacht Club. It's about nine-thirty and *The Money Pit* is dark. Matthews is out or has already turned in. I go on board and bang on the door. There's no sign of stirring, so I bang again. When that still doesn't produce results, I try the handle. The door opens.

Groping around for a light switch, I finally find one. The lights flick on and I become sick to my stomach.

Matthews is stretched out on the floor. He's wearing a pair of khaki shorts and a once-white tennis shirt. The shirt is now soaked through with blood. The cause of the blood is the knife protruding from his back.

A cellular phone is on a table to the right. I pick it up and punch in the police number. Jerry King answers.

"Jer, it's Mason. You'll have to get Griswold. Peter Matthews was murdered. I just found him on his boat. He's docked at the Yacht Club."

King lets out a low whistle. "We're going to overtake D.C. as the murder capital of the world."

"If Griswold has any questions, he can reach me at my apartment tonight or at my office in the morning."

"Okay, Mason."

As I cradle the receiver, evil thoughts and questions suddenly jackhammer my mind. Who had a relationship with Matthews? Who knew I was onto something regarding him? Who has red hair? Who stands to gain from the deaths of Charlie and all the rest of the wives? Only one person.

Driving back to the apartment, I remember how startled she was the night I woke up and found her coming back in. The night Fat Dom was killed. I remembered her being late for Big Bill and Peggy's wedding. That was when Virginia was killed.

I think again about the gold coin missing from my dresser and about who found the typewritten packet that Charlie supposedly meant for me. My feelings for Amanda Kay are in disrepair.

At the apartment, I stand at the bottom of the steps before working up the nerve to climb them. When I finally do, it's as if I'm someone else. Mason Collins is somewhere, but he isn't here. Some other part of my mind has taken over, is moving me one foot at a time and stands there rigid, resigned, unmoved, and unresponsive when Amanda Kay comes up and puts her arms around me.

She drops her arms and looks into my face with a mixture of sorrow and resignation. "What is it, Mason?" she asks quietly. "Just tell me what it is."

"Where were you tonight?" I ask.

"What do you mean, where was I?"

"Peter Matthews was killed tonight, Amanda Kay. Someone stabbed him in the back just the way Fat Dom was stabbed. Where did you go that night I got up and found you gone? That was the night Fat Dom was killed."

Her fist comes to her mouth but no words come out. Finally, all she says is, "Oh, my God!"

"Maybe I should have realized it before now," I go on. "How else would Marlene or Virginia have opened the door, unless it was to let somebody in they trusted completely, somebody in the same boat as them. Another wife."

When Amanda Kay looks up at me, her eyes contain all the troubles of the world. There's hatred there too. Slowly, she speaks in a terrible voice. "Get out, Mason. Get out of my life."

"I'll be back soon. . . ."

I leave, feeling worse than from any beating I've ever had. I'm hollow. Empty. A loneliness I knew only once before squeezes me in its black grip. Back in the jeep, I shiver and feel colder than if I were trapped in an arctic blast.

Proof is the problem. I don't have any, but I know where to go to start to get it. A few minutes later, I'm on Petronia Street, in front of Fat Dom's. Nobody's about, so I walk around back and jimmy the back door. In the living room, I turn on one of the lamps and go over to the painting on the wall that conceals Fat Dom's files, the hidden files that Griswold, like most people, including, I'm fairly sure, the killer, doesn't know are here.

Eventually, I find the trip. The painting slides to the side. My hands are shaking and there's a tightness in my throat as I go through the file drawers until I come across Marti's records.

His folder is thick, and I take it over to the couch and sit down. With great difficulty, I force myself to go through picture after picture, looking for a face that is familiar. At last I come across a photo, and I let out a sigh of the damned as I stare down at a young girl. She has a quietly beautiful face that's still easily recognizable even though she is now a quietly beautiful woman. The last name is Carson and the address on the back is Key Largo, but that's from a long time ago.

I take the picture and go back to the apartment. When I let myself in, Mike Sanders is there.

"Where's Amanda Kay?"

Mike looks sheepish. "Uh, she's lying down. She, uh, doesn't want to see you, Mason."

"It'll only take a minute."

Mike goes into the bedroom. He's back a second later. "She's not there!" Running into the kitchen, he calls out, "She must've slipped out the back!"

Icy fear grips me as I look down at the picture in my still-shaking hand. "Mike, if Betty Donne shows up, arrest her. And for God's sake, don't let her near Amanda Kay!"

My heart sinks. What if Amanda Kay has already gone to her?

I head to the gallery and I let myself in with the keys Betty gave me. She isn't there, and she isn't in the apartment upstairs. She left in a rush. Clothes are scattered about and drawers are half-open. My coin is in one of them. In the top of a closet, I find a red wig.

Downstairs, I check her desk calendar and then her memo pad. A telephone number is written on the pad. Next to it is one word: "Mom!" The exclamation point seems like a cry for help. I dial the number. After several rings, a woman's voice answers. I use the name on the back of the picture.

"Mrs. Carson?" I ask. "Mrs. Carson of twenty-nine Deerfield Road, Key Largo?"

"Yes."

"I am trying to locate your daughter, Betty."

Before I can say another word, the phone hangs up. All I hear is the dial tone. When I redial, there's a busy signal.

I call Griswold. "Will, I know who the killer is."

"Who?"

I sigh. "Betty Donne. I think she killed Matthews as well as Charlie, Marlene, and Virginia. Maybe Fat Dom too."

"Jesus!"

"That's what I thought you'd say."

"Where is she?"

"I don't know. There's something else."

"What's that?"

"Amanda Kay's missing."

"Oh, Christ!"

I try to keep from cracking. "Will, you've got to find Amanda Kay before Betty does!"

"Take it easy, Mason," he says with emotion. "I know what the woman means to you. If she's on this island, we'll find her."

"Thanks," I reply, and hang up, thinking she didn't mean enough to me to believe in her.

Griswold and his men can find either of the women faster than me if they're around Key West. I decide to follow up on a hunch. Once more I climb into the jeep and head north. My only company is terrible thoughts about the ways I betrayed Amanda Kay. First by making love to Betty. Second by not believing in her. The second is worse by a long shot.

■■■■ 52 ■■■■

THE Leeward Trailer Camp is just off Route 1 and toward the south end of Key Largo. A sprawling place, it's come to resemble a weird suburb in Appalachia. Makeshift screened porches, extra bedrooms, and Lord knows what jut out of fronts and sides of trailers like ungainly growths. Even so, the atmosphere is still one of impermanence, of people ready to uproot their lives on a moment's notice. Out front of some trailers are little circles of whitewashed rocks, looking like magic symbols to ward off evil repossessors.

Deerfield Road is a stretch of especially antiquated trailers that look like old rusty diners. No. 29 bravely stands out for having been frequently painted and having a nice little flower garden. Climbing out of the jeep, I stretch aching muscles, hoping after today I won't be making this drive again for a long time. As I look up, a curtain in a window is partly drawn back. The door opens and a woman stands staring at me.

"Hello. You must be Mrs. Carson."

"You're the one who called, aren't you?"

Walking up the path to the door, I realize how much she looks like Betty, a slim, faded blonde with good facial features. Seeing her reminds me of Marti and his picture. It's as if Betty suddenly slips twenty-five years into the future.

"Yes. Yes, I am. My name is Mason Collins and I'm from Key West."

"Well, you can just go back. She's not here."

Mrs. Carson starts shutting the door when I say one word. "Please!"

Pausing indecisively, she stares at me hard for a minute. She must've caught the weariness, despair, sadness, and whatever else is welling up inside me.

"All right, Mr. Collins," she says with painful resignation. "Please come in."

I follow her into the trailer, out of the heat. The front room is small but neat. Window fans do a pretty good job of keeping the place cool.

"Would you like some coffee or tea?"

"Whatever you're having, ma'am."

"I was just about to have a cup of tea."

"I'd like that too."

Flowers are in vases. The kitchen is spotless. A set of encyclopedias and other books line the shelves of a bookcase. The furnishings are old and worn with wear from cleaning as much as from age.

Mrs. Carson comes back carrying a tray with a teapot and two cups and saucers, milk and sugar, and a plate of cookies. She sets the tray down awkwardly.

"I haven't fixed tea for a man since my husband died five years ago. Sugar?"

"One, ma'am."

"Milk?"

"No thanks."

Finally, she sits and wipes a strand of gray hair across her forehead. "I don't know whether I want to know what Betty has done," she starts off. "There has been so much. So much."

"What do you mean?"

"You are with the police, aren't you?"

"No, ma'am. I'm a private investigator."

"She called tonight. She was in a panic. She gets that way when she has done something she shouldn't have. I told her I'd help her if I could."

"You're her mother."

Mrs. Carson pauses and looks at me. "That's not the only reason. You see, I feel responsible. Betty was born with something missing. She's capable of doing terrible things, but afterward, in her own mind, it's as if she hasn't done them. There's this . . . this strange innocence about her."

I quickly realize Mrs. Carson hasn't talked to anybody for a while. Maybe it's just having her daughter crash back into her life, but she gushes forth.

"We first knew Betty was different when she was in junior high school. There was a group of boys at the school who . . . who started talking about her. The boys were boasting about what they did with her with the ruthless exuberance boys that age possess. One day after school, a teacher came upon a group of them with her in an empty classroom.

"Betty's father and I were heartsick. But we tried to be supportive. She was only a young girl. Everyone makes mistakes, and she was so smart and had such a bright future in front of her. Also, she continued to show love and respect for us and seemed truly contrite."

Pausing, she heaves a sigh. "We switched her to a different school, one twenty miles away, where no one knew her. Everything seemed to go well, but then she was caught smoking with other girls, and she began staying out late and not saying where she'd been."

Mrs. Carson's eyes fill with tears, but she doesn't cry. "Finally, the summer she was thirteen, she ran away. After several months, we learned she was in Key West. At our wit's end, we took her to a psychiatrist. You see, Mr. Collins, no matter what she did, she had that innocence. And she'd lie about everything so convincingly that you'd believe almost anything she said.

"She was so bright, the psychiatrist got her a scholarship to boarding school in South Carolina, feeling that a change of environment would be good for her. At first we thought going off to school was the answer. She excelled academically, but then there were incidents of petty thievery toward the end of the year, and Betty was a suspect. Then some girls' clothes were ruined. Someone entered their rooms and urinated on them. It looked as if Betty did that too. The school year ended before the officials knew for sure.

"The next year, there were other incidents that I won't go into, but they involved great cruelty. But she was such an adept liar that she convinced the authorities she wasn't responsible. The summer she was seventeen, she married a terrible young man named George Weller whose family had moved here from Kentucky."

"George Weller!" I exclaim, remembering that cracker park guard.

Mrs. Carson sighs. "Life can be very cruel, Mr. Collins, but you look like a man who knows that. Betty picked up with a lot of very unsavory men and her reputation was ruined. Weller was probably the worst of the terrible people she knew."

Shaking her head at complexities she'd never understand, she went on. "It seemed as if Betty was different people. She could be sweet and kind and she could be wicked. She took a test and was given a scholarship and early admission to the University of Miami.

"Suddenly, she and the Weller boy started coming around with a good bit of money. There were articles in the paper about a pair of young criminals, a man and a woman, who were robbing stores in Miami, but they were never caught. From the descriptions, I . . . I knew it was them, but I couldn't bring myself to turn my daughter over to the police. . . .

"She and Weller separated, but he would drop in and out of her life. Or maybe she dropped in and out of his life."

Looking at me with eyes that could no longer cry, she says, "I should have given her to the police, shouldn't I?"

I don't know what to say. "We all do what we think is best."

"No. Sometimes we know what's best, but we can't bring ourselves to do it."

"Do you have any idea where she might be?"

Betty's mother shakes her head. "She called, but she didn't say much. The one who probably knows is Weller. As I said, they keep in touch."

Standing, I hand her one of my cards. "If you hear from her again, or if you find out where she is, will you please call? I don't want to alarm you, but it's a case of life and death."

"Mr. Collins, I'm well beyond alarm where Betty is concerned. Long ago, I moved into dread."

■ ■ ■ ■ 53 ■ ■ ■ ■

THE little rental boat is chugging over the glades, heading southwest. I was told at the park guard station that Weller is out here somewhere, and I was shown on a map the general vicinity where he's supposed to be. The folks back there were a little suspicious about who I was and why I wanted to see him. At first, I was going to say he was a friend, but I wasn't sure they'd believe me. A man like Weller doesn't have friends. So I told them I'm family. Even Weller has to have that.

Some days can only be pleasant if a puff of arctic wind blasts through the humidity. This is one of them. The air is lying smotheringly low and I'm dripping sweat. The bright sun sits right on my head. Bugs of many species feed indiscriminately on me. None of it improves my state of mind.

After leaving Mrs. Carson, I spent the night in a motel on Key Largo. I called Mike Sanders to see if Amanda Kay had turned up yet. She hadn't. Betty hadn't either. Terrified that Amanda Kay was the last sacrifice on Charlie's funeral pyre, I couldn't sleep.

I hit the glades over an hour ago and am poking around various

A FOOL'S DEATH

channels. Suddenly, I hear a familiar roar. When I turn a bend, I see a powerful boat skipping along. Still a couple of hundred yards away, it's coming my way. As the pilot gets closer, I make out his park guard uniform. I stand and wave. If it isn't Weller, I figure the guy can tell me where I might find him.

The boat slows. Now I make out Weller. After a bit, he recognizes me. I cut off my motor. He does the same when he's about twenty feet off.

"What the fuck are you doin' out here, asshole?" he asks.

"Where's Betty Donne?"

As he approaches, I remember what a nasty, volatile creature he is. No telling what that kind will do. I slip out the .45 from my ankle holster and hold it behind me. If he goes for his gun, I'll blow his goddamn head off.

"You mean Betty *Weller*, fuckhead. Me and Betty married a long time ago."

"Where is she?"

"You know, you ain't very polite. Your dickhead friend was the same way."

My stomach sinks as I think of what happened to Charlie. I also remember what Margie Collins said about a guy in a cop's suit killing Fat Dom. Suddenly, I realize I'm looking at the phantom killer. "So you killed Charlie."

"You got it, fuckhead."

"Why did you kill the wives?"

His hand moves to his gun butt and rests there. Meanwhile, alligators are circling silently around our boats, as if drawing closer to hear what we're saying. It's out-and-out creepy.

"Why, Betty said they all had to die. Betty got them to open up. It was easy as pie."

I'm getting sicker by the minute. "What do you get out of this?"

"Why, half the fortune. You see, Betty is my lawful wife. We never got divorced."

He smiles. "You know why that is, don't you?"

"Why?"

He lets out a loony's laugh. "I'm the only one who could ever handle her. And you know why that is, don't you?"

Curiosity about trying to find some pattern to the psycho's reasoning makes me bite. "Why?"

"I was the only one who knew what she was like and it never mattered to me. Why, Mr. Collins, she's the only woman I ever met who could be as bad as me."

While I stare at the sick fool, he laughs again.

"Whose idea was it to feed Charlie to the gators?"

"Oh, that was me. Betty got him up here. He drove right up to the dock where this here boat was." That crazy laugh comes again. "He thought they were going fishing and was real glad about it. Betty never showed any interest in going fishing with him before."

Weller actually slaps his thigh while laughing at the memory. "You should've seen how surprised he was when I pulled a gun on him. I shot him, but you know, Mr. Collins, your friend wasn't dead when he went in the water and those gators moved in on him. I had a tough time retrieving his hand and foot from those hungry critters."

"Why did you put the gold coin out where he was found?"

"To get the story about his family rolling. Betty thought that up. Nice touch, wasn't it? When you said you wanted to come out to see where he was found, I came out ahead of time and put it where you'd come across it."

The laugh came again. "You didn't disappoint us, Mr. Collins. No, you didn't."

"Why did you kill Peter Matthews?"

His eyes narrow to slits. "He was the one dumb thing Betty ever did."

"What do you mean?"

"Why, she thought she loved him. A weak man like him and she thought she loved him. She only thought up this deal 'cause he was hurting for money. She wanted to keep him out of jail."

He laughs and shakes his head.

"What's so funny?"

He looks up angrily. "A woman as smart as Betty falling for a piece of fluff like him. She was going to cut me out and cut him in. She didn't know I found out, but I did."

"Where's Betty? Is Amanda Kay with her?"

"That doesn't matter, least of all to you."

"Why's that?"

"Because I'm going to kill you."

"That's what I thought you'd say."

He laughs. "Hey, that's pretty good. You know, maybe you should know where Betty is."

He pulls at a fishing line attached to his chair. Slowly, something emerges. Large and covered with muck and saw grass. While pulling it up, he looks grotesque. His eyes are bright. That terrible laughter comes from him as he slowly hauls it higher and higher. The dripping hair is stringy. Muck and strands of saw grass cling to the face, but Betty's head is still recognizable.

Weller's crazy laughter explodes again as he stares down at his trophy. Abruptly his mood turns harsh. "I was gonna just shoot you, but I remember what a prick you were the last time you were here, Collins, so I'm gonna kill you in a more imaginative way."

I smile grimly. Part of me wants to shoot the lunatic right now. Perhaps a more perverted side wants to give him a sporting chance. "I'd like that, cracker."

He flushes. "I'm going to run you down like a dog on a road. But seeing as how I'm a bighearted fella, I'll give you a head start."

He laughs again. There's no way his powerful craft can't overtake my little boat with the ten-horsepower Yamaha.

"Get going," he says, and revs up his engine.

I start the motor and putt-putt away. He takes the craft back up the channel about sixty yards and swings around lazily. As he opens his engine full throttle, I cut off my motor.

The boat roars down, sounding like a jet aircraft. When he's forty yards away I stand. At twenty-five yards off, I raise the gun and fire at his engine, squeezing off shot after shot. Suddenly, a bullet hits his fuel tank. A bright orange ball explodes at the back of the boat, which bucks and veers crazily off course. Whipping up onto a shallow island, it overturns.

Weller is flung into the water. He thrashes and screams. Gators close in on him.

I take my time starting my motor. By the time I get near where Weller went in, he isn't screaming anymore. The water is streaked with blood. In fact, I can't get too close. The gators are busy churning the water around him while finishing up what they started.

▪ ▪ ▪ ▪ 54 ▪ ▪ ▪ ▪

*I*T'S been over a month now since I've been back home. I'm moping around aimlessly. Amanda Kay never calls. She never contacts me. I hope she will but know she won't. I saw her on the street one afternoon, but she crossed to the other side, pretending she didn't see me.

I wrote up my report for Huff, explaining all the intricacies of what had happened. I had gone back to Marti and he confirmed that Betty was the girl he introduced to Charlie. But there are certain things I don't know. I'll never find out what happened during that summer Charlie was down here as a kid.

Huff told me the client was a bank in Philly, the executor of the Donne family estate. Charlie's will was cleared up. Among his papers was found an addendum to his will. He had remembered me. I got his fishing gear and the old Chevy. When I heard, I called Doc Grover and set up a fishing trip with him as a way of celebrating.

Tonight, there's a big going-away party for Amanda Kay. As you can imagine, she's now a very rich lady. She bought herself a good-size yacht to travel around the world, just like she once said she would. The part of her plans for me being on board that boat were obviously canceled. I won't even be at her party, for that matter. Practically everybody on the island is invited to the bash but me. I'll never be at her side again.

I'm going to change my self-pitying routine. Instead of brooding forever, I decide to get on with my life. I'll drive the Chevy over to the Empire Lounge to see whether a certain brunette might like to go to a late dinner after her last show.